SNAP, SPIRIT, MURDER
A GHOST PHOTOGRAPHER MYSTERY

FELICITY GREEN

© Felicity Green, 1st edition 2025

All rights reserved.

No part of this book may be reproduced in any form or by any electronic or mechanical means, including information storage and retrieval systems, without written permission from the author, except for the use of brief quotations in a book review.

Cover Design by Melody Simmons, bookcoversbymelody.com

This book is a work of fiction. Characters, names, places, or incidents are a product of the author's imagination or are used fictitiously. Any resemblance to actual events, locales, or persons, living or dead, is entirely coincidental.

Print ISBN: 978-3-911238-08-3

CHAPTER ONE

My late great-aunt had officially left me two things: a crumbling cottage in the Cotswolds and an old Nikon D40.

I haven't touched a camera since childhood, when my pictures scared me half to death.

But now I was a single mom with two daughters, an absconded criminal husband, and an empty bank account. I didn't know how or if the camera would be of use to me, and I sure as hell wasn't in a hurry to find out.

The cottage, however, was a lifeline. Even if we'd had to abandon what was left of our lives to move across the pond to the village of Fairwyck in England, where I'd spent my early childhood but had repressed most of my memories.

And so I stood in my new—but very old—kitchen on a rainy Tuesday in early May while my daughters were in their tiny attic rooms upstairs bawling their eyes out.

It was the most surreal feeling—and not because of the orange-and-brown-patterned linoleum floor and matching wallpaper from the seventies that gave me vertigo.

This was my life now?

Twenty years ago, I would have laughed in the face of the crazy fortune teller who predicted that at forty-two I would be here, starting fresh. Me? Captain of the cheerleading squad, engaged to football scholarship recipient Steven Grantham? Nope, I would never have imagined myself in this sad, lonely, and humiliating position.

But then I also wouldn't have expected to gain fifty pounds since those days, or that my dreamboat of a husband would turn out to be a cheating con man who'd wreck our family.

As far as my daughters were concerned, this was all my fault, and I had ruined their lives. So even if I wanted to go up the narrow creaky stairs to console them, they wouldn't let me.

This left me busy looking for the cat food.

What nobody had thought to mention was Great-Aunt Ethel's cat. Had it been fending for itself since her death? The small marmalade feline was meowing so loudly that I was sure the neighbors would report me to the RSPCA.

Ethel's clothes were still in her closets, her books on the shelves, and the pantry full of canned food. It didn't look as if anyone had cleared out my great-aunt's stuff. Why would there not be any cat food around?

I was determined to find something to feed the poor thing, even if I had to go to the village shop, which I didn't really have bandwidth for. I just wanted to collapse on the couch with an escapist mystery novel and my secret stash of M&Ms.

Judging by the plaintive cries, the animal would die of hunger before I got back anyway.

Just as I discovered some dusty cans of tuna in the pantry, my cell phone rang.

It was my best friend from home.

"Hi, Sarah."

"Hey, Liv! What's the cottage like? Does it come with prize-winning roses and a cozy fireplace?" She sounded a little too excited. Sarah's only understanding of England came from Regency romance novels and British romcoms.

"Umm. It's…quaint." There was a garden, but it was more of an overgrown meadow littered with sheep dung. "No roses. But a fireplace." I looked toward the pit that appeared to have been blackened by fire since the Dark Ages. I could see it from my vantage point kneeling on the floor as I was dumping the tuna in the bowl because the entire ground floor of my new home was an open-plan kitchen and living room, cabin style.

Mercifully, the cat seemed happy with the tuna, and the meowing stopped.

"I'd say it's more of a fixer-upper." I opened the other can of tuna because I could see that the bowl would need to be refilled soon.

"Oh, hon! You don't have to stay there, you know. Why don't you just sell the cottage and use the money as a down payment for a new home here in Connecticut?"

I snorted. "Do you mean in our old neighborhood? First, I could never afford it. Selling this cottage wouldn't generate enough of a down payment for a two-bedroom in Norwalk."

"No, no, I didn't mean here." Sarah laughed nervously. "You don't want to do that to yourself. You have no idea what everybody is saying about you. It'll be hard to get your reputation back."

My reputation? I bit my lips not to blurt the words aloud. It was completely unfair that our former friends and neighbors didn't fully assign blame where it belonged: to my husband. But it wasn't Sarah's fault; she was just the messenger. At least she was still talking to me, unlike most of my other so-called besties.

"If you ask me, the best thing you can do is get a new

partner. Someone to stick a ring on your finger. That would help you put this whole ugly situation behind you."

What did she mean by that? The last twenty years with my family? That wasn't so much an "ugly situation" as my entire adult life.

I didn't interject, and Sarah kept talking. "Maybe then you could return to our community. My cousin from Hartford is trying to set her widowed neighbor up with someone. I could—"

"Hang on," I finally interrupted her. "I'm not ready to date someone. Let alone get engaged. Steven and I are still married, remember? I can't divorce him in his absence, not even after everything he's done. He has to be gone without a word for some number of years before I can start proceedings…"

I didn't want to get into that. I also didn't want to admit that I couldn't even afford a lawyer right now.

The cat threaded back and forth between my legs, and I bent down to empty the second can of tuna I was holding.

"Anyway, there isn't much I can do with this cottage. Nobody is going to buy it. It's nothing like the British setting you see on TV. An old thatched roof doesn't look so trustworthy up close, let me tell you. I'm just glad it doesn't leak because I can't afford repairs." My mother had lent me the money for our one-way plane tickets, and that still stung.

"It can't be that bad," Sarah said. "What about the furniture? English antiques are worth something."

My gaze traveled from the wonky kitchen table to the faded chintz sofa and armchair of indeterminate color. They were as old as antiques, no question about it, but I doubted even a charity shop would take them.

I sighed. "The only thing of value Great-Aunt Ethel

bequeathed me is a camera. She left me a note with a cryptic remark about getting back to my vocation."

"I didn't know you'd trained as a photographer. Didn't you say you majored in arts?"

"Arts administration, actually. Haven't even touched a camera since I moved away from here. At age eight."

"Oh. Why would your great-aunt—"

"I don't know," I said in exasperation.

Of course, I kind of knew, but I *really* didn't want to get into *that* with Sarah.

"Look, my mom thought she'd done me a favor, getting my great-aunt to put me in her will. She painted a pitiful picture about my plight in the family newsletter, you know. I was mortified. But what was I going to do? We couldn't stay in her one-bedroom condo in that retirement community in Florida. So we're here now, we can't go back, and our home for the foreseeable future is a dump that's going to cost me money to keep up. Money I don't have."

I stopped my rant when I felt tears coming to my eyes. The meowing cat seemed to pick up on my distress. It went quiet. I thought I could see compassion in its slanted, sherry-colored eyes.

Then it just stalked off.

I dove into the pantry and unearthed a tin of corned beef. "Here, kitty, kitty. Sorry, Sarah, I am feeding the cat. Anyway, I'm not sure if I'm worse off than before."

"Why don't you just come home, Liv?"

"I can't. My girls need a roof over their heads. At least they have that."

"Sure. I mean, I don't want to sound negative, but you also need to earn money for food and clothing, right? Starting a photography business with no experience… Is that even realistic?"

"No, of course not." I straightened up from putting the

corned beef in the bowl and giving the returning cat a few strokes. "I already sorted out employment before I got here."

"Is there a museum in Fairwyck?"

"A museum?"

"Or a gallery…umm, I'm not sure what someone with an arts administration degree would do, exactly."

I laughed. "No, no. I have no work experience at all. Nobody is going to hire me for a job like that. And there are no cultural institutions like that here—as far as I know. There's a pub, a tearoom, a shop with a pharmacy and post office, the church, a library, a butcher, and…I think that's it. I just contacted all of them, told them who I was and that I was about to move here with my children, and inquired about any job openings."

Sarah was quiet. "Please don't tell me you plan on working in a butcher shop, Liv."

I swallowed. "Umm, no. The only person who responded was the pub landlady. She needs extra help on Saturday nights."

I could see Sarah crinkle her nose, even though it wasn't a video call. "You're going to be a barmaid?"

"Only part time. The pub landlady was really nice, though, and she asked around. She found out that a local rental agency needs help. There's a high demand for weekend and holiday rentals in the Cotswolds, so apparently there are quite a few of them in Fairwyck and the surrounding area."

"Oh, so you're getting into real estate." Sarah sounded relieved.

"Not…exactly." I wasn't even sure I wanted to correct Sarah's wrong assumption. But why not? I had no reason to lie or to feel ashamed about my situation. "I'm hired to clean the cottages."

The phone line went quiet. "You can't be serious. You want to work as a cleaner?"

Sarah whispered the last word, as if I had told her I planned to sell drugs to children.

"Yes," I said, a little defensively.

"Do you even know how to clean?"

"Of course." We'd always had a cleaner, like everyone else in our neighborhood, but I secretly enjoyed cleaning and keeping the house tidy. There was something satisfying about accomplishing those tasks.

"I understand that this is only meant to be temporary. I certainly won't say anything to anyone here… But there are things that are tough to come back from, Liv."

"What do you mean? Working-class labor is going to give me the devil's mark, or what?" It was a joke, but it masked my annoyance. I needed to make a living. I was glad I'd found work. And I'd rather clean other people's houses than con people out of their money like Steven had done. Now I was the one who was supposed to feel shame?

No.

My husband had pretended he was a successful business adviser, whereas, in fact, he had run a Ponzi scheme, conning many people—our friends and neighbors among them—out of their money. To get the whole thing going, he'd taken out another mortgage on our house and saddled us with extra debts I hadn't even known about. When he'd absconded with his millions, he'd taken his secretary with him—whom he'd been screwing on the side for years.

The FBI had interrogated me like a suspected accessory—and I couldn't even fault them. How blind could a wife have been to not have noticed all of this going on right under her nose?

Yes, I'd been comfortably cushioned in my suburban bubble. I've had blinders on. And that's what I lost sleep over at night. That was on me. Steven was to blame for everything else, though, and the FBI had cleared me of any criminal wrongdoings.

So I didn't care that Sarah was the only "friend" who still talked to me. If she was going to imply that I had been responsible for everything, that I should be ashamed for trying to save what my husband had left of our family, then I was going to speak up.

When I said as much to Sarah, she didn't even deny she felt that way. Worse, she defended everyone who might think the same.

She said that people were right to think that a good wife would have kept her husband on the straight and narrow. "You know, Liv, it's important to stay attractive for our husbands. That's our job. They have work stress and put in many hours to create a great life for us, right? I think they rightly expect us to look trim and presentable."

I shut my eyes. "So you think all this wouldn't have happened if I were still a size six?"

"Well, no, not exactly. I'm just saying Steven might not have strayed."

"So we could both be on an island, sipping cocktails, enjoying our ill-gained fortune?" My sarcasm was entirely lost on Sarah.

"Wouldn't that be better than slumming it in a run-down cottage in England, all alone and fending for yourself?"

"Err, Sarah, I really have to hang up now."

"Okay, speak to you soon?"

I just ended the call. I wouldn't call her back, and I somehow doubted I would hear from her again.

Not all change had to be bad. I mean, I wouldn't go so far as to suggest that my bastard of a husband had done me a favor, but still…

I shuddered to think that only a year ago I had probably been a little like Sarah.

In any case, she was definitely wrong about one thing.

I wasn't by myself. I had my daughters, even though they hated me right now.

"You don't hate me as long as I keep opening cans for you, do you?" I said to the cat, stroking the soft burnt-orange head.

Apparently, I now had a cat too.

CHAPTER TWO

In the end, I persuaded Audrey and Bianca to come downstairs for dinner. I wanted to believe that it was progress, but Audrey only spoke to inform me of a vow of silence. She intended to stick to it until I saw reason and abandoned this crazy plan to start over in England.

Audrey was of the staunch opinion that I was to blame for everything that had happened. Even though she knew her father was under investigation and considered a criminal fugitive by the FBI, she was convinced that it was all just a big mistake. She somehow had gotten it into her head that I had prevented him from taking his family along on his run from the law.

Because she was only nine, she had little concept of how much money our life in a gated community in a Hartford suburb had cost. She didn't understand that we couldn't stay there, where her friends were.

Audrey wasn't even my biggest problem, though.

I had imagined my girls were both crying into their pillows for the last couple of hours.

It turned out, however, that Bianca had used the time to chop off her beautiful long black hair with nail scissors.

She informed me she now wished to be called Blake, and her preferred pronoun was "they."

I considered myself an open and inclusive person, and I encouraged my children to express their true selves, but I had to admit that this came as a complete shock.

Bianca…Blake…had always been a quiet, likable girl. We'd never had any problems with her. It was Audrey who was the headstrong, spirited daughter, much more of a teenager at nine years than Blake had ever been.

This was completely out of the blue, but I recognized it was my problem that I hadn't seen it coming, not theirs. It meant I had work to do on myself, and the thought of taking this on as well threatened to overwhelm me.

I took a few deep breaths. Then I silently vowed to support my eldest's new identity as best as I could. I just had to find a way to tell them I had enrolled them at an all-girls school.

Luckily, I had a few days' grace because the kids wouldn't start school until next week. Until then, I had other things to worry about. Foremost, my new job.

I started early the next morning, shadowing an experienced cleaner by the name of Esme. My new colleague with the light-brown skin and long black braids was very patient, answering my many questions that probably showed I had no work experience whatsoever. Esme looked happy with the results when she asked me to clean a bathroom, though, so I was pleased about that.

When I got home that Wednesday afternoon, my exhaustion had taken on a whole new level. Clearly, I wasn't used to physically demanding work. I was sitting at the kitchen table, drinking a cup of tea and trying to psych myself up to go to the store and rustle up something for dinner, when there was a knock on the door.

I didn't know anyone who would come by, but in my state of fatigue, I just shouted, "Come in!"

Great-Aunt Ethel's cottage was so small that the front door opened directly into the living room, so I didn't have to get up to see the elderly woman enter. She was tall, with chestnut hair in a sort of old-fashioned beehive style, so she had to stoop when she passed through the low door frame.

Despite her dyed hair and regal posture, I would have guessed her to be in her seventies, probably the same age as my great-aunt when she had passed.

"Good afternoon. You must be Liv," the woman said. "My name is Matilda Rutherford, and I'm your next-door neighbor."

"Hi, so nice to meet you." The sight of the basket she held out to me, filled with homemade scones, finally got me off my chair.

I was a big fan of scones, and I imagined this elderly English lady to be a great baker. My stomach rumbled, and I grasped the basket. I somehow managed to make Matilda a cup of tea before stuffing my face with her welcome present.

I had a hard time concealing my disappointment. The scones were dry. My face must have given me away. I know I turned bright red when she said, "Not very good, are they?"

"Umm, I mean, maybe with some butter or cream…"

"That's all right, dear," Matilda said, with her head up high. "I know I'm not a superb cook. My Stanley always said, 'Matilda, darling, you have many talents, but cooking isn't one of them.'"

"Stanley is your husband?"

Matilda nodded. "Ethel used to enjoy my scones, though, especially when she couldn't bake for herself anymore. So I thought I'd make them for you."

"That's very kind. Did you know my great-aunt well?"

"We were best friends."

"Oh, I'm so sorry for your loss." I felt uncomfortable,

because even though Ethel was my relative, I'd hardly known her. Matilda was the one who had really experienced a loss.

Matilda bowed her head with dignity, but the eyes behind the black cat's-eye glasses shone with pain.

"Well, I'm pleased that you and your daughters moved into the cottage. It's nice to have Ethel's family here."

"Oh, it was a lifeline for me and the children," I said. "We didn't have anywhere else to go."

"I imagine you wouldn't have come here otherwise. Ethel told me you were very well off. I guess this cottage isn't on par with your usual living standards."

"Oh. Well, beggars can't be choosers." I had said something similar to Sarah the day before, but now it somehow seemed wrong…ungrateful. "That didn't come out right. Yes, the cottage could do with some updates. I can't really afford repairs right now, but we are so thankful to have a roof over our heads."

Matilda looked around. "I'm not sure if you knew this, but Ethel was sick for years before she passed. She didn't have the energy to take better care of her home."

I winced. I hadn't known that. It made me feel even worse for accepting my great-aunt's gift—and then complaining about it. "Oh, no, I didn't mean to imply—"

Matilda waved it off. "I didn't want to make you feel bad. I'm just offering an explanation. She didn't have a lot of money either, and I told her a few times I'd help with the renovations. Most of it is cosmetic and could be done on the cheap. That's how I spruced up my cottage."

"Really?" I skeptically looked at the broken and stained tiles above the kitchen sink. I had tried to scrub them yesterday, but they didn't look any different.

"Oh yes. I mean, it's not a permanent solution, but if you just want to make the cottage look nicer, I can give you a few tips." She followed my gaze to the tiles. "For example, I used inexpensive tile decals to brighten up my kitchen."

"That sounds like an idea." I smiled at Matilda in appreciation. "So you're into interior decorating?"

"That too. I make my own cleaning products because I'm sensitive to the store-bought stuff. I'm also handy with a hammer and a paintbrush. Refurbishing, painting, woodwork, that kind of stuff. I'm a regular DIY queen, me."

"Wow." I was really impressed. "I wish I had those skills. I can't even assemble flat-pack furniture without suffering a nervous breakdown."

"There's nothing to it," Matilda said in her no-nonsense tone. "I watch all them DIY shows on the telly and just copy what they do. I can show you a few things, if you like. Come over any time."

"I will. Thank you so much."

Stomping feet coming down the narrow stairs diverted our attention to my children.

"Mom!" Audrey said in her most whiney voice. "I'm hungry." Apparently she had forgotten that she wasn't speaking to me.

"I need to go to the store and get groceries. But our neighbor brought scones. Say hi to Matilda."

Audrey and Blake smiled and nodded politely, and I told Matilda my kids' names. Audrey picked up a scone and turned it around in her hand, frowning. "It's got raisins in it. I hate raisins."

"Okay, well then, there's a bag of pretzels in the cupboard, or you're just going to have to wait."

Audrey scrunched up her cute button nose. Blake said, "Why don't we get the groceries? The store isn't far, is it?"

"That would be wonderful." I smiled and described the short walk to the village shop. Blake and a visibly disgruntled Audrey left to get groceries.

"I see you have your hands full with them, but Blake seems like a responsible child."

"Yes. She…they are. Do you have any children? Grandchildren?"

Matilda shook her head. "Stanley and I weren't blessed."

"I'm sorry to hear that."

"That's all right." She waved it off but seemed sad.

I didn't know what to say. "Oh, then you have time for all your DIY projects."

"True."

I have a habit of filling silences with chatter, so I blabbered on. "Love your hair, by the way. Do you color it yourself as well?"

"Oh no, that's the only exception I make. My Stanley always loved my hair, you see. I have a standing appointment with my hairdresser so it looks like it always used to."

Matilda certainly seemed to adore her husband.

My neighbor started coughing and pulled an inhaler out of her skirt pocket.

"Everything all right?" I asked, concerned.

"Oh yes, just my asthma playing up. You don't have any pets, by any chance?"

At that moment, the marmalade cat made its presence known. It must have slunk through the door when the kids left. Now it was meowing loudly, as if to complain that we hadn't noticed it.

"Only Ethel's cat." I got up to get the last of the corned beef out of the pantry, cursing myself for having forgotten to tell the children to get cat food. "I keep forgetting that I now have to feed three hungry mouths."

"What do you mean, Ethel's cat?"

I straightened up from putting the corned beef in the bowl and saw that Matilda was looking at the cat with a frown.

"It keeps coming by. I assumed it was Ethel's."

Matilda shook her head. "Ethel didn't have a cat."

"Oh, you sneaky one," I berated the cat who was wolfing down the food. "You have a home and come here for seconds. Does it belong to one of the other neighbors?"

Matilda shook her head, her eyes still on the cat.

"No. No, I've never seen it before, but…"

She slowly got up from the table and moved around to get a better look at the reddish-orange feline with the white-tipped tail and paws.

She had me a little worried. "Is there something wrong with it, do you think?"

The cat had finished its meal in record time and sat on its hind paws. It started to clean itself unselfconsciously.

"Ethel didn't have a cat," Matilda said slowly. "But this cat certainly looks a lot like Ethel."

I raised my eyebrows. "What do you mean?"

"Do you remember what your great-aunt's hair looked like before it turned gray?"

That was easy. I had a few very distinct memories of Ethel from when I was younger. "Red. She had glossy long red hair."

Matilda nodded, still staring at the cat. "Yes. Her hair color was exactly the same as the cat's coat. A kind of burnt orange. And her eyes…they shone golden amber too, didn't they?"

"Hmm." Matilda was right. There was a similarity between the cat and Ethel, but what was she trying to get at? "I have the same eye color. It runs in the family. My mother has it too. Neither of us inherited the red hair, though. Mom's is dark brown like mine, just finer. Well, it used to be. It's more salt and pepper now."

Matilda studied me. "You do look a lot like Calista, now you mention it."

I kept forgetting that the older inhabitants of Fairwyck

had all known my mother once upon a time. Well, and me, as a child.

"But that cat…" Matilda's gaze went back to it, and she shook her head. "You know what, there are photo albums at the bottom of the bookshelf in the living room. Do you mind getting the cream one?"

"Um, no, hang on…" I walked over to the bookshelf. It was still full of Ethel's books. I hadn't had time to go through them yet, to make space for my own. At the bottom, I found the photo album Matilda had mentioned.

I brought it over to the kitchen. My neighbor was still rooted on the spot, her eyes on the cat.

"Would you open it up? There should be a picture of Ethel when she was younger."

I put the album on the kitchen table and opened it to a big photo of three young women with linked arms. The tall one with the chestnut beehive was undoubtedly Matilda. There was another shorter young woman with a mop of brown curls. And then there was Great-Aunt Ethel. She was much younger than in my memory, with her burnt-orange hair in a straight, long, seventies cut, matching the young women's clothing style.

Now I remembered something else. Ethel had had a blond streak in her hair, right at the front. As a girl, I had always assumed it was gray, because Ethel had seemed old to me. It had to have been a colored highlight, though. Had she kept the same hairstyle for decades with a standing appointment at the hairdresser's, just like her best friend?

But Matilda told me that Ethel had been born with it. "It's actually a rare genetic condition," she explained. "It's called a Mallen streak."

"Oh." I looked from the photo to the cat. There was white on her chest, paws, and tail-tip, so I hadn't really paid any attention to the white streak behind its ear.

But now that I had the picture to compare, I could see a resemblance. It wasn't even just the eyes, the marmalade coat, and the Mallen streak. It was the face too.

I had to agree with Matilda.

This cat, which apparently didn't belong to anyone and had just turned up here after Ethel's death, looked exactly like my great-aunt.

CHAPTER THREE

I hoped that Matilda's visit would be a good start to settling down in Fairwyck.

I tried not to let the fact that she had made a rather abrupt exit worry me. It could have been because of her asthma acting up. Or she might have been freaked out about Ethel the cat, as I had named the feline.

The similarities to my late great-aunt and the fact that this cat seemed to have turned up out of nowhere notwithstanding, I couldn't quite believe that the feline was a reincarnation of Ethel. That would be crazy, right?

In any case, I thought we'd had a pleasant chat, and Matilda seemed eager to connect with Ethel's family.

I didn't hear from her again for the rest of the week, however. I had intended to pay her a visit and bring her something homemade, like a casserole. My culinary skills weren't exactly stellar, but that hadn't stopped Matilda either.

Time got away from me, though, because I was really busy. If I wasn't cleaning other people's houses, I was trying to sort out our own. We hadn't brought over a lot of stuff, but I still had to decide what to do with Matilda's things. Most evenings, I was so tired that I didn't get around to doing very much at all besides feeding myself and my children.

So I never made that casserole to cement the bonding with my neighbor.

I also wasn't off to a great start with anyone else in the village.

I'd already turned our other neighbor against us, it seemed. Her larger house was on the other side of my garden. In fact, her property was almost double the size of mine, so it bordered on Matilda's garden as well. I had seen an elderly lady with gray hair peering out behind her curtains a couple of times, but she hadn't come out and introduced herself.

One evening, I called for Ethel the cat because I really wanted to go to bed, and I preferred her to be indoors at night.

As I was calling the cat and trying to avoid stepping in sheep dung—why was that even in our garden? I had seen no sheep around—I saw Ethel on the other side of the fence, in the neighbor's garden, completely ignoring me.

The neighbor clearly didn't appreciate her presence. Possibly alerted by my calls, she came out from behind her curtains for once. She stomped out the back door, shooing the cat away.

I introduced myself, but instead of giving her name, she just asked if the cat was mine.

I shrugged. "It kind of came with the cottage."

The little round lady squinted her eyes, peering at me over the fence. "Ethel didn't have a cat."

"So I heard." I called the cat again, but she had settled in the vegetable patch and was cleaning herself blithely.

"Nice to meet you," I said, trying to make an effort. "And your name is…?"

"Phyllis Bishop."

"Okay. We'd love to get to know you, Phyllis. Come over for a cup of tea anytime you like."

She just squinted some more and then turned to run toward the cat, attempting to shoo her away.

It looked slightly comical, but I managed not to laugh.

The cat got up and stretched, in no hurry whatsoever. Then she stared at Phyllis Bishop, who was stomping at the ground, with what could only be described as derision in her golden eyes.

Ethel the cat hissed, turned around, and hightailed it out of there through a hole in the fence. I returned to the kitchen door, eyes trained on the ground so I wouldn't accidentally step on sheep dung. When I looked up, Phyllis had disappeared into her house.

"So we don't like her, do we?" I asked when I opened the door wide to let the cat in, but Ethel seemed more interested in finding her bowl than communicating with me. If she really was reincarnated Ethel, she had forgotten my great-aunt's good manners.

I was looking forward to my shift in the pub on Saturday night because cleaning was a bit of a lonely job now that I could work by myself. I'd forgotten to exchange numbers with Esme.

My boss at the rental agency, owner Judith Winters, was a little intimidating. She had a brisk way about her, seemed so spunky, and was always made up to the nines. In fact, she looked like Anna Nicole Smith in her heyday, dressed up as a businesswoman.

These were the only women, aside from Phyllis and Matilda, that I'd met in Fairwyck. So I hadn't really struck up a friendship with anyone since moving here, and I had high hopes that the job at the pub would bring me into contact with more people.

Since I had Saturday morning and afternoon off, I

suggested to my children that we should explore the village. So far, we had only been to the grocery store.

Blake pointed out that exploring Fairwyck would take us all of ten minutes, since there wasn't much more to see than the few shops.

That wasn't strictly true. Although the village was small, narrow cobblestoned alleys separated the houses, meandering this way and that, leading you to unexpected little gems of regional old architecture. There was a brook that bordered the village and then the beautiful surrounding rolling hills of the Cotswolds.

But we didn't get around to any of that because, to our delight, it turned out that the second Saturday of each month was a busy market day for Fairwyck. The village green was full of market stalls selling everything from fresh produce to local honey to arts and crafts. And best of all, there was a food truck that served coffee and pastries.

I didn't even say anything when Blake ordered a coffee too. And when I got Audrey a chocolate croissant, I saw her smile for the first time since we'd arrived in England.

We looked at the art stalls, and I saw a lot of things that I would have loved—if we'd only had the money!

I decided we could splurge a little when we all expressed delight in an inexpensive art print. For the first time since our move, we agreed on something—and the print seemed like a symbol for a first significant step. I was carrying the rolled-up print in one hand and my coffee in the other when someone bumped into me. The coffee spilled all over the precious commodity I'd just purchased.

Livid, I turned around, firing off a few swear words at the man. He apologized profusely.

"We just bought this," I screamed, as I furiously tried to get the coffee off the print.

"I'm so sorry. I'll buy you another one." The man was

tall and handsome, with dark hair and brown eyes, giving off his best puppy-dog impression. I was not having it.

"It was one of a kind. My children and I picked it out together, and I paid for it with the last of my cash. So thanks for that."

Looking around for Audrey and Blake, I saw they were hiding between two stalls, clearly mortified that I was making a scene.

"Again, so sorry!" The man put his hand on his heart. "Where did you buy it? Marco's stall? I know he won't have one that's exactly the same, but he often does variations, so maybe there'll be something else that you and your children like?"

"That's not the point." I almost cried. Our day out was clearly ruined. Why was this all so difficult? Couldn't my family and I catch a break for once?

"May I?" The man carefully took the rolled-up print out of my hands. He removed the rest of the excess liquid with tissues. Then he unrolled it. He put it on top of Marco's stall, and the stain on the other side was not even noticeable.

I turned bright red. Now I really felt like an idiot. Everyone was looking at me. "I think it's fine," the man said unnecessarily. "But I'll still buy you another one, if you like."

I tried to hold my head up high. "Like I said, we were only interested in that one. It holds special meaning for us. We'll keep it, as it's not completely ruined."

Even though I wanted to do nothing more than run away, I took my time, carefully rolling up the print, fastening it again, and strolling toward the street. I nodded toward my children, who slunk behind me.

We hastened home without saying a word.

Blake and Audrey went up to their rooms, and when

they were out of earshot, I allowed myself to cry a few tears.

The art print that had seemed a symbol of a fresh start was now just a reminder of how I had failed as a mother yet again. I really wished nothing more than to do something right for our family for once.

CHAPTER FOUR

My mood picked up when I arrived at the Owl and Oak pub for my shift that evening.

Proprietor Ellie Bullwart had been the only person to respond to my desperate search for employment. We had spoken on the phone a couple of times but hadn't met in person yet. She was exactly like I'd pictured her. Warm, with a halo of blond hair. She was even dressed in a butter-yellow dress.

We hugged, and I just knew we were friends already.

I was really trying to like her husband, Jason, too. But the burly man with short-cropped hair didn't make it easy. He'd grunted in my direction instead of saying hello, clearly more interested in the game of darts he was playing with his mates.

Maybe I was judging him too harshly, I told myself. The Bullwarts had hired me because they needed help, and tonight was my turn to man the bar. For all I knew, Jason had been working his large behind off all week. He might be due for some time off, and it wasn't for me to judge whether his wife could have deserved a break too.

After a while, Jason ambled over, studying me. "I

expected the help to look different. We usually hire students and the like. How old are you?"

I was taken aback, and Ellie noticed, so she quickly put in, "I told you Liv is a single mom."

"Yeah, but you didn't say she was an *old* mom."

My eyes widened.

"I mean, you look good for your age, don't get me wrong, luv." Just when I thought Jason's comments couldn't get any worse, he went on. "But you've got to lose the mom look if you want to make tips on a Saturday night. A little cleavage goes a long way." He wasn't talking to my face as he said that. "You've the knockers for it."

"Jason!" Ellie chided, her cheeks turning red.

He held up his hands. "Just trying to help."

Still looking at my chest, he walked backward and returned to his friends.

"I'm so sorry," Ellie stuttered.

"I really, really, appreciate this job, Ellie." I finally found my words. "I do desperately need the money. But he can't say that kind of stuff to me, you understand?"

"I know, I know. I'll talk to him."

Luckily, it got busy fast, and Jason stayed away from the bar. Ellie and I were run off our feet, but I wasn't unhappy about that. The time went by quickly, and I didn't have to deal with Jason.

There were a few regulars Ellie introduced me to. It wasn't difficult to serve drinks, and I also quickly picked up on how to use the till. Pulling pints took me a little longer to learn. I had a patient customer to practice on, though.

It was this old guy with lots of gray facial hair and aviator-style sunglasses. He wore an IPS uniform. Trying to figure out that acronym drove me crazy until I finally asked Ellie when we had a brief lull.

"International Parcel Services," she said.

"What's his story?" I assumed he was a regular too.

But Ellie didn't know him. "He isn't local. He has recently been in here on Saturday nights, drowning his sorrow, it feels like."

Then she pointed at the door. "Hey, it's your relatives."

"What?" An older woman with dyed-blond hair and a colorful caftan waltzed into the pub, followed by a mousy-looking willowy thirty-something. No, on second look, she wasn't exactly mousy. Her brown trench coat, slightly hunched figure, messy topknot, and old-fashioned glasses just made it seem that way. There was a pretty girl underneath.

"Your relatives," Ellie repeated. "Ethel's sister, Gina. Her daughter, Emerald."

I stared at Ellie, then at the two women, in disbelief.

I'd had no idea that I had more relatives in Fairwyck. My mom hadn't mentioned it. I couldn't remember Gina from when I was younger either.

And why hadn't they been by the cottage? Wasn't it strange that I had been in Fairwyck a week and they hadn't introduced themselves?

Maybe they wanted to rectify that today. It was possible they'd heard I was working here. But while I was busy serving first the sad IPS guy and then some young people at one end of the bar, my relatives went to Ellie and ordered from her.

Ellie had just put the requested two glasses of white wine on the counter when a commotion near the dart board caught my attention. It looked as if Jason and his mates were getting riled up about something. They kept looking and pointing at the bar.

Jason walked over just as Gina was about to pay. "We don't want the likes of you in here."

"Jason!" Ellie turned bright red again.

"You know how I feel about those witches, Ellie!"

"And you know how I feel about discrimination," Ellie

said. "Gina and Emerald probably want to say hi to Liv. I will not turn them away."

"Liv? Who's Liv?"

Ellie pointed at me, which I only saw out of the corner of my eye, as I was busy taking payment from the young people.

"Oh. The MILF." Then he changed his tone. "Why would they want to say hi to her?"

"Because Gina is Liv's great-aunt."

"She's American." Jason sounded like he thought Ellie was pulling his leg.

"Yes, the great-niece from America, who inherited Ethel Seven's cottage. She used to live here. I went to primary school with her, just two years behind. I told you this! Don't you ever listen?"

I heard a lot of cussing. The IPS guy chose that moment to knock over his beer. I didn't see Gina's or Emerald's reaction. By the time I had wiped away the beer, poured a new one for the IPS guy, and served a bunch of other people, Jason was back with his pals, and Gina and Emerald were nowhere to be seen.

It was ten o'clock, and the big rush seemed to be over. The pub was almost empty.

Ellie told me I could go home. She sounded friendly, but it wasn't hard to detect the note of false cheer in her voice.

Jason gave me the stink-eye when I left.

I felt I had done a decent job and that I had bonded with Ellie, but I wasn't sure I would be asked back the following week. It wasn't fair, but I wasn't sure I wanted to work for someone like Jason anyway. If only I didn't need the money so badly! I vowed to do an extra good job cleaning so I wouldn't have to rely on the pub job.

My hope to make friends certainly had been dashed. Instead, I had learned that there were people close to me, family, who had been actively avoiding me. I really didn't understand why.

When I got home, I didn't even have anyone to tell my woes to, other than Ethel the cat. At least she answered with a sad meow and let me stroke her.

CHAPTER FIVE

Sunday was my busiest cleaning day yet because it was change-over day in most of the cottages.

Monday was supposed to be my day off, which worked out well, because I could drive the children on their first day of school.

It was the longest drive I'd taken thus far in the old Fiat I'd inherited from my great-aunt. We'd intended to drive to Cirencester for a shopping trip on Saturday afternoon. After the epic fail of the visit to the market that morning, we'd canceled that plan.

To my surprise, the old car handled the drive well. Still, Audrey commented on how embarrassing it was to arrive in a rust bucket and asked to be dropped off a block away.

"It might have been a concern back home," I tried to reassure her, "but this is a state school, honey. Other students are used to parents driving old cars."

I saw Audrey's horrified look in the back mirror. "You enrolled me in a public school?"

"Private schools are expensive. It isn't that bad—in fact, it's normal here. I actually went to this school as a kid. Look, here we are." I pulled up in front of the school.

"Ummm, Mom," Blake said. "If you went here, didn't you know the students wear uniforms?"

That's when I remembered *why* we'd planned to go shopping in Cirencester on Saturday.

"Yes. Yes, I knew that. I wanted to buy—"

"Mom…is this an all-girls school?" Blake's voice shook.

I undid my seatbelt. "Kind of. They have a boys school too, but it's in a separate building. Let's go in and find the principal's office."

The principal was very understanding when I told her we'd only arrived in the UK a week ago and hadn't had time to sort out uniforms. She even named a store in Cirencester where we could buy them. "I can point you toward secondhand options too."

I could tell Audrey was mortified, so I just thanked her and smiled.

Then I wished my kids a nice first day at school, but they both looked as if I was leaving them for the Grim Reaper to collect.

I wanted to drive to Cirencester and buy a set of uniforms right away, but when I got into the car, my phone rang. It was Judith.

"I know it's supposed to be your day off, but do you mind working today?"

"Um, no, not at all." I had been looking forward to tackling my long to-do list. But those uniforms wouldn't be cheap, so an extra shift wouldn't hurt.

"Great," Judith said quickly. "I'd like you to clean your neighbor's cottage, Matilda Rutherford. Did you know her?"

"Yes, she came over and introduced herself last week," I said, a little confused. Judith's agency was for holiday rentals. As far as I knew, they didn't provide cleaning services for anyone else. And why was she talking about Matilda in the past tense?

"Okay, great. There's a key under the planter next to the front door—"

"Is Matilda all right?" I interrupted my boss. "She seemed healthy last week, even talked about her homemade organic cleaning products. I'd have thought she cleaned her own home. She's not sick, is she?"

Judith seemed unsure of how to respond for once.

"It's not that I mind at all," I hurried to say. "I'm happy to clean her cottage."

"Matilda passed away a few days ago. Haven't you heard?"

Now it was my turn to be stunned into silence.

"Her niece Tracy is inheriting the cottage. She wants to rent it out and list it with us. She asked me to have it cleaned as soon as possible."

"I'm sorry," I stuttered. "I hadn't heard. This is a bit of a shock. What happened? When did she pass?"

"Saturday night, I think. I don't know exactly. She was old, wasn't she?"

"She seemed pretty spry to me when she came by with homemade scones the other day."

"I don't know what to tell you." Judith seemed in a hurry, and I didn't want to annoy her.

"Okay, um, no worries, I can clean the cottage."

"Make it a deep clean. I'll pay you overtime, of course. Oh, and change the sheets, towels, and everything, will you?"

"Of course, not a problem." It suddenly occurred to me that Matilda might have died in that bed, so I wasn't exactly looking forward to that task. "Um, there is no *special* cleaning involved, is there?"

"Special cleaning?" Judith asked impatiently.

"Like…blood."

"Oh. No. No, I don't think so. Tracy didn't mention it. Like I said, she probably passed away from old age."

"Hmm."

"If you need anything, just call me."

"Okay…"

Judith had already hung up.

All the way back home, my head was spinning with the new information about Matilda's death. And what about her husband, Stanley? The way Matilda had talked about him had given me the impression that Stanley was still alive. But going through what I remembered from our conversation, I realized she had also sounded like a single lady living by herself. If Matilda's niece stood to inherit the cottage, then I must have misunderstood my neighbor. Maybe Matilda had recently been widowed.

I drove past Matilda's cottage to get home. I had noticed nothing different about it in the last couple of days. I'd been at the pub on Saturday night, and I'd been busy, but I felt guilty for being so self-involved that my neighbor's death had just completely passed me by.

I changed into work clothes and walked over to the Rutherford cottage. Picking up the key from under the planter and just letting myself in felt like an intrusion.

That feeling got worse when I saw a half-empty cup of tea on a coaster next to the armchair. A paperback with a bookmark in it lay next to it—the half-naked guy in a kilt suggested it was a romance novel. A red shawl was casually thrown over the back of the armchair.

It looked as if Matilda had just been here and had gotten up only moments ago. I was half convinced Judith had made a mistake. Matilda probably wasn't dead. Someone else had passed away, someone who wasn't my neighbor.

"Matilda?" I called out, first quietly, then a little louder. I went upstairs, but nobody was up there.

The bed was made, however. Whatever had happened to Matilda—and now I could no longer pretend nothing had happened—she hadn't died in her bed. I was actually a little relieved, remembering that I had to change the sheets. It wouldn't be so bad because they looked fresh to me.

A look in the bathroom told me that Matilda was a tidy and clean person. The bathroom had a pleasant lavender smell. It had probably only recently been cleaned with one of Matilda's organic homemade cleaning products.

There was a spare bedroom with a desk in it, and that could have used a dusting, but other than that, I couldn't really see a reason for getting someone in here so urgently.

I returned to the living room. With a lump in my throat, I folded the shawl. I wasn't sure where to put it. In the end, I walked back upstairs and put it in the closet. I changed the sheets, brought the dirty linen downstairs into the kitchen, and stuffed everything in the washing machine. There was a duster on top of it, and I grabbed it.

After dusting the living room, I put the novel back on the bookshelf. I left the bookmark in. My chest tightened at the thought that Matilda wouldn't get to finish her book.

I brought the mug into the kitchen and washed it. As I was drying it, I noticed the pretty design on the tiles. I remembered Matilda had told me she'd used decals. You couldn't tell at first sight that they weren't Moroccan tiles. I was really impressed.

I put the mug and other dishes from the drying rack into the cupboard. Then I looked for the cleaning products. I found a bunch of empty bottles under the sink. Some were all-purpose bottles, neatly labeled. I found homemade furniture polish, a descaler, and tablets for the toilet. An unlabeled bottle was empty and gave off a lavender scent. I also found several bottles of strong chemicals, store-bought bleach and floor cleaners. All of them were empty.

I was a little surprised. Maybe Matilda had occasionally used the potent stuff when the organic cleaning products hadn't cut it, but I remembered her saying something about being sensitive to those products.

I wasn't sure what to do. The other rental cottages had cleaning caddies with products. I got my phone out, only to discover that the battery had died. But I didn't really want to call my boss and complain about not having all the tools to do my job anyway. Not during my trial period.

So I went home and got my own. As I was gathering supplies, my gaze fell on the Nikon that I had put on the top kitchen shelf.

It occurred to me I could quickly take a few pictures of the tiles and some of the DIY projects Matilda had told me about. She *had* invited me to come by and look at everything. Maybe I wouldn't have the chance again, and I really liked that tile design.

Before I could listen to the inner voice that had forbidden me to take pictures for the last thirty-four years, I quickly picked up the camera along with the bag of cleaning supplies.

By the time I got back to Matilda's kitchen, I had lost my nerve already.

I would finish all the cleaning first, I decided. After all, that was what I was being paid for. I dusted the rooms upstairs, vacuumed the entire house, polished the furniture, and cleaned the bathroom, even though it didn't need it.

All the while, I paid attention to Matilda's DIY projects. There was furniture that had presumably been bought secondhand, sanded, refinished, and repainted. She had also hung wall art to cover cracks in the walls. She had spackled and painted first, but you could still tell where those imperfect bits of wall were if you took down some of the pictures.

Matilda had a different taste in wall art than me, but I was impressed by what she had done. It made me so sad that I could only get to know her through her home—now that it was too late to get better acquainted in person.

She seemed to be into quotes and sayings, even had embroidered Bible verses framed.

In the living room, there were a bunch of sofa cushions embroidered with proverbs or clichéd sayings, like *Live Laugh Love* and *Carpe diem—You only live once*. Considering Matilda had just passed, they didn't seem so contrived to me.

The kitchen was the last room left to clean.

My gaze fell on the camera that I had deposited next to the cleaning supplies on the small kitchen table. I didn't want to pick it up, but something compelled me to. Maybe I needed to commemorate Matilda, the unique stamp she had put on her home, before it was made to look impersonal and rented out to affluent weekenders. She had deliberately and lovingly chosen everything to make her home look nicer. She had taken the time to learn DIY skills, and then she had carefully budgeted her home improvements.

I no longer felt like an intruder—I thought Matilda would have liked me to take pictures to remember her home.

Starting in the living room, I took photos of the end tables and an old bureau that I assumed Matilda had restored. I had dusted the picture frames on the bureau and the mantlepiece earlier without really paying attention to them. One of them was of Matilda in a wedding dress —I recognized her as the young woman from the photo in Ethel's picture album—together with a very handsome man who I presumed to be Stanley. There were two, three more pictures of Stanley as a young man, but no recent ones. The other photos were of a girl with curly reddish-blond hair and very blue eyes. She had a round face and freckles.

I went to the kitchen to take pictures of the tiles next.

So far, I purposely hadn't checked the images on the digital display. A part of me didn't want to look at them.

But then I told myself that I was being silly.

As a seven- or eight-year-old child, I had been blessed with a lot of imagination. I had loved taking pictures, and I had experimented a lot. I'd probably created something that wasn't there with light and shadow. At least, that's how my mother had explained it to me.

Now, as an adult, I was inclined to believe her—even though my inner kid had prevented me from getting into the same situation again all these years. It had felt safer not to risk it.

It was finally time to get over that. What had the shock of what Steven had done taught me? That turning a blind eye to something, repressing something, has never done anyone any good. I was much better off facing whatever made me uncomfortable.

I took a big breath and lifted the camera.

When I clicked the button to show me the photos on the display, I felt transported back in time. I was suddenly eight-year-old Liv again, shivering and terrified.

The last picture I had taken appeared on the screen. The sink and the tiles.

And there was something else, something that definitely hadn't been in the room when I'd pressed the camera button.

This time, nobody, not myself or my mother, could convince me that it was a smudge or a weird shadow.

The thing in the picture was definitely a person. A tall, slim woman in a skirt and a blouse with a chestnut beehive.

She was bent over as if in pain, and I could only see part of her face.

But I knew who it was, all the same. Matilda Rutherford.

"Who do we have here?" a male voice said behind me.

I screamed.

CHAPTER SIX

The person who had startled me into almost dropping the camera and suffering a heart attack was a detective inspector with the Gloucestershire police.

He told me he'd been born and raised in Fairwyck before he divulged his name. DI Farrow.

I explained to him I had been hired to clean Matilda Rutherford's cottage.

"Doesn't look like you were cleaning to me." He pointed at the camera.

"Oh, that. I was taking a picture of the tiles. Matilda had mentioned them to me as a DIY project, and I really liked the decals, so…"

I trailed off when I saw DI Farrow's face.

"The woman isn't even buried yet, and you break in here to take pictures of her tiles?"

"I didn't break in. I was hired—"

"Not from here, are you?" DI Farrow interrupted me.

"Originally, yes, but I've lived in the US for the last thirty-four years. I came here with my children and moved in next door, into my great-aunt Ethel's cottage."

DI Farrow looked me over, and there was a funny expression in his eyes. I could have sworn his whiskers—a Poirotesque mustache—quivered with excitement.

"I know who you are." He dragged the phrase out with his broad Gloucestershire accent.

"Well, yes, because I told you. My name is Liv Grantham, and I work for—"

"You're Calista's daughter."

"Um…yes. Do you know my mother?" He was probably the same age as my mom.

"I knew her well. Once upon a time." Farrow stroked his mustache. "How is Calista? I tried to keep in touch, and I still check up on her from time to time, which has been a lot harder since she quit Facebook."

"What?" That sounded more like stalking than keeping in touch. "She's well. Enjoys retirement in Florida."

"Oh, yes, I knew that. Been single since your stepfather passed a few years back, has she?"

I was too taken aback by the question to answer right away, and then DI Farrow stunned me even more with his next comment.

"It's a real shame Calista's life choices led to this. Raising a criminal daughter?" He shook his head and tutted. "I heard about your difficulties with the law."

I huffed. "A criminal? You mean my husband?"

"Sure. Your husband, you…I made some inquiries. The FBI doesn't believe that a husband can hide this level of con-artistry from his wife. I have to say I agree."

I'd known Fairwyck was the kind of place where gossip traveled fast, but this was next level. "Actually, you'll find that the FBI cleared me of any—"

"Yes, well, you might've pulled the wool over the FBI's eyes. Like mother, like daughter, huh? That isn't going to work here."

"Look, I don't know what kind of problem you have with my mother, but I hardly think this…"

"You can tell your mother not everything is better in the United States. A humble Gloucestershire detective inspector might just prove himself more capable than the high-and-mighty FBI by taking decisive action. I'm not going to let breaking and entering slide."

Lost for words, I just stood there, staring at DI Farrow, open-mouthed.

"You probably thought the old lady had a few coins under her mattress." He took out handcuffs and made a move to put them around my wrists.

I held up my hands. "Let's back up. Like I said, my boss, Judith from Winters Letting Agency, called me and asked me to come here to clean the cottage. She said Matilda's niece Tracy had hired WLA to list the cottage and deep clean it. I didn't break in. Judith told me where to find the key."

"Nice try, young lady. Why would Tracy do anything like that? It's not her cottage yet. Matilda Rutherford's death is still under investigation. And you seem like a good suspect to me."

"What? Are you crazy? Now you're accusing me of murder?" My voice sounded shrill.

"It's suspicious enough you turned up here, after you and your mother wanted nothing to do with this place for decades. Now your neighbor—"

"I inherited my great-aunt's—"

"Liv Grantham, I'm arresting you for the murder of… Hey!"

Instinct took over, and I freed myself from his grip before he could put the cuffs on. I moved around him and ran toward the front door.

Right into the arms of the stranger who had caused me

to make a scene at the market on Saturday. "Wow," he said. "We have to stop bumping into each other like this."

"Stop that woman, Rees," said DI Farrow. "I was about to arrest her for the murder of Matilda Rutherford, and she was trying to run. If that doesn't scream guilty, I don't know what does. I caught her here, probably getting rid of evidence."

"For the hundredth time, I was here because my employer, Judith Winters, asked me to come. I work for WLA as a cleaner. I didn't even know Matilda had passed. She introduced herself to me once—this was a few days ago. Other than that, I didn't know her. What reason would I have to murder her?" I said in exasperation.

"To rob her—" DI Farrow offered, but I interrupted him before he could come up with any more ridiculous speculations.

"Besides, Judith said Matilda died on Saturday evening, and I was in the pub at that time."

"Like yer drink, do yer?" DI Farrow shook his head disapprovingly.

"I was working," I said tersely. "Just ask Ellie Bullwart."

"We'll check your alibi. Don't worry. But first you'll come to the station with us."

The other man came to my rescue. "Why don't you put in a call to the Bullwarts, boss? It's an easy enough alibi to check. And ring Judith too. I'll watch the suspect for you."

DI Farrow grumbled a bit but eventually went outside to make the calls, but not without warning Rees. "Watch out. She's a slippery one, just like her mother."

It looked as if Rees's lips twitched when he said, "Oh, don't worry, boss. I'll make sure she doesn't run away again."

"Does this situation amuse you?" I asked, barely able to control my anger.

My "rescuer" was clearly trying to keep a straight face.

"No, of course not." His voice softened. "Look, I'm sure it'll straighten itself out. DI Farrow is a little overly zealous."

I was about to launch into a tirade that the DI's treatment of me seemed hugely unfair—he appeared to have a bee in his bonnet about my mother—but the handsome police officer interrupted me.

"Now you don't need to convince me. I'm sure you had nothing to do with Matilda's death."

"There's absolutely no reason for me to kill her. I barely knew her."

"And DI Farrow is going to figure that out. I've learned it's better to let him get to it in his own time."

I folded my arms and squinted up at him. "So you're what…a DI as well?"

"A sergeant, DS Jamie Rees. I'm sorry I haven't formally introduced myself. Somehow, we just blew past that."

"Liv Grantham," I said.

"I hope everything is all right with your art print?"

"It's fine. I overreacted." I sighed. "It's just that my children and I are having a difficult time, and that print was the first thing we agreed upon since moving here." I didn't know why I felt the need to explain myself.

"What happened to Matilda?" I had to ask. "Judith didn't know how she died, but I had the impression that she passed peacefully. I thought it was strange, because Matilda appeared healthy and spry when she visited me last week. Now it seems as if you're treating it like a suspicious death?"

DS Rees nodded. "She died of an asthma attack. Her brother couldn't get through to her on the phone on Saturday evening, which struck him as unusual. He got worried, came by around nine o'clock, and found her on the kitchen floor. We thought nothing of it at first, but then there were some irregularities. They're still being analyzed, so I can't say any more about that."

I put my hand over my heart. "Oh no. Poor Matilda. Why would anybody want to kill her?"

DS Rees shrugged. "That's what we're trying to find out. Like you said, who would have a motive to kill Matilda Rutherford? We can't think of anyone. Which is why Farrow is grasping at straws. But if it helps, I don't believe you did it, especially if your alibi checks out."

He smiled, and the many tiny lines around his eyes crinkled, which I had to admit looked very attractive. I caught myself wondering how old DS Rees was. Probably not much younger than me. I hadn't spotted a wedding ring, but that didn't have to mean anything. He could still be in a committed relationship. Actually, it would be weird if a woman hadn't snapped him up. He was handsome, incredibly nice, and well mannered, and he had a good, respectable job.

Not that I was ready to date. I'd only ever dated one man in my life, and that had turned into a colossal disaster. There wasn't a lot I could shield my children from, but I would not make the mistake of bringing the wrong man into my life again. I'd rather not have a man in it at all.

I wouldn't have to worry about any of that with DS Rees, though, so it was pointless mulling this over. I hadn't made the best first impression and very much doubted that he would want to ask me out. He most likely had me filed away as "crazy American lady who likes to make a scene" or "wrong place at the wrong time woman."

DI Farrow came back into the cottage. He didn't look pleased. "It seems as if Mrs. Grantham here has an alibi for Saturday. I couldn't reach Judith Winters." He clasped his arms behind his back and bounced a little on his toes while studying me.

"I'm going to let you go…for now. I'll keep my eyes on you, Mrs. Grantham. Don't leave town."

I would have rolled my eyes if I wasn't a little scared.

What if DI Farrow really arrested me? If he didn't see reason? What would happen to my children?

I went back home in a bit of a state.

I thought preparing a lasagna for dinner that evening would take my mind off things, but it wasn't really working. I messed up the bechamel sauce by forgetting to stir, so it turned out lumpy and burned. Then I was out of milk.

Contemplating whether I should make spaghetti Bolognese with the meat sauce instead, or something completely different, took the rest of the energy out of me. Defeated, I sat down at the kitchen table, trying not to cry, instead of getting on with things.

The day was going so horribly wrong… Who was I kidding? The whole last week, ever since our arrival in England, had gone horribly wrong…and I couldn't even make a decent dinner for my kids.

That's when I remembered I hadn't arranged whether I'd pick them up from school or not. And that I'd planned to buy their school uniforms today. And that I should at least have milk in the fridge for breakfast tomorrow…

Now the tears were falling.

At least I didn't feel self-conscious blubbering away, my head in my hands, because nobody was there to witness my minor breakdown.

Wrong—a loud meow tore me away from my little pity party.

Ethel the cat had somehow appeared in the kitchen—hadn't I closed the front door? Maybe she'd been upstairs, in one of the bedrooms, snoozing.

She looked at me as if to say "What's the matter, love?"

In fact, I could almost hear her say that in my head, as

if I suddenly remembered how Great-Aunt Ethel used to talk.

"You know, I'm really trying my best here," I complained to the cat. "Don't you think I deserve a little break? Is the universe trying to punish me for something, do you think? I knew something was up with Steven. I probably chose not to notice it because it was easier that way. There's no way I could have known about his business dealings, how many people he'd conned out of money. But if I'd have shown a little interest in our personal finances, maybe I'd have caught on to the fact that he'd taken out a second mortgage and borrowed money to get this pyramid scheme started. And the affair with his secretary? Do you know, I was secretly glad he was less demanding in the bedroom. Maybe I didn't want to see."

"Meow."

Great, I was talking to a cat about my nonexistent sex life and my financial problems. That was some serious lonely spinster territory. Maybe I ought to try a therapist instead.

I didn't actually believe that Ethel the cat was a special case because she may have been my great-aunt reincarnated, did I?

That would definitely mean I'd need a therapist.

I sighed, gave Ethel the cat some cuddles and food—which was probably what she'd wanted all along—and dusted myself off.

Ethel shed little hair, so it was more of a metaphorical gesture.

There was no point in moping.

I'd pick up the kids from school, drive to Cirencester to get the uniforms, and get groceries on the way back.

I could do this.

How much worse could this day get, right?

CHAPTER SEVEN

Oh boy.
Never put the question "how much worse can this get" out there for the universe to show you what she's got.

When I got to the school, Audrey and Blake weren't there. They must have taken the bus home. I decided they would be fine there and that it would be more important for them to have uniforms tomorrow. If I drove back to pick them up, we wouldn't make it to the shop in time.

When I got to the shop in Cirencester, it was already closed. Should have probably checked opening times.

At least I managed to grab a few essentials from the supermarket, but when I finally arrived back at the cottage, where my children's sullen faces awaited me, it turned out that the meat sauce I'd left out to cool was completely gone.

"Ethel!" The cat was still cleaning its whiskers.

I found a jar of tomato sauce in the pantry, and as I was heating it up and boiling the pasta, I asked Audrey and Blake how their day had been.

Blake clamped their mouth shut, and Audrey said, "Oh, fantastic! Everyone wanted to be my friend. I just haven't decided who I want to hang out with." Her blue eyes were glistening suspiciously, betraying her words. My heart broke a little.

"Well, it was only the first day. It's always weird starting somewhere fresh. For me too." I almost told them about the near arrest, but then thought better of it. If they had been in a different mood, they might have laughed about it. I didn't want them to worry.

"Okay, who's hungry?"

We'd just sat down to eat when someone knocked on the door.

"Get started without me," I said to the kids. "I'll get the door."

I silently prayed our guest wasn't DI Farrow, coming to handcuff me in front of my children.

When I opened the door and saw two women instead of Gloucestershire's answer to Poirot, I wasn't sure if I should be relieved.

"Gina? Emerald?" I remembered the names Ellie had told me on Saturday night.

"Liv!" Great-Aunt Gina opened her arms. She had a shaggy mane of dyed-blond hair and wore a similar caftan to the one she'd sported on Saturday. Myriad gemstone necklaces and bracelets added even more sparkle and color.

I awkwardly leaned into the hug. Gina had a pleasant scent—a mix of flowers and herbs. She held on a little too long for my comfort level, so I really got a whiff.

Well, who was I kidding? My comfort level really was zero. I tried to remember Great-Aunt Gina from childhood but totally drew a blank. I also wished my mother, or anyone, really, would have told me I had family in Fairwyck.

Then there was the mysterious fact that they had waited more than a week to come by and introduce themselves…

It suddenly occurred to me they might think I'd been the rude relative, waiting for me to come by and pay them a visit.

"I'm so sorry we're only meeting like this now," I said, after shaking Emerald's hand. "To be honest, I had no idea that you…well, existed." I laughed, and it sounded a little tinny. "I was a little kid when we left here, and I don't remember a lot. Nobody mentioned you. My mother said nothing."

"Oh, don't worry, love," Gina said, waltzing into the cottage and somehow taking up a lot of space for a small woman.

She enthusiastically greeted my children, who were in the awkward position of having spaghetti hanging from their lips while being hugged.

"I didn't live in these parts when you were a child, Liv. I traveled a lot," Gina expounded. "So it's no surprise you don't remember me. Emerald wasn't even born then. I'm only a few years older than your mom, even though I'm her aunt. Later, your mother tried to keep you away from the family. That's why she moved to the US with you."

"Umm, no, she always sent letters and then the newsletter." I felt the need to defend Mom.

"I like what you've done with the place." Gina changed the topic and pointed at the fine art print on the wall. It was the only thing that we'd changed downstairs since moving in, so I wasn't sure if her comment had been ironic, or even acerbic.

"Ummm, anyway, nice to make your acquaintance now. Why don't you have a seat?"

"Thank you." Gina plunked herself down on the sofa. Emerald sat next to her.

I made tea before joining them in the living room area.

"So, Emerald, what do you do?" I asked, putting the mug down in front of the shy but friendly young woman with the honey-colored braid.

"I'm a librarian." Emerald seemed to light up from the inside, much like the gemstone she was named after—a name that had seemed unsuitable for the plain woman until now. "I actually run the local library," she explained proudly. "It's small, with a disproportionately large children's section. But I love it."

"That's so great," I genuinely enthused. "My children love to read, and me too. We'll come by sometime."

"Yes, that's great," Gina interrupted, "but it's not what we've come to talk to you about, dear."

"Oh?" I said, taking a sip of tea. "Is there something specific you wanted to discuss?"

My heart started beating faster, and I wrapped both hands tightly around my mug to stop them from shaking.

I was sure that Gina would say the cottage really belonged to them, that Great-Aunt Ethel had no business bequeathing it to me, since they were the closest relatives. And I was just someone related by blood but who hadn't even known her, who hadn't bothered to come and visit her once in the last thirty-four years.

They would tell me they would contest the will and sue me—and then what would I do? I couldn't even afford a lawyer to get the divorce proceedings started. I wouldn't be able to pay one to battle this out in court with Gina and Emerald.

What would happen next? My kids and I would be without a home, unable to afford plane tickets to the US, stranded in a foreign country, forced to live in the streets…

I worked myself up to such a degree that my ears were ringing.

So at first I thought I'd misheard when Great-Aunt Gina finally came out with the reason for their visit.

I coughed and leaned forward. "Say that again?"

"You're in grave danger, Liv. Something terrible is going to happen to you."

CHAPTER EIGHT

I was tempted to throw Gina and Emerald out.

It had been one hell of a day, and the last things I needed were mysterious, vague threats from hostile relatives.

I got up slowly, trying to control my breathing.

"Listen," I said. "We don't know each other. I'm sorry about that. I would like nothing more than to have family in Fairwyck, to make it easier for us to settle here. Which, let me tell you, has not been going too well. I understand if you don't agree with Ethel's decision to leave the cottage to me, but this is our home, the only home that we have. We need it. You're welcome here anytime, if you would like us to get to know each other. But turning up out of the blue, making threats—"

"Oh, honey, no," Gina interrupted. "You've got this all wrong. You're welcome to the cottage. We don't want it."

"Ethel did the right thing, making you her heir," Emerald reassured me in her quiet voice.

I was stumped. "But…why didn't you introduce yourselves before?"

"We thought you might not be interested in meeting us," Gina said. "You never contacted us."

"I always wanted a cousin," Emerald said and smiled.

"Okay, but…" I was confused. "What about the threat?"

"I wasn't threatening you," Gina said with a chuckle. "I was only warning you."

I blinked. Wasn't that the same thing?

"My mother read your cards," Emerald put in, as if that would explain anything.

"My cards?"

"Yes, honey, tarot cards," Gina said. "That's what I do." She looked at Emerald. "It's worse than I thought."

I sat back down and exhaled slowly. "You read tarot cards and believe that one of them suggested I might be in danger? Okay, got it."

My great-aunt's outfit and general appearance suddenly made sense. She was one of those New-Age people who believed in crystals and oils and, apparently, tarot cards. She wasn't dangerous, just kooky.

I'd clearly overreacted. "Sorry. I don't know why, but Mom never mentioned you."

"Clairvoyance is my mother's special gift," Emerald put in. "You know, like all of the Seven women have special gifts?"

"Sure. Mine is eating a whole large pizza by myself." I laughed, suddenly feeling in a silly mood after the day I'd had and having misread the situation with my relatives. "What's your special gift, Emerald?"

My cousin appeared alarmed instead of amused. She turned to Gina. "Could it be that she doesn't know?"

"Told you. Calista has always feared our abilities. She pretended they didn't exist. And that's why she moved away with you, Liv. She wanted to keep all of this from you."

"Yes, but how is that even possible?" Emerald wondered out loud. "Liv's special gift would have made itself known to her, no matter where in the world they were or what her mother did."

"It's easy to repress things, not see what you don't want to see. Humans are very good at that."

Emerald shook her head. "Still, I couldn't imagine pretending I couldn't hear the books."

Gina laughed. "There are plenty of people who are taking pills for that. With the right drugs in your system, you can shut yourself off from anything. For a time. It'll wear you down eventually, but still…" She eyed me. "Does your mother have you on any kind of medication?"

I drew my brows together. "I'm a grown woman. My mother has very little influence over me at this point in my life, and she's never force-fed me pills, no. Um, this is all very interesting, but I was about to have dinner with my kids. So maybe we can continue this conversation another time?"

I made a move to get up, but my children—apparently done with their pasta—had snuck up on us and were sitting cross-legged on the living room floor, gawking at our relatives.

"I'd like to know more about these special abilities that run in our family," Blake said.

Gina smiled at them. "Sure, but you strike me as the kind of sensitive person who already knows what I'm talking about."

Blake turned bright red, and I had to wonder what else I didn't know about them.

"What do I have?" Audrey asked excitedly, sounding like a little kid for the first time in a long while.

I leaned back in my chair. What was the harm in Gina and Emerald telling a few amusing stories about tarot cards and Wiccan spells, or whatnot?

"You'll find out, love," Gina said. "But I have a feeling that it has something to do with animals." She winked at Audrey.

My youngest looked thoughtful. I didn't think she was particularly interested in animals, not like most kids who were forever asking their family for pets. Gina had probably thought it would be a good guess for someone Audrey's age, bless her.

"So, Gina, your special…um, gift is clairvoyance?" I picked up my tea from the side table and took a sip.

"That's right, similar to your mother."

My mom was a no-nonsense person who'd never had time for woo-woo-type stuff, but I didn't argue. I was really just making conversation for my children's sake. "And you read tarot cards?"

"That's my preferred method, yes."

"And you, Emerald?"

"Books talk to me."

"Sure." I didn't say that most people would call that reading. It was oddly relaxing to talk nonsense, because, lately, everything had felt heavy.

"Clearly, there's so much we need to talk about, but what's most important right now is what the cards told me about you, Liv," Gina said.

"I thought you weren't supposed to draw cards for someone else?" Blake asked.

"That's right." Gina gave Blake a brilliant smile, as if they were a star student. "I was reading my own cards when something disconcerting came up." Her blue eyes became cloudy, fading to a dark gray.

"Is there a card with my name on it?" I joked, trying to hang on to the lightheartedness.

Gina stayed serious. "No, of course not. But I got the impression that the card stood for close female relatives, and I immediately thought of you, Liv."

"We're not close, though," I couldn't help but object. "You're my mother's aunt, and we hardly know each other."

"You're the closest female relatives I have around."

"Except for Emerald." I strained to produce a smile.

"Oh, believe me, I would know if this card pertained to my daughter."

"Could it be about…Audrey or Blake?"

"Not me," Blake quipped. "Not female."

"Am I in danger?" Audrey squeaked.

I immediately regretted mentioning my kids. "Of course not, sweetheart. I'll bet nobody is in danger. Tarot is just some silly game."

Emerald looked as if she wanted to object, but Gina put a hand on her arm to stop her.

"My intuition is usually right," Gina said. "I had the distinct impression the card was about you."

"Okay, you're the expert. What card was it?" I tried to recall the little information I had gained about tarot cards from movies, TV series, and books. "I hope not…Death."

"Death would be a card I'd expect to see in your situation," Gina said. "It symbolizes the ending of a major phase or an aspect of your life. You're just starting over after a few things ended in a major way. It's a card that signifies renewal and transformation. If you were to draw your own cards, there'd be a good chance Death would come up."

"Five of Pentacles could also be one," Emerald piped up.

"Absolutely. Material misfortunes, loss of funds, unemployment, solitude, poverty," Gina listed.

"Gee, thanks." I grumbled. I was glad there wasn't a tarot deck around to rub it in.

"Three of Swords could be another one. You've been betrayed, you're lonely, your heart has been broken…"

"Okay, okay," I stopped Gina. "What card *did* I get?"

"Yes, you're quite right, it won't do to speculate," Gina agreed. "The thing to remember is that one card, and its general meaning, isn't going to say much. We need to interpret it, and that depends on the individual and how the cards are in relation to each other."

I imagined that interpretation was key—the reason most people thought such readings were accurate.

"So one card that related to you, I think, was the Tower. It just means that coming here is going to shake up your world. Your world view is going to change, in a very literal sense. I think this is about your gift. It'll make itself known. This time, you won't be able to ignore it. And it'll change your world, more so than what has already happened with your husband."

"Yes, true, my world could not be any more shaken right now."

"But then we also had the Five of Swords, the Ten of Swords, and the Devil," Gina said. "I mean, that's violence, hate, death, facing your enemy. That's not good, Liv." She looked at me sternly, as if it was my fault.

"No, it doesn't sound good. A lot of swords and the devil. Who wants that? Not me, thank you very much."

"Exactly," Gina said.

Emerald exhaled in relief. "We're so glad you understand. We weren't sure, you know, with your mother and everything, how open you'd be to our warning."

Blake had been typing away furiously on their phone. "Oh my god, Mom," they said, then jumped up and came over to my armchair. "Look how brutal." I saw fear in their big sherry-colored eyes.

I looked at the screen. The tarot card with the man prone on the floor, ten swords stabbed in his back, was not a pretty sight, I agreed. But I downplayed my shock.

"Don't worry, honey. Like Gina said, these cards are

open to interpretation. They're not meant to be taken literally. It's not like someone is actually going to stab me with a ton of broadswords, right?"

My tone was pointed and my smile a little forced when I looked at my relatives opposite me on the sofa.

They did not get my message.

"Wellll…" Gina began. "Maybe there *will* be brutal violence, considering the other cards. I mean, when you take this card together with the—"

"Okay," I said and got up. "Thank you so much for your visit. And the warning, of course."

When Gina and Emerald didn't get up right away but only looked at each other with a mix of confusion and disappointment, I said, "We've had a hell of day and could all do with an early night. Next time, call, and we can have dinner together. How does that sound?"

Mentally I added: It doesn't sound good to me, and if I can find an excuse to get out of it, I'll use it.

They still didn't get up.

"Kids, can you say goodbye to Gina and Emerald and then get started tidying the kitchen? I'll escort our guests to the door."

My children, bless them, did as they were told without rolling their eyes.

Emerald stood and made not-so-subtle signs at Gina, who took her sweet time making her way to the door. I almost pushed them out, followed them, and closed the door behind me.

"What gives you the right to just come here and spew this nonsense—"

"Oh dearie me," Gina said and turned to Emerald. "I told you her mother poisoned her."

"My mother did nothing of the sort," I whisper-shouted angrily. "She has nothing to do with this!"

Emerald put a hand on my arm. "Listen, Liv, I know this sounds scary, and you might—"

I shook off her hand. "This isn't about me. You scared my children with your violence and hatred and so on, and those graphic depictions. They've been through enough. They don't need to be traumatized by this. Now you've planted the seed in their heads that something will happen to me. I'm the only one they have after what my husband did." Tears sprang to my eyes, and I furiously blinked them away.

Gina and Emerald seemed a little sheepish. "We didn't think of that, Liv. We're sorry," Emerald said.

"Yes, but even so, wouldn't you rather know someone or something is coming for you?" Gina insisted. "Even though it's scary, you'd want the warning and the truth, right? Isn't closing your eyes to something like that what got you into this mess?"

"You make it sound like it's my fault, and I don't appreciate that," I said in an icy voice. "But yes, I would rather know the truth. If we were talking about facts. If you knew something concrete, I'd want you to tell me—not my children, mind you—so I can deal with it. But what you're doing is superstitious fear-mongering."

"No, but—" Emerald tried to interject.

Gina stopped her. "I'm sorry you see it that way. It was nice meeting you."

She took her daughter by the arm, who was a little more reticent to leave. "You know how it is, love. You can't force anyone to—"

I didn't hear the rest, as I was already back in the cottage.

I helped the kids in the kitchen and talked about other things, trying to get their minds off the tarot cards. When Audrey was in bed and Blake in their room, I sat in the living room, staring at the phone.

I wanted to call my mother and ask her about Gina and this ESP thing running in our family. When my relatives had been sitting here on the couch, I had been adamant that they were talking nonsense. I had defended my mother.

But now I wasn't so sure. There were things in my childhood that had scared me, and my mother had protected me from them, that much I knew. She had done a very good job at keeping those old demons at bay, and I had always appreciated that.

My husband's actions and everything that had happened after had made me change my mind about repressing unpleasant truths. I now knew that they had a way of coming back with a vengeance. Gina was right, I'd rather be in the know. But was I just telling myself that? Old habits die hard. Evidently, I still wasn't ready to confront some things.

Blake saved me from fretting any longer about it.

They came down the stairs, their phone in their hand. "Mom, didn't Gina and Emerald talk about the Tower card? Look. How horrible!"

On the phone screen, there was a depiction of a medieval tower. Lightning was striking the top, and stones were crumbling. People were jumping down, escaping the horrors up top, just to plunge to their deaths. Their faces showed pure agony.

I shuddered.

"The image is horrifying, but didn't Gina say that this card meant something good? Like, we already have this disaster behind us, and we're starting anew."

Blake looked at me skeptically. "Do these people look like they'll get a chance for a new beginning? Even if they survive, they'll be traumatized for life."

My heart broke a little. I carefully put my arm around

my child and waited to gauge their reaction. Blake leaned in, and I properly took them into my arms like I had done when they were a little girl. It seemed like yesterday. When our world had still been whole, and we hadn't even known how precious everything was.

At that time, Steven had already been putting his Ponzi scheme in motion. But the fact that our happy life together had merely been an illusion would never change how I felt back then. Saved, loved, blessed.

I honestly couldn't say if I'd go back in time to take all of those memories away from Blake and Audrey, to ruin my children's childhoods, just for the sake of facing the truth. Because the truth was intensely painful, and I was okay with the fact that it hurt me. My kids, however, were a different story.

In that way, I could understand what my mother had done. In some ways, I was probably more like her than I'd ever care to admit.

"Promise me you won't obsess over this tarot thing, okay?"

Blake tilted their head. "I just find the cards fascinating. Especially the drawings."

They were a talented artist and loved to draw.

"I get that. I'm not saying you can't look at the illustrations. But what Gina said about them… We've already gone through so much. We don't even know Gina and Emerald. I don't believe they're in a position where they could get a good reading on us, if you know what I mean? And even if there's something to it, if these cards really predict awful things to come… Unfortunately, you know better than most kids your age that there are bad things in the world. Sometimes we encounter them. All we can do is deal with them to the best of our abilities as they come up. Maybe it's better not to know these things in advance, because if we were worried about everything that might go wrong, we couldn't live our lives, could we? I'd like to keep a bit of optimism that our new lives here will be okay."

"Yes, I'd like that too." Blake was quiet for a moment, then they slipped out from under my embrace to look at me. "So, Mom, you really don't know what Gina and Emerald were talking about when they mentioned the special gifts that run in our family?"

"No," I said, a little too quickly. "I mean, you know your grandmother. Does she strike you as someone who would wield some secret paranormal powers?"

That made Blake giggle. "No." They got serious again, looked down, and played with a loose thread in their pajama pants. "But…what powers could they be talking about, do you think?"

"I'm not sure. Clairvoyance. I don't know, maybe something else ESP, like telekinesis. Or dreams that come true. Something like that?"

"Ah." They seemed a little relieved. "Okay."

"It's past your bedtime, sweetheart," I reminded them. "Why don't you turn in?"

"Yes, I will. Good night."

"'Night."

I waited until the stairs stopped creaking. Then I went to the kitchen and grabbed the camera from the shelf.

I couldn't claim that I had forgotten about the photos I took in Matilda's house, but I had certainly been busy enough to put them out of my mind.

After the conversations with my relatives and Blake, I could no longer put off looking at what had appeared in the pictures.

I booted up my laptop and inserted the camera's SD card to download the images.

My heart was going a mile a minute when I finally clicked on the last one.

With the photo blown up to the size of my laptop screen, there was no mistaking what or who had been in Matilda's kitchen as I was taking the picture.

Bile rose in my throat when I realized that everything Gina and Emerald had said was true.

CHAPTER NINE

The entity in the photo was Matilda Rutherford.

She was a little blurry compared to the sharp outlines of the rest of the kitchen—the old-fashioned AGA cooker, the sink, the laminate countertop, the tiles with the Moroccan design.

I couldn't make out her facial expression. But I definitely recognized the chestnut beehive, the cat's-eye glasses, the thin lips painted coral. The sensible oatmeal-colored skirt with a matching blouse might have even been the same outfit she had worn on the day of her visit.

There was no doubt—I had somehow captured my neighbor's ghost on camera.

She had been right there, in the kitchen, directly in front of me.

It should have spooked me. Instead, I was freaked out by something else.

I'd never seen an actual dead person I recognized in my photos before, but this wasn't the first time I'd captured an otherworldly entity.

There had been blurs, smudges, and weird shadows in

my pictures for as long as I could remember. Only that wasn't saying a lot, because I couldn't recall much.

I had been in love with photography from a young age. There were kids who collected stickers or cards, others who were mad about bugs, some who ran around in a tutu all day long practicing pirouettes. My childhood obsession had been photography.

Someone gave me a camera for my sixth birthday. I was forever taking pictures with that thing, it seemed like; but in reality, probably not so much. It wasn't like today, where people take a thousand photos a minute with digital cameras and smartphones. That camera was analog, a simple press-and-click Nikon with thirty-odd pictures on the film roll. We had to take it to the shop to have it developed. Sometimes we'd leave it for ages, and I forgot what pictures I had taken, making me even more excited to get the photographs back.

I'd cherished that feeling of opening the thick envelope —it was like coming downstairs on Christmas morning.

At first, everyone was proud of me. I was their talented little photographer. But after a while, my pictures didn't come out right. They had blemishes. Something I hadn't noticed when I had taken the picture.

"Make sure your thumb isn't in front of the lens," my mother would say. Or "Keep the lens clean."

I was little, so I rarely had the patience or sometimes even the words to reason with her, but I was sure I had done everything right when taking the pictures. At some point, after paying a lot of money to develop all the photographs, my mother became convinced that there had to be something in the camera—a speck of dust or dirt— that caused the smudges and blurs in my photos. She took the camera away from me.

I cried often after that, missing my camera like a limb.

Some relative—maybe even Great-Aunt Ethel—took pity on me and gave me a new camera for Christmas when I was eight. Even though my mother said nothing, I had the distinct impression that she was furious about it. In fact, she hardly spoke a word that Christmas, and the tension was palpable. Adults always think children don't notice what's going on, but of course they do. Since I knew it was somehow all my fault, the guilt I felt almost overshadowed my joy about the present.

I carefully took pictures when my mother wasn't looking and soon had a full film roll. My mom wouldn't have taken the film to get it developed, so I took money out of my piggy bank. I hid the pictures under the floorboards in my room. Not all of them had blemishes, but some did. If I squinted, they sometimes looked like people. I tried to not do that. But I took my photos out at night to study them. After a while, I got a feeling for composition and got rather good at being a photographer.

I got another feeling too—something that didn't have to do with the technical aspects of photography, but more with what was in them. It almost felt like I was compelled to take a picture sometimes, as if motives were choosing me, not the other way around. It was exhilarating and scary at the same time.

Pretty soon, all my photos had what I'd called entities in them. And one day, the thing I saw in one of my pictures scared me so much that I screamed.

Earlier, I had run to the shop after school to pick up my envelope. I'd stuffed it in my schoolbag without looking at the pictures because I'd had to rush home. That night, in bed, I had finally looked at them.

Instead of a blemish, a shape, or a vaguely human blur, there was an actual person in my photo. An irate old lady with the sort of piercing blue eyes that looked right into your soul. Her mouth was twisted in an angry snarl.

Worst of all, I was a hundred percent certain that the old woman hadn't been there when I had taken the picture. Nobody had been there but me.

It was a photo of my bedroom, taken from almost exactly the same vantage point I had now, sitting on my bed.

I stared at the empty air at the foot of my bed, then again at the photograph. That scary woman could be there, in that spot, right now, could have always been there, watching me with that hateful glare, while I was blithely unaware and felt safe by myself.

I was so petrified I couldn't move a muscle.

My mother must have heard my scream, and she came rushing into my room. Eventually she roused me from my near-catatonic state, but all I could do was shake and cry and mutter, "She's watching me."

Mom might not have understood what I was trying to say, but she found the picture on my bed. And then she found all the other photos under the floorboards with blurred and shadowy things in them.

Dead things.

Dead things that were all around me, apparently, but that nobody else could perceive. Only I could capture them with my camera.

My mother moved with me to the United States the next day. At least that's what my memory tells me, even though it couldn't have happened quite that quickly in reality. That's what it felt like, though. Friends and family, everyone and everything I had taken for granted, like children do, were suddenly far away. Even though my mother diligently kept up with letters—and later set up a monthly family newsletter—we never came back to the UK to visit.

As much of a shock as the sudden move had been, I assimilated. My mother fell in love with and married a wealthy dentist, and we had the kind of life where we could buy anything we wanted. We never bought a camera again, though. In the US, I was a different kind of Liv, a Liv who wasn't a photographer. Not taking pictures hadn't even been a big deal until smartphones became ubiquitous.

I'd somehow avoided taking pictures with my phone camera too, claiming not to be a "selfie person." I probably had fewer pictures of my children than most people, but I had always made sure we had portraits taken or asked for copies of other people's pics from parties and get-togethers, so there were still plenty.

At some point, my phobia of taking photographs became a trait of my mine in its own right, divorced from the root cause. I hadn't completely forgotten about those scary pictures from my childhood, but my talent for burying unpleasant stuff deep in my subconscious helped. I hadn't even noticed that it meant I'd repressed a lot of my childhood along with it.

For so long, that had seemed a small price to pay. Now that I was at an age where I could see that half my life had run like sand through my fingers, I wasn't so sure about that anymore.

I picked up the phone and dialed my mother's number.

"Nice to hear from you, Liv. I was wondering when you'd call."

"It has been a crazy few days, Mom. The girls started school today..." I saw absolutely no reason to tell her about the uniforms because something like that would never happen to her. And then I remembered it was wrong of me to say "the girls." How on earth would I explain to my mother that Bianca was Blake now? I wasn't ready to tackle that yet.

"Liv? Are you still there?"

"Yes, yes. Sorry. I'm tired. I've started my cleaning job, which has been absolutely exhausting, and today I had to clean my neighbor's house. A friend of Great-Aunt Ethel's. You probably know her, Matilda Rutherford?"

"Ah, yes."

"She came by last week and introduced herself. Nice lady. So it turns out, she passed away on Saturday night. And today I had to clean her home." I stopped because I noticed I was rambling. I didn't know how to tell my mom what I wanted to tell her.

"Okay. Well, I'm sorry to hear about Mrs. Rutherford."

I waited a beat. But she didn't comment on the fact that a recently departed neighbor could particularly be a problem for me.

"Then we had unexpected visitors this evening. Gina and Emerald."

"I see. How's Gina doing?"

"She seemed fine. Rather eccentric, but I guess that's normal?"

"Oh that. Yes."

"Mom! You never told me I had another great-aunt. Did you even know about her daughter? That they live here?"

"Of course. I've kept up correspondence with our family; you know that. I'm perfectly aware that Gina has a daughter named Emerald. Librarian, isn't she?"

Her calm and collected responses made me feel like pulling my hair out. "So why didn't you tell me?"

"Didn't I? I'm sure I would have mentioned—"

"Don't you think it would have been nice for us to get a family welcome in a country we know nothing about?"

"Now you're exaggerating, dear. It is not like you're a stranger in Fairwyck. You grew up there."

"I was eight. I remember little. And Gina said that she wasn't around when I was younger. I wouldn't even have been able to recall her. I just think it would have been nice—"

"I don't see why you make it sound like it's my responsibility. I've always attempted to stay in touch, and you could have done the same."

I pinched the bridge of my nose. "But you didn't tell me…" I stopped myself. There was no point. This conversation would just go around in circles. I tried a different tactic. Something I had become an expert at avoiding, especially with my mom.

Direct confrontation.

"I thought maybe you didn't want me to get to know Gina and Emerald because you were a bit, I don't know, embarrassed about them? Their…worldview is a little different from yours."

"Is it?"

"Yes. I don't know what Aunt Gina was like when you were younger, but now she comes across as very woo-woo. Emerald too. Gina reads tarot cards, and she came here specifically to warn me because the cards told her something about me. I'm in grave danger, apparently."

"Oh, she's still doing that? How tedious. I do remember her going on about things like that when we were younger. Before she went traveling after graduation, and I was only what…fourteen. After that, I didn't see much of her. She's my aunt, but just a few years older than me, remember? There's this big age gap between your grandmother and Aunt Ethel, and another six years between Ethel and Gina—"

I interrupted her babbling. "They told me it ran in our family."

My mother was suspiciously quiet. She didn't ask what I meant.

"They claimed that it's in our blood, passed down to female relatives."

My mother sighed.

"Mom?"

"Yes, yes, there's something like that."

"Like ESP? A talent for clairvoyance, telekinesis, telepathy?"

"I suppose so."

"Do you have a talent like that?"

"Of course not." She said it as if I'd asked her if she had lice.

"But I do?" I closed my eyes and held my breath.

"I don't know, darling, do you?"

"Mom!"

"What? You're forty-two years old. You would know by now if you had any propensity for…that."

She had a point. I still wished she would tell me, though.

"Gina said that you didn't want to know about any of this, that you suppressed your…gift…and mine too."

"She would say that. Gina was always very gung-ho about it. She couldn't understand that some Seven women just want to lead normal lives. Like you and me."

I felt like I hadn't been given much of a choice, but I didn't say that.

I was a mother too, and I knew the urge to protect my children all too well. If my kids started seeing ghosts in their photos, I don't know what I'd do. I would go to some lengths so they'd feel less scared, to be sure.

I had my doubts that pretending none of this existed was the right strategy, but I'd used a similar tactic to pretend our fairytale life was still intact for many years. My mother might have modeled this unhealthy behavior for me. Even so, it meant I wasn't in a position to throw stones.

I must have been quiet for a longer than I'd realized, because my mother started talking in a tone that I didn't quite recognize.

"Look, of course I feared that something like this would happen upon your return to England. I've kept you at arm's length from your relatives…an ocean's length, if you will…just to keep you from that nonsense. And I knew if I reconnected properly with Aunt Ethel, asked her to put you in her will, and you went back there… Let's say I knew the trade-off would be that you might learn about this family affliction of ours. But you needed help, and Aunt Ethel was more than willing to give it. I had nobody else to turn to. This was all I could do for you. I admit I might have refrained from getting you and Gina together, hoping you would be spared finding out about it a little longer."

I was speechless. That was some admission. "So…what exactly is this family affliction?"

"Well, like you said. ESP. Supernatural abilities, if you want to call it that. There have been stories passed along about the women in our family. Ancient stories. Mostly legends, I'd imagine. I don't really know much about it. And remember that Gina might make too much of this. I wouldn't believe everything she says. She always had a flair for aggrandizement."

"What kind of ability did Aunt Ethel have?"

"I really don't know, darling. And I've got to go now. My program comes on in a minute."

"Okay. Well, maybe we can—"

"Nice to talk to you. Give my grandchildren a kiss. Bye now."

I'd wanted to ask her about DI Farrow, but she was adamant about ending the call. "Bye, Mom."

I held the phone in my hand for a little while longer, staring into the deep pit of the cold fireplace.

I was so tired, my brain refused to make sense of all the information I'd gotten today, all the old memories that had resurfaced.

I rubbed my face. Going to bed was my only recourse for the time being. The only problem was that sleep wouldn't come.

I just lay in my bed, staring at the dark ceiling beams.

It was ridiculous, but I was suddenly wide awake.

There was only one thing to do.

I got up, pulled on a cardigan over my PJs, and went downstairs to fetch the camera.

I needed to return to the cottage next door and take more pictures of Matilda's ghost.

CHAPTER TEN

"Mom? Mom!"

"Go away," I mumbled and swatted at whoever was trying to get me to open my eyes. I couldn't have fallen asleep longer than a minute ago.

"Mom, wake up!" Blake's voice sounded urgent, so I did my best to crawl out of the dark pit of blissful unconsciousness.

I pried my eyes open just a slit. "Something wrong?"

"Mom, you overslept. We have to get ready for school."

"Hmm?" I blinked and tried to locate my alarm clock. There it was. Oh no.

I scrambled out of bed, shoving my matted dark hair out of my face. Where was the way to the bathroom again? Knocking my head against one of those bloody low ceiling beams, I stopped in my tracks and put my hand on the sore spot. "Ouch."

"Don't you have to go to work, Mom?"

"Yes! Blake, get some cereal and milk for the three of us, will you? And do you know how the coffee machine works?"

"Will you be mad if I say yes? And if I make coffee, can I have some too?"

I sighed. "All right. I'll be down in a minute."

After splashing water in my face, pulling my hair into a ponytail, and throwing on jeans and a T-shirt, I grabbed socks and rushed downstairs.

Audrey and Blake were already eating breakfast, and the coffee was ready. "I'm so sorry. You'll have to take the bus today."

Audrey looked as if she was about to cry. "Buses are disgusting and have millions of germs from all the dirty people."

"Honey, it's a school bus. Most kids around here take the bus to school. Remember, we talked about that?"

Audrey pulled a face. "I thought you were trying to scare us. You know, a consequence for misbehavior. Go to your room without dinner. Ride the bus to school. That kind of thing."

"Taking the bus to school is normal, not a punishment," I said, my mouth full of cereal, while pulling on my socks. "I wanted to drive you the first couple of days, but that's just not possible today."

"Mom, what about the school uniforms?" Blake sounded anxious.

"I'd rather wear my own clothes," Audrey said. "The uniforms look really unflattering, and everyone loves my style."

Blake gave their little sister a pitying smile.

"I know, I'm sorry. The shop was closed yesterday. I'll pick you up from school today, and we'll get the uniforms. Promise!"

"Can you let the school know, please?" Blake said. "One teacher tried to give me points for detention—"

"On your first day?" I was outraged. "That's not fair.

It's my fault. I'll call the principal." I gulped down a large sip of coffee. "Okay, go, or you'll miss the bus."

"I haven't brushed my teeth," Audrey said.

"Hang on." I found my purse, rummaged around until I found sugar-free chewing gum, and handed it to her. "You'd better hurry. Love you. Bye!"

When the kids were out the door, I put the dirty dishes in the sink and poured the rest of the coffee into a thermos.

I double checked the location of the cottage I was supposed to clean today on the village map I had pinned to the fridge. It wasn't that far, but because I was running late, I took the car.

The cottage had a key safe outside the door, like most of the WLA properties. After I'd let myself in, I called the school principal about the uniforms. "We'll try to get them today," I promised.

"All right, but it would be in your children's interests to dress like everyone else as soon as possible," the principal advised. "I understand neither of them is having the easiest time fitting in, and it might help if—"

"What do you mean?" I interrupted the woman.

"They are a little different—"

"Umm, yes, Bianca wanting to be called Blake is new to me too. I might have chosen a different school for them, although this is the closest one. Blake has been through a lot, and I don't know if this is a reaction to everything that has happened, like a temporary identity crisis, or not. I just think it's important to stay open and supportive—"

"Of course, of course. We are an inclusive school. We want to support Blake, and the other students certainly seem to do that."

"Oh, so there's no bullying going on or anything like that?" I was a little relieved, because I had to admit I'd been worried about that.

"No, quite the opposite, I'm afraid."

"What?"

"Well, it seems Blake has become somewhat of an inspiration. We are experiencing an epidemic of name and gender changes… We like to be open, but it's getting a little confusing for the teachers—"

"If Blake is a role model for others, that's fantastic, isn't it?"

"Not all the other teachers think so, I'm afraid… ummm… And then I don't think Blake is comfortable with the role of a leader."

"That might be true. I'll talk to them."

"Okay. I'm more worried about Audrey, though."

"Really? She told me she's made a lot of new friends."

"Audrey clearly feels our school is a few steps down from her previous one, and she is letting everyone know that, including the teachers. She's been bragging about her wealthy upbringing, and this has led other students to… let's say fact-check her claims. It didn't take long for them to find out about Audrey's father…and now there's a rumor going around that Mr. Grantham is a mob shark at large."

"Oh my god. No, no, his criminal activities have nothing to do with the mob…" I sank down onto a chair by the kitchen table.

"I believe uniforms would help them blend in better. Help calm things down."

"I understand. We'll get the uniforms after work today. Speaking of my job, I really have to go now. Thank you and goodbye."

I hung up, then sat there, slumped on the chair.

The new information about my children's problems at school swirled together with my other concerns in my exhausted brain.

Being a single mom, starting over, and making ends

meet was hard. It felt like I wasn't very good at this juggling act, where all the balls were made of glass, so precarious that I couldn't drop anything. It was difficult enough, so I needed to stay on top of my game.

Being up all night staring at pictures of my neighbor's ghost clearly wasn't the best way to spend my precious resting hours.

Yes, DI Farrow had it in for me, and he considered me a suspect in Matilda's murder, but did I actually need to be worried about it? I was innocent; I had an alibi, and justice surely would prevail.

It wasn't my job to figure out who the killer was. If I was skeptical about Farrow's ability as an investigating officer, there was always DS Rees, who seemed like a reasonable and smart man.

I should just keep my nose out of the investigation and worry about my own problems, of which there clearly were many. I didn't need to add finding Matilda's actual killer to my overflowing plate.

On the other hand, having the unique ability to photograph ghosts was kind of hard to ignore. Last night, I'd felt compelled to go to the cottage next door, to find out what it meant.

There was a possibility my ghost photos were imprints of the past. Maybe that old woman in my childhood bedroom hadn't been watching me at all. Perhaps I hadn't photographed a ghost but somehow captured someone from the past on celluloid.

All my life I'd been scared of the other interpretation, that we were all constantly surrounded by dead people and that my pictures were photographic evidence of that. If that were true, I had to contemplate how *aware* those ghosts were.

Had the scary old woman really stared at me with vitriol? Had she known about my ability to sense her?

If so, what was Matilda's ghost capable of? There was a small possibility my dead neighbor could remember her killer and I could communicate with her in some way, getting her to pass on this vital piece of information.

Last night, it had seemed probable. In the wee hours of the night, I'd believed in the gifts of the Seven women, in their paranormal powers. It had made sense to me that I'd have a unique ability for a purpose, and what else could the purpose be than helping the ghosts I could see in my very own special way?

Something that had merely scared the heck out of me until now had become a gift. I could not run away from it, if there was even the slightest chance Matilda's killer could be brought to justice.

As silly as it felt now, in stark daylight, I'd spoken to Matilda in her cottage, asked her ghost to remember her killer and reveal their identity to me. I'd explained to her I could see her with my camera and invited her to communicate with me through those pictures. Then I'd just snapped away in the cottage, moving from room to room.

Matilda's ghost was in all of my photos, pointing at cushions and wall art. Pointing at words, literally giving me a message.

I'd felt exhilarated until I'd tried to decipher that message at home. To my frustration, it wasn't clear what words Matilda pointed at exactly, and every time I blew up the photo to zoom in, it became too blurry to read.

I'd stared at the pixelated images until my eyes hurt. At some point, I'd given up and gone to sleep.

I didn't want to ignore Matilda and give up on her. Clearly, my great-aunt had left me the camera because she'd believed in my gift. It had to be the vocation she'd mentioned in her note. And I'd come to England with the intention of never hiding my head in the sand again. I couldn't in all good conscience squeeze my eyes shut and pretend I didn't have the ability to look beyond the veil any longer. Especially if it meant helping my neighbor—and getting DI Farrow off my back.

But it was something else I had to take on, and right now I didn't feel physically able to bear it. I had the very real feeling of crumbling under all the weight on my shoulders.

Nonetheless, I got up from that chair, dragged myself to the counter where I'd put my bag down, and got my thermos out.

I couldn't do anything for Matilda right now. I was on the clock, and without this job, we wouldn't survive. That was priority number one, and everything else just had to fall in line.

So for the next couple of hours I'd focus on cleaning this cottage. Then I'd pick up the kids and get those bloody uniforms. I'd feed my children dinner and talk to them about how they were doing at school.

If I had any bandwidth left, I'd worry about Matilda's murder then. One thing at a time. That was the only way I could function right now. That and coffee.

I drained my thermos and got to work.

Thanks to my focus-on-the-most-immediate-priority method, I managed to stay sane that morning. It felt a little like I was a coffee-fueled automaton, going through the motions, but it worked.

Things started to look up at lunchtime. I grabbed a sandwich from the village shop, and on my way out I ran into DS Rees, or Jamie, as he'd insisted I call him. He had a late shift that day and was also picking up a sandwich and a soda from the shop before driving to Cirencester, where the police station was.

He'd suggested we take a walk together, enjoying the unusually sunny May day. It was a very pleasant half hour, during which I learned that Jamie was separated from his wife, who'd changed her mind about wanting children and went traveling to Australia.

"This was three years ago." Jamie laughed. "She hasn't returned to the UK yet, but at some point she should, so we can sort out the divorce."

"You don't seem too broken up about the whole thing—if you don't mind me saying."

Jamie shrugged. "I was at first. I really wanted a family. But she wasn't the one. I should have realized that sooner. Now I'm actually glad it turned out this way."

"I know a little something about that." I told Jamie about my husband, but kept it brief. I was having far too much of a good time, and Steven had already ruined enough of my life.

We walked across a bridge to the other side of the little brook on the edge of Fairwyck and strolled back to where I'd parked my car close to the village shop. I could have spent another hour with Jamie, but I had to get back to work.

I was in a much better mood and did my afternoon cleaning tasks with fresh energy.

But the best thing about the day was that I had what I thought were really good chats with my children about their problems at school. For the first time, I felt like I could maybe handle this single-mom thing.

When I went to bed that night, I was completely exhausted and thought I'd fall asleep immediately. Instead, my thoughts returned to Matilda.

Pondering her message brought me wide awake again. Sighing, I got back up. I knew how it was going to go, and there was no point in dragging it out.

I went downstairs and plugged in the small printer I had purchased on sale in the department store in Cirencester, where we'd finally gotten the school uniforms that afternoon.

I printed out the pictures I'd snapped last night. My plan was to take them to the cottage next door, hold the photographs up next to the relevant cushion or wall art, and hopefully identify the right words, so I could get Matilda's message.

Much like the night before, my heart pounded when I let myself into the cottage under the cover of darkness. As far as I knew, I was still DI Farrow's prime suspect, and he had already found me at the scene of the crime once. However unlikely it was that he'd turn up here this late in the evening, I would be hard pressed to find an excuse for being caught in Matilda's house again.

Yesterday, I'd been fueled by a mix of fear and adrenaline at the thought of figuring out what it meant that ghosts showed up in my photographs. That had been heightened when Matilda had seemed willing and able to communicate with me. I'd been in and out of the house in a quarter of an hour, snapping away furiously, then rushed home to decode the message.

Tonight I was thinking a little more clearly. I also worried it would take me a while to figure out what Matilda wanted to tell me.

Then I remembered that my cleaning products were still in the kitchen—unless DI Farrow had confiscated them… No, they were still there. I gathered them and put them on the kitchen table. It would be a poor excuse for breaking and entering, but it was better than nothing.

I pulled the printed pictures out of my tote bag. Looking at the image of the tall, slim woman with the beehive reminded me that Matilda most likely was here now too, even though I couldn't see her with the naked eye.

The atmosphere in the cottage shifted. I shivered.

"Hi, Matilda," I said hoarsely. I felt self-conscious, but not acknowledging her presence seemed even more wrong.

I felt the urge to take pictures, just to reassure myself where Matilda was. My neighbor seemed to welcome me here, but still. Her ghost could be breathing down my neck right now, or I could walk right through her. That thought freaked me out a little.

I'd left the camera at home, though. So I shook off the feeling and got started.

It wasn't that easy to identify the words Matilda had pointed at, so I borrowed a pen from the kitchen to jot down a couple of possibilities. I figured I might be able to puzzle the different options out until I came up with the most likely message. Looking at the digital photos on my laptop would help as well, because I'd saved them in order. In my hurry, I had messed up the printouts, so everything was a bit pell-mell.

There was an embroidered cushion with the crude image of a bird—possibly a dove—and what I assumed to be roses. The embroidered Bible verse said *Seek first the Kingdom of God*, and I was pretty sure that Matilda had pointed at the word *seek*. This was definitely the first picture I'd taken.

Then Matilda had shown me a lino print—possibly from the same local artist we'd bought ours from—that said *Stay close to people who feel like sunshine*. I was pretty sure Matilda's finger pointed at the word *close*.

Less clear to me was what word Matilda had wanted me to use from the wall art that said *Let your smile change the world, but don't let the world change your smile*. *World*? Or *change*?

I noted both words on the printout, then went into the kitchen. There was a wooden painted sign next to the fridge that said *Live Love Laugh*, and I was almost certain that Matilda indicated that the word *love* was the important one.

I was just jotting that word down when I heard a noise.

I froze.

There was someone at the front door.

Panicked, I threw pen and printouts into the tote bag that hung off my shoulder. I quickly grabbed one of my cleaning products and stuck it in the bag too. I had just picked up my glass cleaner when a stylish young woman entered the kitchen.

"What are you doing here?"

CHAPTER ELEVEN

The young woman in the kitchen looked out of place.

Her spice-orange cashmere sweater and matching knit skirt exuded class. I was struck by a pang of envy when I recognized the designer as Gabriela Hearst. The feeling was gone quickly, just a burst of nostalgic longing for my former life, where I might have worn something exactly like it on an ordinary Tuesday night.

I didn't really have any regrets about having sold all my designer clothes. In fact, I might have owned the same Ralph Lauren crocodile-stamped belt this lady was sporting right now, and I couldn't say that I had missed it so far.

There was something else that seemed familiar about the woman, but I couldn't put my finger on it. Long glossy-brown hair, a perfect manicure, understated gold jewelry… The only thing about her that wasn't classy and perfect was her Kelly green eyes. They looked like contacts.

I was so overwhelmed by the minutiae of her out-of-place presence that I forgot to be scared. Also, my brain was busy trying to come up with a reason she was here—who was this woman?

The lady wasn't concerned with introducing herself, though. She looked me up and down with cool eyes. "Who are you, and what are you doing here?"

"Umm, I was supposed to clean the cottage the other day." I held up the bottle of glass cleaner as evidence. "I used my own products, and then DI Farrow came to tell me that Matilda's death was being investigated, and I forgot about my supplies. I just came by to pick them up."

The woman narrowed her eyes. "You're the next-door neighbor, aren't you? The one who broke in the other day? The police told me. You're a suspect in my aunt's murder."

She took a phone out of her Luis Vuitton purse, most likely to call the police. She seemed more annoyed rather than overly concerned that she might have stumbled upon a dangerous criminal.

"You must be Matilda's niece Tracy?" I hurried to say. "You asked Judith Winters to have the cottage cleaned—I'm her employee, and she sent me. You know I had a reason to be here."

"I asked Judith, that's true. I plan on listing the cottage with her, and she said she could do a deep clean. But I obviously didn't mean right away! My aunt's things are still in here, and the police tell me this is a crime scene, so—"

"Then there must be a misunderstanding. Judith asked me—"

"You can drop the innocent act," Tracy interrupted me in a harsh voice. "I know what this is all about. The jewels. Did Matilda tell you about them, and then you planned to steal them? Did my aunt catch you? Is that why she had to die?"

I shook my head in confusion. "Jewels? No, I—"

"Or you killed her, trying to make it look like an accident, so you could come here and search for the jewelry?

Maybe Judith told you I planned to list the cottage with her, and you used it as an excuse." She pointed at the rest of my cleaning products on the kitchen table.

"That's ridiculous. I don't know anything about any jewels." I was getting mad. What was wrong with these villagers that they came up with the most absurd accusations? "The police confirmed my alibi. I was working at the pub on Saturday night when Matilda was killed. They should have also checked with Judith by now. I was just doing my job. And I forgot about my cleaning products, so I thought I'd quickly pick them up. I'm on a tight budget right now, and—"

"Oh, yes, I heard you're broke. You must be desperate. Maybe so desperate that you came in to look for the jewelry again tonight?" Tracy glared at me with those disturbingly green eyes.

"For the last time, I know nothing about any jewelry. And if you check with the police, I'm sure they'll confirm I'm not even a suspect anymore."

"Yes, I will. I'm calling them right now." Tracy held the phone to her ear.

I closed my eyes in resignation. My hope was that DI Farrow would tell her I wasn't a murderer or a thief.

I didn't like my odds, though. My return to the scene of the crime might just be welcome proof of his earlier theory. That provincial wannabe-Poirot would probably jump on Tracy's suggestion that I was after Matilda's jewels.

We spoke no more while we waited for the police to arrive. Tracy seemed busy with her phone. I put the rest of my cleaning supplies in my tote bag.

Just a couple of minutes later, the front door opened. To my relief, the person who came into the kitchen wasn't DI Farrow, but DS Rees. I had to stop myself from throwing my arms around his neck. "Jamie!" I called and then went bright red.

"I just came to pick up my cleaning stuff," I continued sheepishly. "I know I shouldn't have just come in, but—"

"I insist you arrest her, officer," Tracy interrupted. She still seemed self-assured, but I thought I heard her voice shake a little.

For the first time since being caught by her, I didn't feel outrage at her unfair accusations. I even had a little empathy. Tracy had just lost her aunt. The killer was still at large. She had to have been scared to find me in her aunt's kitchen. Of course, she'd jump at any opportunity for a motive.

"I'm sorry if I scared you," I offered.

She raised her chin. "That's what you're sorry for? The jewelry belongs to me, and if you took it—"

"I didn't take anything! I did nothing…" I looked at Jamie for help.

He took pity on me. "Ms. Grantham has an alibi for the time of Matilda's murder."

"But you have to admit that it's very suspicious she keeps turning up here. Breaking in at night!" Tracy got worked up, and her clipped upper-class accent slipped a bit. "My aunt's jewels are missing." She repeated her accusations to Jamie.

He thought for a moment. "Did she specifically leave the jewels to you? Were they in the will?"

Tracy shook her head in irritation. "She left everything to me. So, by definition, the jewels too."

"Could she have given them away before she passed?" Jamie asked.

"They were her husband's heirlooms. She would never have given them away or even sold them. My aunt was devoted to Stanley."

I believed that—even from the brief conversation I'd

had with Matilda, I had gotten that impression. She'd even made me think he was still alive.

"If you're sure, and if you can't find them anywhere, report them stolen," Jamie advised. "But…has the paperwork for the will even gone through? I guess what I'm trying to say is, are they yours to report stolen yet?"

"No, I guess not, but—"

"I'd wait. This is all very fresh. I imagine it must be painful to lose a beloved aunt in such a manner. You haven't even been through all of your aunt's things yet, have you? The jewels might still turn up." Jamie seemed uncertain. "On the other hand, they could be a motive for the murder, so maybe we should—"

"No, you're right," Tracy interrupted him. Her smile, revealing perfect white teeth, seemed halfhearted, but who could blame her? Like Jamie said, this all had to be very painful for her. Everyone dealt with grief differently. It wasn't my place to judge her for the way she had spoken to me or handled the whole situation—especially considering that I had entered Matilda's home without permission. Well, technically, I was sure I had Matilda's ghost's permission, but Tracy didn't know that.

"I'll have a proper look for them. Maybe I overreacted, thinking they might've been motive for murder." She paused. "I guess I'm latching on to anything to make sense of this."

"I understand." Jamie's tone was gentle. I too softened toward Tracy, but my empathy only lasted a short moment, until she said, "I still think you should arrest Ms. Grantham, Officer. I'll check with Judith to verify her story. Maybe it really was a misunderstanding. But there's no excuse for her to have been here tonight. She scared me half to death. No matter what her reason, she broke in, and she ought to be arrested for that."

My eyes widened in shock when Jamie said, "Okay, I'll take her with me."

"No, you can't—" I didn't have time to protest before Tracy made the situation even worse.

"I also think you should check her bag, just to make sure she didn't take anything that doesn't belong to her."

I froze and clutched my tote bag against my chest. It contained the cleaning supplies, but there were also the printouts. Countless photographs that showed Tracy's recently departed aunt as if she were alive and kicking in her home.

Jamie didn't miss the panic in my eyes—it was probably written all over my face. He furrowed his brow. I could tell that he had considered me innocent so far but was now changing his mind. I clearly had something to hide.

I would make it worse if I objected to Tracy's request. I tried my best to smooth out my expression. "Sure, no problem." I mustered up a smile and passed the tote bag to Jamie.

He took some bottles back out, moved smaller items around in the bag, then pulled out half a page from the stack of printouts.

I didn't dare breathe. My heart was racing, and I felt light-headed.

Jamie cocked his head to get a better look at the image. A deep line appeared between his brows.

"What's this?" he asked.

CHAPTER TWELVE

I fought against the impulse to snatch the tote bag out of Jamie's hands.

"Just photos. I brought them along in my bag here. It's just paper…" I stuttered and pulled myself together. "Personal documents."

Tracy had her arms folded across her chest and glared at me. She clearly thought I had something to hide.

I silently pleaded with Jamie. He must have seen something in my eyes. "Okay, yes."

"Nothing from my aunt's home? Are you sure?" Tracy turned toward Jamie.

"No. Just the cleaning products and printouts of photographs." He handed me the bag. "Now, if you'd please come with me, Ms. Grantham?"

His serious tone made it sound as if he was really going to take me to the station. I didn't dare protest, though. I just wanted to get myself and my photographs out of this house, away from Matilda's niece.

I followed Jamie outside. He stayed silent while we walked to the car, where he opened the passenger door for me.

Looking toward my home, where my children were sleeping in their beds, I asked with a shaky voice, "You're not really going to arrest me, are you? My kids—"

He sighed. "Just get in. We're taking a little drive." When I still hesitated, he added. "I think we should talk, don't you?"

I didn't want to, but I clearly had no other choice. I had to explain myself to Jamie somehow. Otherwise, I might be in real trouble. What would become of my children if they woke up tomorrow and I wasn't there? Worse, if the police kept me detained for longer? Would they get to my mother somehow? Would Social Services take them in?

I was suddenly terrified.

By the time Jamie had walked around the car, sat down behind the wheel, and pulled off the curb, I was shaking in my seat.

Jamie noticed. "Are you okay?"

I tried hard not to sob. "Not...not really."

He drove down a side road and parked the car again. Then he carefully put a hand on my shoulder. "Everything's going to be fine."

Now I started to cry. I was so embarrassed, and Jamie clearly didn't know what to do with himself. He made a move to put his arm around me to comfort me, but then thought better of it, probably thinking it wasn't appropriate behavior, considering he was an officer of the law and I was technically his detainee.

Could all of this get any more messed up? I furiously wiped at my tears, trying to get a grip so we could finally have a talk and end this whole awkward situation.

"Sorry," I said. "I was just thinking about my kids. They have nobody else here. If I get in trouble..." I bit my lip. Then I continued. "I know it was wrong of me to just go into Matilda's house to pick up my stuff. Please, please, don't arrest me for breaking and entering."

Jamie sighed. "I won't arrest you. I just said it to appease Ms. Martens and defuse the situation. As far as I'm concerned, you're not a suspect. DI Farrow has a different opinion, but the fact is that you have an alibi. Many people saw you in the pub during the time Matilda died. Even if you'd been able to set some sort of asthma-inducing death trap in advance, why would you? Anyone can see that you're trying your best to have a fresh start. You're hardworking and trying to provide for your family… Why would you jeopardize this second chance by killing your neighbor—whom you hardly know?

"It's common knowledge that Matilda Rutherford wasn't well off. This is the first time I've heard about valuables…but jewelry might also have sentimental value, which could be the case here. If you'd wanted to kill a neighbor for valuable things to pawn, you would have done away with the other one, Phyllis Bishop." He shook his head. "No. I really don't think you did it."

Relief at hearing him say that made me slightly dizzy. "Thank you. You don't know what it means to me to hear a reasonable—"

"So why do you have photos of Matilda Rutherford on your person? Countless photos of her in her home?" Jamie shook his head. "You said she visited you once, and you had never been to her house before. You've got to explain this to me."

I didn't know how, so we sat there in silence for at least five minutes.

"Liv…" Jamie sighed again. "I don't want to arrest you. I really don't. But these photos—"

"I took them after she died," I blurted out, closing my eyes. I didn't want to see his facial expression. "Apparently, I have some sort of special form of ESP. I didn't know about it. Or it would be more accurate to say I had repressed my memory of it." I tried to explain to Jamie what had happened during my childhood, how my mother and I had basically run away from our supernatural talents and suppressed them ever since.

The problem was, however matter-of-fact I attempted to be, it still sounded completely insane.

"I'd basically forgotten about all of this. Then we met our relatives, Gina and Emerald Seven. They told us about a family affliction…"

Jamie finally responded. "Of course, I've heard of the Seven witches. Fairwyck is a small place, and people talk. I just haven't…I mean, I never took it seriously. I thought Gina's, um, business, was founded on theatrics. If people are gullible enough to believe in that sort of thing…" He waved a hand.

"I guess *you* don't believe in that sort of thing?" I said, defeated.

I felt like a fool. I probably should have made something up about the pictures. He'd demanded an honest answer, though, and I'd attempted to give it to him.

"That you took pictures of Matilda's ghost?" His acerbic tone said it all. "No, I don't believe that, Liv. Can you blame me? Who would?"

In a way, it might be better that Jamie didn't believe me. But some part of me wanted him to, was even mad that he didn't.

I opened my tote bag and tugged at the wad of printouts. "Here, look at them." I shoved them under his nose. "It's undoubtedly Matilda in the pictures, no?"

Jamie took the printouts, and, to his credit, examined them one by one. We were parked near a streetlamp, but it was not the best light. Still, the person in the pictures couldn't have been mistaken for anyone else.

"What's she pointing at?" Jamie asked.

"Words. I think she's trying to tell me something. A message that might lead to the killer."

Jamie looked at me with raised eyebrows and passed the printouts back to me. I stuffed them in my bag.

"You must have taken them before she died. Why did you lie about not having been in her house before?" He didn't say it in an accusatory tone.

I still got defensive.

"I didn't. I swear, I'd never been in there before. I took them the other night. The day I cleaned Matilda's cottage, the day DI Farrow came in and told me her home was a crime scene? That's when I took the first picture of her. Like I said, I hadn't touched a camera in years, but my aunt left me that Nikon, and that was the first time I used it. To take pictures of the tiles because I liked the decal design so much. When I realized it was Matilda's ghost in the picture, I went back the other night and took a bunch more. She was in all of them, and—"

"Don't tell me this was the second time you broke into Matilda's cottage!"

Fiddlesticks. "Umm… Okay, yes, I did. Wouldn't you have done the same? I could hardly believe what I was seeing—like you don't believe it—and I had to find out if it was a fluke or if…if…"

"If you could really take pictures of ghosts?" Jamie averted his eyes.

"Yes." I took a deep breath. "I can show you the digital copies. They have time stamps on them."

"That's not proof. That could easily be manipulated." He turned to look at me again. Now he seemed angry. "In fact, all these pictures could be doctored. It's easy to do nowadays. What I can't figure out is why you'd do such a thing!"

"Because I didn't. I didn't manipulate anything," I cried in exasperation. "I'm trying to tell you the truth, a truth I haven't been able to admit to myself my entire life. But I see it was a mistake."

"Yes," he said. He sounded sad.

Silence reigned in the car again. We didn't look at each other.

Eventually, I couldn't take it any longer. "So what are you going to do, Officer? Are you going to arrest me? For breaking and entering, tampering with evidence, ghost photo fraud?" I tried to sound flippant, but I didn't quite manage it.

"No," he sighed, and started the engine. "I'll drive you home."

When he parked in front of my house, Jamie said. "Look, I know you've been through a lot. I don't know why you told me this…why you have these pictures or what they mean…but my gut still tells me you didn't murder anyone. That you're an honest woman. I like you, Liv. Just…I have to think about all of this. I have to focus on who killed Matilda Rutherford. I have to solve this case, and I can't…" He trailed off and added quietly, "This is all a bit much."

"Yes," I answered. "I know the feeling."

I got out of the car and walked up to the cottage.

Maybe I should have been grateful to Jamie for not arresting me. It probably wasn't fair to him, but I was still really disappointed.

Lost in thought, I entered the cottage.

My mood changed immediately when I saw my children huddled together on the living room floor, crying.

Alarmed, I rushed toward them. "What's wrong?"

That's when I saw the brick and the broken glass of the living room window.

CHAPTER THIRTEEN

It was almost two in the morning when Blake and Audrey finally fell asleep.

I'd coaxed them away from the traumatic scene of the crime, first to the kitchen to make them cocoa, and later to my room, where we'd talked, read stories, and snuggled up.

They'd fallen asleep in my bed—which didn't really have enough space for two people, let alone three. I'd climb the narrow second flight of stairs to the tiny attic rooms to catch a few hours' sleep in Blake's bed later.

But first I had to take care of the mess downstairs. It was time for me to face the attack. I didn't think I was overly dramatic when I called it that.

Luckily, nobody had been hurt, but it could have gone a different way. I had left the light on downstairs, and for all the brick thrower had known, there could have been someone in the living room in danger of getting hit by the brick or cut by the glass.

I stared at the shards under the broken window, my arms wrapped around my body. Shivering, I thought of the terrifying possibility that one of my children could have been injured.

Of course, I was the most likely victim of the attack—maybe I would have been on the couch if I hadn't gone over to Matilda Rutherford's cottage. Blake and Audrey had been asleep in their beds, and they'd both woken up from the sound of the breaking window and a car speeding off.

Wracked by pangs of guilt for leaving them alone in the first place, I carefully removed the heavy brick from amid the shards and saw that a message was attached to it.

I stepped back into the kitchen to remove the note. It said *Criminals get out*.

Word must have gotten around the village that I was a suspect in Matilda's murder. Or did people think I was an accessory to my husband's crimes, just like DI Farrow did? It seemed as if the whole village already knew about what had happened to my family, anyway.

It was probably a bit of both. They assumed I was already a criminal, someone who had defrauded a lot of hardworking people of their money, and that there wasn't a big leap from that to murder.

It was only human nature, I supposed. People didn't want to believe that neighbors, whom they knew and trusted, would be capable of such a horrific crime. In a village as small as Fairwyck, where everyone knew each other, an outsider with an alleged sketchy past naturally would be the first murder suspect.

It wasn't really my fault. First of all, it was unfair to be found guilty of my husband's crimes by association. I should have handled things differently, yes, but I had done nothing illegal. I'd turned a blind eye, but if I had seen proof of Steven's fraudulent activities, I wouldn't have hidden it from the authorities.

I also had nothing to do with Matilda's death, and it

was an unfortunate coincidence that I had gotten entangled in the whole mess. Even more unlucky was the mere fact that the first murder in Fairwyck since the Dark Ages had been committed less than a week after our arrival—and right next door to us.

I still felt responsible, having dragged my children to England and right into this mess. I had to find a way to protect them. They had been through so much. We were at the end of our rope. We had no other choice than to stay here, no matter what anyone thought of me. I had to make this work somehow, and I didn't know how much more my kids could take.

As I was sweeping up the glass shards, I went through all the options in my head about what I could do to improve our situation. If I hadn't been nearly arrested tonight, I might have called the police to report it. In fact, I knew that I should report it. But DI Farrow had it in for me, and I'd burned my bridges with DS Rees. At best, Jamie thought I was crazy. At worst, he suspected I was making stuff up to cover something up.

Right now, as things were, the police wouldn't help me. That meant reporting the incident also wouldn't help my kids. They'd get questioned, which might add to their trauma. And the whole thing would probably draw even more attention to us, as word inevitably got around in Fairwyck. That would make matters worse.

I took apart some cardboard boxes that were still stacked in one corner of the living room from the move. After rummaging around the kitchen for a bit, I found a roll of duct tape. I did a poor job of boarding up the window, but it would have to do.

Completely exhausted, I sank down at the kitchen table and checked my phone for window repair companies in the area. My plan was to call one first thing tomorrow, even though I had no idea if I could pay them.

A cup of tea would have been great right about now, but I didn't feel I had the energy to make it. I was able to manage to get my secret stash of M&Ms out of the cupboard and sit back down.

I popped one after another M&M into my mouth, and by the time the bag was empty, I had a plan.

Matilda's murder had to be solved as soon as possible. If the real killer was behind bars, people wouldn't suspect me anymore. Then attention would shift away from us, and my kids and I could finally move on.

If the police weren't capable of catching the killer, and nobody believed that I could help—if nobody believed *in me*—then there was only one thing to be done.

I didn't know how I could handle it on top of everything else, but I just had to swing it somehow.

I had to solve this crime myself.

CHAPTER FOURTEEN

After only a few hours of sleep and coming off a serious case of sugar coma, I faced more than a few doubts that I could pull off my plan.

First of all, how would I even find time to do it? I had my hands full with looking after the kids and doing a stellar job at work. Neglecting my job and playing detective wasn't an option.

Last night, in the state I had been in, I'd somehow felt equipped to find Matilda's killer. After all, I had read enough mystery novels and seen enough crime TV shows to know how it was done.

In the cold light of day, feeling sluggish and burned out on top of being insanely busy and overwhelmed, my brain was ready to check out.

I couldn't come up with anything that made sense.

The police had no clue who the killer was, so how the hell would I ever figure it out? More frustrating, the only avenue I had, deciphering Matilda's message, was closed off to me. I couldn't break into her cottage again. If I was caught one more time by the police, there would be no leniency. Whatever I did, it had to be beyond reproach.

Still, Matilda's message was the best clue, so that evening, after the children went to bed, I got the photos out again. I tried to connect the few words I had identified yesterday evening, but nothing made much sense.

Seek probably told me I should seek the murderer, or maybe even pointed to where I could find him or her. It could also mean the killer was looking for something.

Then there was *close* and *love*—those seemed more useful clues. I had the distinct feeling Matilda wanted to let me know the killer was close to her. Maybe they lived close by? They had a close connection? There was love involved, which made me think of Stanley.

In one more picture, I had discovered *change* or *world*, but those words were too random. They didn't spark any ideas.

There were still other words to be identified, but I just couldn't make them out in the blurry zoomed-in pictures on my desktop, no matter how hard I tried. It was immensely frustrating, and I was very close to throwing all caution to the wind and breaking into Matilda's cottage again.

Just to get my mind off the mystery, I got out Ethel's photo albums. It was the only other aspect of Matilda's life I could glean. I poured over the photos of young Ethel and her friends Matilda and Phyllis. In one picture, there was the same handsome man I had seen in a photo frame in Matilda's living room—it had to be Stanley.

It was an interesting picture, and I looked at it for a long while. Matilda, Stanley, and Phyllis were sitting at a table. Stanley, in the middle, was turned toward Matilda and touching her hand. His charming smile was clearly directed at Matilda.

And then there was Phyllis, who looked adoringly up to Stanley.

A loud meow drew my attention away from the photo album.

It was Ethel the cat, at the back door. I got up to let her in. "Hi, Ethel," I greeted her, relieved—I hadn't seen her since last night. Maybe she had been scared off by whoever had broken the window.

Now she hungrily fell upon the bowl of cat food. I gave her some water and told her about my problems.

I didn't expect her to understand me, but I had nobody else to talk to. The only human I'd wanted to confide in—Jamie Rees—had let me down. I'd foolishly thought we'd forged a connection and that I could trust him. I would not make the mistake of disclosing my secret and unburdening myself to another person.

Ethel might not have been able to reassure me with words, but she jumped onto my lap for a cuddle after I returned to the sofa. That was almost as good.

"That's enough now," I finally told her, lifting her and setting her down on the sofa cushion next to me. "I should go to bed, but I really wanted to make progress, find clues about motives for Matilda's murder." With a sigh, I closed the photo album I had already studied twice.

Ethel jumped down and sauntered over to the bookshelf. I followed her to slide the photo album back in.

"Do you think there are others with photos of Matilda?" I thought out loud. "It's likely, since she and Ethel were best friends." I picked another album at random, pulled it out, and started to take it to the sofa, but Ethel protested.

"What is it?" I asked.

The cat was rubbing her cheek against the spine of some books on the shelf above the photo albums.

"Maybe you shouldn't rub against those. I'm not sure if I'll keep them." Something occurred to me. "I could sell them to secondhand book sites, I guess. They might not bring in much, but every little bit counts."

The cat gave a long meow. Then it touched the spines with its paw. "We won't get any money if you scratch them," I admonished her.

Ethel looked at me with her golden eyes. The expression clearly said something like "Don't you get it? How daft are you?"

"All right, all right, you want me to take these books down, I understand," I grumbled. I felt silly obliging a cat.

The books were time-traveling romances, but nice hardcover ones. I wondered if I really could sell them. They looked all right from the outside, and I thumbed through the pages.

That's when I discovered the thin paper stuck between them. I took it out. It was old-fashioned, cheap stationary. Small writing in faded ink covered the back and front.

I checked the other two books as well and found more of the letters. They were all addressed to Matilda and didn't have dates on them. The signature at the bottom clearly said Phyllis. When I started reading them, I was shocked. My heart rate sped up.

The words were pure venom.

Phyllis and Matilda hadn't simply fallen out—Matilda clearly had hurt Phyllis greatly.

The letters spoke of a malicious betrayal.

There was no love lost between these two former best friends.

On the contrary, the letters were hate mail. I had no idea why Ethel had them. Had Matilda given them to her? Maybe accidentally, when lending her these books? I'd seen a lot of books of this genre on Matilda's bookshelf. Or had my great-aunt intercepted them so that Matilda never got to read the vicious words?

All I knew was: Phyllis Bishop had hated Matilda and wanted her dead.

CHAPTER FIFTEEN

I had the next morning off, but after tossing and turning all night, I got up early anyway.

It felt good to make the kids a proper pancake breakfast and send them off to school well fed and on time.

Next, I did a bit of housework, even though the sight of the badly boarded-up window depressed me. I gave up on my earlier plan to call around for someone to fix the broken glass pane.

Fairwyck was a small English village, and people conducted their business differently here. I wanted to take advantage of that, despite—or maybe because of—the anonymous threat last night. People saw me as an outsider. I couldn't change how they perceived me, but I could stop acting like a suburban American.

Instead of doing a big shopping run at the next large Tesco, I walked to the village shop. It was the type of village hub that sold essentials from tea and toast to toilet paper and canned tomatoes. The shop doubled as a post office—you just purchased stamps or posted parcels at the shop counter. A couple of steps led to a nook that housed the pharmacy.

I entered and called out a friendly good morning. After throwing a couple of items in my shopping basket, I got in line at the counter. There were two customers in front of me, but the cashier didn't seem to be in any hurry. The middle-aged woman with a short platinum-blond perm seemed the chatty type. I didn't complain because it suited my plan.

When it was my turn, I slowly put out the items for her to scan. Her name tag said Michelle, so I greeted her by that name and introduced myself. "I only recently moved here. Maybe you knew my aunt, Ethel Seven?"

"Oh, yes, sure, everyone knew Ethel." She held the packet of spaghetti in her hand like she'd forgotten to scan it. Her eyes shone with enthusiasm, as if she couldn't believe her luck that I'd provided her with gossip fodder for the rest of the week.

"I didn't know her very well, unfortunately." I grimaced. "My mother, Calista Seven, she's also from here?"

Michelle just nodded vigorously.

"Well, she moved to the States with me when I was little, and I never had the opportunity to visit. Maybe you know what it's like. When parents are estranged from relatives, you don't really think to make the effort."

I didn't mind casting my mother as the villain if it ingratiated me with the villagers. It seemed to work. Michelle told me about a bunch of cousins on her father's side who only lived about twenty miles away but whom she hadn't even met.

Smiling sympathetically, I said, "It's not your fault, right? But I feel guilty now, let me tell you. My great-aunt left me her cottage when she died, and I'm incredibly grateful. I'm not sure if you heard, but my husband deserted my children and me, and he left us in a real bind."

Michelle's big eyes became even rounder. Luckily, there

was nobody waiting to be served behind me, so I didn't feel the need to hurry. I doubted Michelle would have hurried this along, anyway. I knew I had her on my side when I gave her the morsel she'd longed to hear: Steven's affair with his secretary.

"I wonder if she convinced him to steal and lie," Michelle said excitedly. "I had a husband in my twenties. He was seduced by another woman. He wouldn't have left me if it hadn't been for her."

"Then you understand. Anyway, it taught me a lesson. Since I missed the boat with Great-Aunt Ethel, I really want to connect with my other relatives. I met them briefly the other day, but I don't know where they live. Gina and Emerald Seven. Would you be able to tell me?"

"Of course. Everyone knows Gina. She's a different cup of tea to our Ethel, though." Michelle scrunched her nose and leaned over the counter to whisper. "People think she's a witch."

"A witch?" I laughed. "Sounds amusing. I just want to make an effort, you know."

"Of course. I see that. Just…you know. You'll find other friends in Fairwyck soon, I'm sure."

Michelle finished ringing up my items, then wrote down Gina's address and instructions to get to there.

I thanked her profusely. "Oh, one other thing. My window broke last night. Can you recommend someone who'd be able to fix it?"

"Well, there's one person who does that sort of thing, but I'm not sure…" Her round cheeks colored.

"What? Would he not come to my house?" Were there people in Fairwyck really that bothered about my outsider status?

"It's just… The person is Matilda Rutherford's brother. Luther Martens."

"Oh." Now it was my turn to blush. Gossip about me

being a suspect in Matilda's murder was clearly making the rounds, even though Michelle didn't seem to believe it. Otherwise, she wouldn't have been so friendly. I decided to quash those rumors.

"DS Rees assured me last night that I was off the suspect list. I have an alibi, after all. The police just had to do their due diligence."

"Oh, good."

"Is Luther Martens Tracy's father?" I asked.

"Oh, you've met Matilda's niece?"

I just nodded.

"Well, yes, he is."

"And he's a handyman?" Tracy didn't look like she came from a working-class background, but then, why shouldn't she move up in the world?

Michelle interpreted my surprise correctly, because she said, "You wouldn't know it, looking at Tracy now, would you? She's changed a lot. Used to work here." She nodded toward the small pharmacy part of the shop. A stooped elderly man in a white lab coat was busy cataloging something behind the counter. I really couldn't picture Tracy working there. I would love to know what she was doing now.

Before I could ask, someone else I knew came into the shop.

My antagonistic neighbor, Phyllis Bishop. The little round lady didn't greet Michelle or me, just squinted and pulled a face before she turned left to walk up the steps into the pharmacy.

I had the photograph of the curly-haired young woman in my mind's eye, looking up adoringly at Stanley Rutherford. Michelle's voice pulled me out of my reverie. "That's weird. Phyllis usually only comes in on Tuesday mornings."

"Oh, really?" I asked, still looking in Phyllis's direction.

The woman was quietly arguing with the pharmacist, it seemed.

"Yes, like clockwork. She is very particular, Phyllis is. Comes in for her weekly shopping—and she always gets the same things, I could list them for you if you'd like—and at the end of the month she fills her prescription for beta blockers. High blood pressure. Typical for Type A personalities like her. And she used to be the principal of a school nearby. That would be a stressful job. Anyway, she's been retired for a while now."

"Well, it looks like she's jumbled up her days." It was easy to get everything mixed up when your former best friend and neighbor got killed. Especially if you'd wished a horrible death on them for decades and might even have something to do with the murder.

I turned to face Michelle. "I've got to go. Thank you very much for the friendly chat and your help."

"No worries. I look forward to seeing you around."

I brought the groceries home, put everything away, and had a fortifying cup of coffee before I set out to visit my mysterious relatives.

CHAPTER SIXTEEN

Michelle had sent me to the Sacred Salmon Inn. As far as I knew, Gina didn't run an inn. When I'd been looking for employment, I hadn't come across an establishment with that name in the area either.

Now I stood in front of a run-down building just outside Fairwyck. The sign with the bloated salmon on it was so faded, the writing was barely legible. The inn clearly hadn't been in business for a long while. It certainly didn't look as if anyone lived there. Had Michelle been pulling my leg?

Only one side of the building resembled an actual wall, with a dark timber frame and formerly white-washed plaster. The rest looked as if rubble had been cobbled together with no regard to ninety-degree angles. Perhaps levels hadn't been invented at the time of construction. There was an extension that seemed newer, possibly Edwardian or Victorian. It all looked wonky, like the pieces didn't quite fit together. I had a suspicion everything was only holding up thanks to the dense net of climbing plants that had been allowed free rein.

With the village out of view behind a hill, woods blocking my view of whatever lay farther down the narrow country lane, no human being in sight, and the old sign with the salmon swinging creakily in the wind, I felt temporarily transported into one of the less pleasant Grimm fairy tales.

I swallowed and fought the impulse to run back home. Mustering up some courage, I walked past the boarded-up entrance and around the newer extension, where I found a second door.

"Gina? Emerald?" I called hesitantly. "Anyone home?"

Reluctantly, I banged a doorknocker in the shape of the Green Man against the peeling paint.

"All right, all right, I'm coming," a voice called.

It was familiar.

The door swung open, and my great-aunt beamed at me. "Liv! What a surprise. What brings you here? Come in, come in."

I resisted the temptation to ask if her cards hadn't given her a clue about my visit today. "It's my day off, and I went for a walk. Someone told me you live here, and when I saw the house, I thought I'd knock."

Gina smiled knowingly, as if she was aware of my fib but didn't mind it. I quickly added, "What an unusual home. It's a bit…um…" I struggled to put the nightmarish fairytale quality into nicer words.

"Isn't it wonderful?" Gina gushed. "I dreamed of living here as a child. Did you know the Sacred Salmon used to be the most haunted inn in England?"

"No," I said slowly, hugging myself for comfort and protection. "How…interesting."

"Yes. And when the owner put the inn up for sale, I knew I had to move heaven and earth to buy it. We've been living here, gosh, let's see, for over twenty years."

Poor Emerald had grown up here? My eyes roamed

over the Gothic wallpaper, black-velvet curtains, and oppressive dark-wood furniture. No wonder my cousin was a little eccentric.

"Let's go through here." Great-Aunt Gina led the way. "We use the original kitchen and taproom as a living area."

I didn't know what to say. I'd thought of Ethel's cottage as rustic, but basic and quaint would probably be a better description, especially compared to the room I was in now.

The tables and benches had been cobbled together with roughly hewn planks, the walls were exposed stonework, and the low-hanging ceiling beams were blackened by centuries of smoke from the enormous fireplace. The smell of unwashed patrons and spilled ale was still hanging in the air.

Gina made us tea and brought the tray over to where I was carefully perched on the edge of a bench. "We rarely receive visitors here. But you're family, so I'm making an exception. There's a darling Victorian parlor in the extension, where I hold séances and read cards. Our bedrooms are also in the extension. We like to spend time here, though, in the original part of the inn, to soak up the atmosphere. The Sacred Salmon has been here since the twelfth century. Isn't that astonishing?"

I just nodded. The most astonishing part to me was that it was still somehow standing, even though it clearly hadn't been renovated since then.

"We couldn't sleep in the inn rooms upstairs. We wouldn't get a wink in, let alone forty. That's how badly haunted they are. They've been left exactly as they were when we moved in. There's still some paranormal activity in the extension, and it can get a little too much for Emmy at times. She periodically moves out to recalibrate and take a breather."

"Makes sense. Doesn't it ever get to be too much for you?"

"Sometimes," Gina smiled. "But what I do is often aided by spirits. So I'm grateful for them. I can do things here that I can't do anywhere else, because they aren't really part of my gift. This is a special place, though." She looked around admiringly. "It's good for my business."

"I see."

"I know—why don't you bring your camera next time you come for a visit?" Gina's face lit up. "I'd love to see what some of our housemates look like in a photograph."

"Umm, maybe." I shuddered at the thought. "If you don't mind, I wanted to talk a little about Ethel," I said, eager to change the subject. "I found an old photo album with pictures of her when she was younger."

"Of course, darling." Gina poured the tea and offered milk and sugar. "What do you want to know?"

"I knew Matilda Rutherford was Ethel's good friend. I recognized a young Matilda in many of the pictures. But there's a third person in them, and if I'm not mistaken, it's my other neighbor, Phyllis Bishop. Do you know anything about their friendship?" I blew into the tea.

"Sure. The trio used to be inseparable—until Matilda stole Phyllis's boyfriend." Gina pointed invitingly at a plate of delicious-looking lemon bars. My mouth watered, and I almost stretched my hand out to take one. A silly notion of witches and not eating their food came into my head, though. Maybe it was due to all the fairytale associations that were popping into my head.

I really shouldn't have paid any attention to the fact that some villagers were a little wary of Gina and Emerald.

Gina was eccentric, no doubt about it—and Emerald was a little kooky too. Gina even played up her esoteric persona, probably for the purpose of marketing her business. Plus, they lived in this spooky house. No wonder the villagers considered them to be witches.

I *knew* they were witches…or something like that. I had

to acknowledge their abilities, now that I'd embraced my own. Finding myself on the receiving end of a witch hunt would make me more sympathetic to my relatives too.

So why was I afraid of them? Maybe some residual wariness had to do with the fact that I still thought it suspicious Gina and Emerald hadn't introduced themselves right away when I'd moved here. And I couldn't help but wonder if they weren't bitter about being left out of Great-Aunt Ethel's will.

Especially now that I had seen their home. Gina might love it here and benefit from living in a haunted inn. But it sounded as if Emerald didn't quite feel the same way, and I couldn't blame her. It was also normal that someone wouldn't want to live with their mother forever.

Great-Aunt Ethel's cottage wasn't much, but for a young single woman who had a decent income and could invest in renovations, it would have been a convenient windfall. With no other relatives around, I imagined Emerald had counted on it—until I came along.

I didn't feel I could quite trust my relatives, so even though my mouth watered, I didn't touch the lemon bars.

Back to the topic at hand. "I'm surprised that Ethel stayed friends with Matilda—and both shunned Phyllis later, if I understand correctly. Ethel seemed to have been on Matilda's side, even though Matilda stole Phyllis's partner."

"It wasn't that black and white. Stanley and Phyllis weren't in a serious relationship. Yes, they got together first, but they also still dated other people. It was the seventies! I was still young at the time all of this happened, but I remember I used to be fascinated with what Ethel and her friends were up to." Gina giggled. "Phyllis used to be a happy and bubbly sort of girl, by all accounts. I heard she was a little needy, though. When Stanley chose Matilda over her, Phyllis turned bitter and resentful. And she never recovered. She never dated another man, just focused on her career as a teacher and later as a principal. She even bought that bigger cottage next to Ethel and Matilda so she could brag about how well off she was."

Gina paused, as if considering whether she should say more. "If you ask me, she also bought it so she could spy on them, and thus feed her hatred. It's sad, really, how she let the whole thing ruin the rest of her life."

I thought about the letters I'd found. They fit with everything Gina said. The police believed Matilda had had no enemies. But they were wrong. There was one person who had definitely hated her.

Her neighbor, former friend, and arch rival. Phyllis Bishop.

CHAPTER SEVENTEEN

I ate one of the lemon bars in the end, and it was so good that bewitchment would have been a small price to pay.

But after that, I couldn't get away from the creepy inn fast enough. The building itself was one reason, and Gina's constant probing about my children's paranormal gifts didn't help.

My great-aunt's line of questioning freaked me out. I'd only recently acknowledged my own paranormal abilities. I couldn't handle it if my kids discovered something like this about themselves in the near future. And I feared it would be too much for them too, after everything that had happened.

I didn't want to make the same mistake as my mother, so I probably should prepare them. But I really wanted to put that at the bottom of my long to-do list right now.

The most pressing thing on it was finding Matilda's killer so we could all move on and settle here in Fairwyck, and that was also the reason I wanted to get home as soon as possible.

My talk with Gina had cemented my suspicion that Phyllis Bishop could be responsible for Matilda's death.

On my way back home, I gave Jamie Rees a call. I couldn't really blame him for being skeptical about my ghost photographs. But this wasn't about me. Matilda's murderer needed to be identified, and I had important information.

Jamie picked up immediately, but his greeting was cautious, and there was an awkward silence before I blurted out, "I have a pretty good idea who murdered Matilda Rutherford. Her neighbor, Phyllis Bishop. She had a personal vendetta against Matilda because she was convinced her former best friend stole the love of her life, Stanley Rutherford, and—"

"Hang on, Liv," Jamie interrupted me. "You're not honestly trying to tell me a little old lady killed her neighbor because of a love squabble eons ago. I understand you want the actual killer behind bars, but you're grasping at straws here."

"No, it's true! I've been asking around, and I have this on good authority."

Jamie groaned. "Please tell me you haven't been playing detective."

I hesitated. "Well…"

"Liv, listen to me. You've got to stay out of this." Jamie sounded very earnest, and I had to swallow. "You're not doing yourself any favors. Don't get involved. You're on thin ice with Farrow as it is."

"You don't understand. This is personal. I need the real culprit behind bars so my kids and I can move on. I have a good hunch that Phyllis did it. Someone threatened me—" I was just about to tell him about the brick thrown through my window, but Jamie interrupted me.

"A hunch? You mean like a psychic vision?" His voice turned cold.

"No, not exactly." His skepticism raised my hackles, though. What if it was? If my gift was more akin to Gina's, for example. "Does it matter? I'm telling you—"

"Something like that isn't actual evidence, Liv. You're making things worse for yourself. If I were you, I'd keep my head down and stop the supernatural mumbo-jumbo."

"Is that right?" I couldn't keep the hurt out of my voice.

Jamie sighed. "Just let us do our jobs, okay? You'll be all right. Believe me, I want you to come out of this on the other side." He hesitated for a moment. "I really like you. And I was hoping, when all of this is over, I could ask you out."

"If I manage not to make a fool of myself in the meantime, you mean? Keep my head down and not draw too much attention to myself?" I knew I sounded angry, but I couldn't help it. That's the kind of person I'd always been. I'd always stayed small and played nice so nobody would think anything bad of me. After what had happened with Steven, I was done with that. And I'd happily pass on any man who wanted me to be an unobtrusive-wife character. Even if he was as handsome as DS Jamie Rees.

Before Jamie could respond, I said, "You know what, we've only spent a bit of time together, and maybe you don't know me as well as you think. Chances are, if you did, you wouldn't like me as much as you think. And that's okay."

I hung up, seething all the way back to the cottage.

When I had calmed down a bit, I did consider that one thing Jamie had mentioned was actually a valid point. He hadn't dissuaded me from my theory that Phyllis Bishop was the killer. But the feud between the two former best friends had been going on for ages. Why murder Matilda now?

In her hate letter, Phyllis had promised Matilda that

she would get revenge, even if it took her fifty years. But why wait that long?

Possibly, she'd wanted to wait until Stanley passed away. The bitter old spinster might have held out hope that Stanley would change his mind eventually. She wouldn't have wanted to do anything to tarnish her reputation and give Stanley a reason to reject her a second time.

I resolved to find out when exactly Matilda had become a widow. When we'd first talked in my kitchen, Matilda had spoken about her husband as if he were still alive. I couldn't imagine he'd been gone that long. But the strange thing was that there weren't any pictures of an older Stanley in Matilda's cottage, which meant he'd passed away many years ago.

The only other thing that had changed recently was Ethel's death, but I didn't quite understand how that could have made a difference. Had Phyllis maybe held out for a renewal of her friendship with Ethel? Or had Matilda been more vulnerable without her friend next door? Was this connected to a special Seven skill that might have protected Matilda?

I'd never asked Gina about Ethel's paranormal talent. It was something else I needed to find out.

All these questions were driving me bonkers. When I saw our boarded-up living room window, I knew I should take care of that too, but I didn't know how.

Frustrated, I decided to face at least one challenge head on.

I marched outside, crossed the garden and the low fence, and knocked on Phyllis's back door.

Yes, she might be a murderous criminal, but she didn't hold a bitter grudge against me, did she? Plus, she was an old lady. What could she do to me?

When she opened the door, her face like thunder, I smiled sweetly. "Hi, we haven't formally introduced ourselves, so I thought I'd remedy that. I'm Liv Grantham, Ethel's great-niece, and I moved in next door with my children Blake and Audrey—"

"You're trespassing," Phyllis said.

"Well, I thought it would be easier to walk across the gardens, instead of all the way around—"

"You're just like your bloody cat, aren't you? Get off my property."

"Um…sorry if our cat bothers you. She just turned up when we moved in. I thought maybe you'd seen her around here before?"

"Well, the filthy animal is not allowed to poop in my garden. If it happens again, I'll call the police."

"Okay. I have a question for you. Do you know when Matilda Rutherford's funeral will be?" I bravely tried to follow through with my plan of playing innocent. "I thought you, as her neighbor, might know."

"Hell would freeze over before I'd go to four-eyes's funeral." Phyllis squinted menacingly.

"I see. Did you not get on—"

"But I'll happily go to yours, which is going to happen soon if you don't get off my property." She opened the door a little wider and lifted the rolling pin she had been hiding behind her back.

I took a step back and held up my hands. "All right, all right, I understand. I was just trying to be friendly. And, to be honest, the murder next door freaked me out. I thought if we paid more attention to our neighbors, something terrible like this could be prevented. But I wasn't even home that night. I was working at the pub, and my children were home alone. Did you see anything that evening, by any chance?"

Phyllis turned very red in the face. She stepped outside the door and swung the rolling pin. It should have looked comical, this round, gray-haired old lady with a prune face threatening me like that. But her small beady eyes told me she meant serious business. I had really riled her up. "Didn't I tell you—"

"Nice to meet you, bye!" I shouted and ran away, jumped across the fence—which probably looked even more comical than the rolling pin–swinging spinster—and sprinted to my back door.

Panting, I closed it behind me and sank down onto the floor.

As I was catching my breath, certainty settled in my gut. Phyllis Bishop was out of control. Resentment and thoughts of revenge had consumed her until she had turned into a cold-blooded murderer.

I was more sure than ever that she'd killed Matilda Rutherford.

CHAPTER EIGHTEEN

Adrenaline was still pumping through my veins, so I thought it was as good a time as any to call Luther Martens.

I found his number in the yellow pages, where he advertised his roofing company. Michelle had reassured me he did all sorts of repairs around the house and rarely turned a job down.

He answered on the first ring. "Mr. Martens? My name is Liv Grantham, and I've been told you may be able to help me. Someone broke my living room window, and I need a new glass pane."

I held my breath, waiting for a negative reaction to hearing my name.

But Luther Martens either didn't know who I was or it didn't bother him to take the person who was suspected to have murdered his sister on as a client. He sounded eager to help me out. "You know what? I have half an hour of my lunch break left. Why don't I come over and take the measurements, so we can get you sorted as soon as possible?"

"That would be wonderful. Thank you." I gave him

my address, and there was a slight pause in the conversation. I was bracing myself for a reaction again, thinking Luther had finally caught on to who I was.

But he only said he'd be right over.

Luther's mentioning of his lunch break made me notice my grumbling stomach and that I'd had nothing to eat but pancakes and a lemon bar today.

I'd just wolfed down half of a sandwich when there was a knock on the door. I wiped my mouth with a napkin and let Luther Martens in.

He was tall, with a mop of curly red hair and light blue eyes. He had a big mustache and a pleasant, freckled face. Luther reminded me of someone, but I couldn't think of whom.

He looked at me with open curiosity when he shook my hand. "Ms. Grantham, nice to meet you."

"Please, call me Liv."

"Luther." He pointed at the boarded-up window. "I take it that's it?"

I just nodded.

"I'm going to have to take the cardboard off, I'm afraid, to take accurate measurements."

I was a little embarrassed about the poor job I'd make of it and tried to compensate with a joke. "No worries. My nine-year-old can probably board it up better than me."

Luther smiled. "You have kids?"

"Two."

"I have a daughter. She's all grown up now, though."

"Oh yeah, um, I met her. Tracy, right?"

Luther nodded while inspecting the wooden window frame. Since he didn't mention it, I figured Tracy hadn't told him about my run-in with her at Matilda's cottage.

Luther wrote something down with a pencil in a notepad he'd pulled from his tool belt. Then he said in a casual tone, "You must've seen her next door."

"Yes…" I hesitated. I wasn't sure what was appropriate to say, since the man had come to fix my window. I decided to speak from the heart. "My deepest sympathies for your loss. Matilda was your sister, wasn't she?"

"Yes. Thank you." Luther rubbed his chin. "We weren't that close. She was a few years older than me, and…well, I left Fairwyck for several years and missed quite a bit of Tracy's childhood. Matilda never approved of that. We spoke on the phone every Saturday night for a quick catch-up, but aside from that didn't spend a lot of time together. It's still upsetting, though, for her to die so suddenly."

"Of course! And in that manner… It must have been a shock. I'm so sorry."

Luther smiled. "That's kind of you to say. It's my daughter I'm concerned about, really. She was Matilda's goddaughter, and they had a special relationship."

He pulled a measuring tape from his tool belt and began to measure the window.

"Oh yes, I gathered that. Matilda left everything to Tracy, didn't she?"

"She doesn't have any other relatives. I know she left Tracy the cottage. Although I seem to remember Matilda told me something about bequeathing money to the Postal Workers Benevolent Fund. Her husband Stanley worked as a mail carrier."

"Oh, right! When I spoke to Matilda the one time, shortly after we moved in here, she mentioned Stanley, and it sounded to me as if he was still alive. I only realized later that he must have passed away quite a few years ago. Sorry to ask you this, but it's been puzzling me. When did Matilda become a widow?"

Luther gave her a funny look, then turned his attention to his notebook to write down the measurements. He turned bright red when he mumbled, "Um, Matilda has been on her own for a few decades. She always considered herself married to Stanley, though. Even after all these years, after everything, she remained enamored of him…" Luther had stopped writing, staring blankly at the page, lost in thought.

Then he shook his head as if he wanted to clear his mind. "Anyway, Liv, I'm afraid you'll need a new window frame. This one is really old, and the wood is rotting. I could put a new window pane in, of course. But it might not hold up very long."

"What?" Suddenly, the circumstances of Matilda Rutherford's death seemed much less important. "Oh no. How much is that going to cost?"

"It depends on the material. I can get you a few estimates. I'd recommend a modern PVC frame. They're reasonably priced, easy to maintain, and durable. It's an excellent investment."

"Okay…" My stomach clenched at the thought of getting the money together for this expense.

Luther smiled sympathetically. "Is some of the glass pane maybe salvageable? I could take it off your hands, give you a discount on the new pane. What happened to it?"

"No, it's gone, I'm afraid. Completely shattered. Someone threw a brick through it."

Luther's baby-blue eyes widened. "What?"

"It seems like we're not welcome in the village, and someone wanted to let us know." I shrugged, but I couldn't stop the tears from springing to my eyes.

"Liv, I'm so sorry. Villagers can sometimes be…" He took a deep breath. "They gossip. One reason I left Fairwyck temporarily. I wish I wouldn't have, that I hadn't given a damn about what people said. I made a mistake, and I should have owned up to it and then lived with the consequences. The bigger mistake was to leave Tracy here alone with her mother. Really, it was cowardly of me to run away. I've been trying to make up for it since my return, but Tracy was fifteen then, and my ex-wife had just passed away. I'd missed her entire childhood and left her to go through the worst of her mother's illness without my support. Now I give her everything she wants, but I can never fully make up for the past."

"I'm sorry to hear that. And I hear what you're saying. I'm not going to let the village gossipy types drive me away. But there's vicious talk…and then there's a brick through the window. Apart from the fact that I can't really afford the repairs, I'm scared for my children."

Luther nodded vigorously. His eyes bulged and his face turned red. "That's not on. What a horrible thing to do! If I'd catch—" A beeping sound interrupted him.

He rolled up his sleeve to look at a device that looked like a watch. "My high blood pressure is high." He smiled at me, chagrined. "I'm not supposed to get worked up. Tracy makes me wear this so I can always monitor it."

He got a bottle of pills from his tool belt. "Could I trouble you for a glass of water?"

"Of course." I sprinted to the kitchen to get the water, feeling bad for getting him into this state. "I hope you're okay," I said, passing him the glass.

"Oh yes, no worries. I just haven't taken my pill yet today, and this reminded me." He put it in his mouth and swallowed it with a sip of water.

"Thank you so much." He set the glass down on the coffee table. "I have to go, but I'll get back to you with estimates for the new window. Do you have an email address? That's easiest."

He got out his phone and passed it to me so I could add the email to my contact details.

When I pressed the save button and closed the contacts, I saw his phone background. There were apps in front of the girl's face, but I recognized it right away. It was the same picture Matilda had framed in her cottage.

Suddenly, it hit me. Luther had seemed familiar because he looked like the girl in the picture. "Oh, is that Tracy?" I blurted out, passing the phone back to him.

"What? Oh, the background picture. Yes. When she was little."

"I saw the same picture at Matilda's," I explained. "But I didn't recognize Tracy. She has changed so much."

Luther's expression turned troubled—more troubled than he'd seemed by his sister's death or by his health problems.

"Yes," he said. "I really have to go."

Without looking me in the eye, he waved and disappeared through the front door.

CHAPTER NINETEEN

The next day, I finished work at two p.m., so I had plenty of time to continue my investigation. If anything, it took my mind off worrying about finding the money to pay for the new window. Luther had sent me estimates, and I'd opted for the cheapest one, but it was still more than I could afford right now. I would have to ask my mother for a loan again.

Procrastinating on that uncomfortable conversation, I thought about ways to find out more about Phyllis Bishop. In the end, I used a trick out of my suburban American housewife arsenal.

A quick trip to the village shop revealed that Phyllis Bishop was fond of Chelsea buns.

I told Michelle I planned to pay my neighbor a visit and wanted to bring something she liked. "I have the impression that Phyllis isn't the most welcoming person," I said. "She hasn't introduced herself so far."

Michelle snorted. "I don't think anyone has dared to darken her doorstep in a long while. The milkman refuses to deliver to her. I have it on good authority that postal service workers leave parcels on the doorstep, ring the doorbell, and then leg it, like they do when there's a vicious dog in the house."

That explained why I'd seen the gray-bearded IPS guy from the pub lurking around recently. He was probably psyching himself up to deliver a parcel to Mrs. Bishop. "Well, I should at least try. She's my neighbor, after all, and I don't want to get off on the wrong foot. Imagine living next door to someone for years and hating the sight of that person."

That gave Michelle an opening. "You wouldn't be the first. Rumor has it Phyllis and Matilda couldn't stand each other. Phyllis always called her names, like poor man's Princess Margaret or four-eyes. If you ask me, she could use a set of glasses herself, the way she always squints. I don't think she's being rude when she ignores people in the street. She just doesn't recognize them. But she's too vain to get glasses."

"Phyllis and Matilda hated each other, huh?" I brought the conversation back to what interested me. "Why do you think that is? I was under the impression they used to be best friends when they were younger. My great-aunt Ethel too. They used to be a trio. I found old photo albums."

"Really? I don't know anything about that."

"Oh." I was a little disappointed. I would have thought the feud and its origins were common knowledge. But then, Michelle was quite a bit younger than everyone involved.

My visit to the village shop wasn't a total flop, though, because I found out about Phyllis's favorite treat and could put my plan into action.

Instead of buying the packaged Chelsea buns of a mediocre brand, I drove to the big Tesco and purchased half a dozen from the bakery. I had to supplement yesterday's shopping anyway, as the village shop wasn't as well stocked and was overall more expensive.

I went the extra mile and bought nice-looking paper napkins on sale, as well as a card with flowers on the front.

When I got home, I found a small basket in Ethel's pantry, padded it with the napkins, and arranged the Chelsea buns in an appetizing display.

Then I wrote the note. "It was a little forward of me to just turn up on your back doorstep. Please chalk it up to cultural differences. I grew up here, but many years of living in the States must have done away with my manners and all sense of propriety."

I paused. Was I laying it on a bit thick? Phyllis Bishop didn't strike me as someone with a sense of sarcasm, so it was probably all right. I would merely confirm her prejudice about Americans being brash and unrestrained.

I put pen to paper again. "I just wanted to be neighborly. Please accept these freshly baked Chelsea buns as an apology—and maybe a fresh start?

"Your new neighbors, Liv, Blake, and Audrey."

I walked all the way around, down the road and then onto the parallel road to Phyllis Bishop's sidewalk. I waved at the IPS man, who was doing a poor job of hiding behind a lamppost. He ran off in a panic.

It reminded me of the postal workers' strategy Michelle had told me about. I placed the basket with the Chelsea buns on the doorstep, rang the doorbell, and ran away.

At home, I pushed the bag with the supermarket bakery logo far down into the trash can, feeling guilty about passing off the high-quality baked goods as my own.

Funny, in my old world, I wouldn't have thought twice about it. Everyone was doing it. Moms in my former neighborhood would rather get their nails done than stand in the kitchen all day and produce a hundred muffins for the school bake sale. It was a sanctioned lie—you bought the best and presented them as your own.

Everyone would talk about how much they loved baking—but they never did it. It was the same with gardening. You'd show up with stylish gloves to prune roses in the front yard, but it wasn't exactly a secret that the gardener did the actual work.

Even though I was more than disenchanted with my former sisters in the gated-community trenches, this wasn't something I blamed them for. Attempting to do anything yourself was futile because there was no way you could meet the high standards of perfection. I could never have styled my unruly dark tresses in a way that measured up, so I had to go to the hairdresser for my weekly blow-out. And I definitely couldn't have produced anything in the kitchen that would have passed muster.

Life in Fairwyck was a world apart, and it was astounding that I had adapted so quickly. The truth was, I felt much more comfortable with my hair long and in a ponytail, rather than having to coif the curls into sleek styles. I didn't want to be the person who'd fit into my old community anymore. With tears in my eyes, I thought about Matilda's dry scones. That had been a genuine gesture and counted so much more than the ton of overpriced cupcakes I had distributed in my old neighborhood.

I told myself that Phyllis's case was an exception. My Chelsea buns had to impress. They needed to hit the right note. For just one day, I had to step into that suburban American housewife persona, because it reminded Phyllis that I was not my great-aunt.

Plus, I figured if she was used to the village shop variety of her favorite treat, she would love the luxury version. If she thought I'd really baked them, she might hope to be on the receiving end of this talent of mine again and actually deign to extend a neighborly hand across the garden fence, so to speak.

My strategy paid off. I got a phone call that evening when the kids and I were sitting down for dinner.

"Maybe I judged you a little quickly," Phyllis admitted. "I certainly enjoyed the buns."

"I'm so glad," I said and waited with bated breath. I was really after a chance to visit Phyllis so I could find out more about how to nail her for Matilda's death.

"Why don't you and your daughters come over for tea tomorrow afternoon?"

"Oh, um…" I could hardly believe my luck that cantankerous Phyllis had turned around so quickly…but I also hadn't expected Audrey and Blake to be included in the invite.

"I do have to get something off my chest, to be honest." Phyllis sounded exhausted, as if she had been battling with the decision to let someone into her confidence for a while. By all accounts, Phyllis had alienated herself from all her acquaintances, so she probably had nobody to talk to. My friendly gesture had come at just the right time.

What had been weighing on Phyllis Bishop? Was she going to confess to murder? I'd rather not have the kids present for that, but I couldn't very well start negotiating on the rare occasion she extended an invitation to somebody.

"Of course we'll come," I blurted. "It would be a pleasure."

"Fantastic! I'll see you at four." She hung up before I could say that I wasn't sure Audrey and Blake could make it.

But then I decided I would bring the children along after all. They would put Phyllis at ease. I didn't want to give her a reason to change her mind at the last minute.

The next day, I picked up the kids from school so we would make it on time. They were pleased to see me but were less enthusiastic when I told them about the invitation.

"I really wanted to draw this afternoon," Blake said. "I have this cool idea."

"Take your sketchbook. You can excuse yourself during the conversation and say you feel inspired to draw the teapot or something. I'm sure Phyllis will find it charming."

"The grumpy old lady next door?" Audrey said incredulously. "She reminds me of the witch from Hansel and Gretel. She always stares at me as if she wants to stick me into her oven."

I got the chills thinking that I had been reminded of the same fairy tale yesterday. Shaking off the feeling, I said, "Listen, she hung up before I could say you kids can't make it. It would be rude to turn up by myself. Just come along. We probably won't stay long—it's just a neighborly gesture."

"Okay, but I'm bringing my sketch pad," Blake said.

Audrey reluctantly agreed too, but only because I promised ice cream for dessert after dinner that night.

The kids dropped off their school bags, Blake got their drawing pad and pencil, and it was already time for our visit.

So as not to ruffle the old lady's feathers again, we walked down the road and around to the parallel road to knock at the front door.

I was feeling more and more queasy, as if my intuition was telling me I was making a big mistake. Yesterday I'd felt so clever with my little high-end baked goods trick. Now I wasn't so sure.

It was vital to talk to the murder suspect because I had nothing I could bring to the police. Phyllis Bishop would have to give me something that would warrant an investigation. So if I was to succeed in my plan to catch Matilda's murderer as quickly as possible, I had no choice but to accept her invitation.

But if I really believed Phyllis was a killer, what was I doing leading my kids into the lion's den?

As we waited at Phyllis's front door, I was ready to puke. I seriously considered telling my children not to eat or drink anything since I was getting completely paranoid. This time I wasn't worried about a witch's spell like in Gina's case. It just occurred to me that there could be an actual possibility that Phyllis would poison us.

"If anything tastes funny…" I whispered. I didn't get to finish, though. Phyllis Bishop yanked open the door, looked left and right, and then waved us in.

"Come in, come in. I've been jittery with nerves since I decided to tell you. I don't think I can stand it any longer."

I hardly recognized the old lady. She really did look like a bag of nerves, not the surly pit bull she'd represented herself as so far.

We followed her into the living room. Tea cups had been set out on the coffee table, and a steaming teapot stood in the middle. There was a plate with store-bought shortbread. Either our neighbor had already demolished the Chelsea buns, or she didn't plan on sharing them with us.

Phyllis pointed at the sofa and chairs with flowery chintz covers in muted rose and brown tones. The rest of the living room was beige—walls, carpet, cushions, tablecloth.

We all took a seat and looked at Phyllis expectantly. She perched on the edge of an armchair and put a hand on her heart.

"I thought I wouldn't say anything. I thought I could do this. Usually, I handle everything by myself; I've never needed anyone. But ever since I called you and decided to unburden myself, I've been feeling worse by the hour. This is weighing on me. I really need to tell someone, and I'm so glad you're here."

Oh my god. The woman was going to confess to murder in front of my children. What had I done? I was way, way out of my depth.

CHAPTER TWENTY

Audrey surprised me by taking charge of the conversation.

"Mrs. Bishop, you don't look so good," she said with a frown. "Here, why don't you eat a cookie? I always feel better after I've eaten something sweet."

She passed the plate of shortbread to our elderly neighbor, who absentmindedly took one and put it into her mouth.

I smiled gratefully at my youngest daughter, and, taking her lead, poured Phyllis a cup of tea. "Milk and sugar, Mrs. Bishop?"

"What? Umm, yes, three sugars, please."

I dumped three heaping spoonfuls of sugar into the tea and stirred, then passed the cup to the old lady.

She took a few fortifying sips, which seemed to help. "Yes, as I was saying, I really need to tell someone. I saw Matilda's killer the other night." Her hands were so jittery, the tea spilled on the saucer, and she set it back down on the table.

I had literally been holding on to the edge of my seat,

so I didn't know if I should be disappointed or relieved that Phyllis didn't out herself as the murderer.

"Yes." Phyllis hung her head. "I'm ashamed to say that I didn't want to help the police catch Matilda's killer. There has been bad blood between us, you see."

"I heard something about that. My great-aunt has photos of the three of you when you were younger, so I wondered what had happened…" I trailed off. I didn't want to say too much, to remind Phyllis that Stanley had left her, in case she got self-conscious. We needed to stay on topic.

"Yes, we were best friends before Matilda stole my boyfriend. Stanley was the love of my life, and Matilda married him, knowing it would break my heart. I used to think she did it on purpose." She leaned forward, and I could see her eyes glitter with tears. "That she couldn't bear to see me happy. To add insult to injury, Ethel sided with her. I had nobody, and I stayed lonely all my life. I used to blame it all on Matilda."

"It sounds as if you changed your mind about that," Blake said perceptively. "Did you forgive her in the end?"

Mrs. Bishop's expression turned grim, and she shook her head. "No. I could never do that. Whether or not she meant to, Matilda ruined my life by stealing Stanley away. But…" She nibbled on a shortbread cookie. "She called after Ethel passed away, Matilda did. She hadn't tried to reach out in a long while, but I guess Ethel's death made her lonely too."

"What did you talk about?" I asked curiously.

"I didn't." Phyllis shrugged. "I just couldn't. I picked up, intending to tell Matilda to stop calling, but I never got a word out. She told me some things. About her DIY projects. Her family. She worried about her niece, said she'd changed so much, worried about her brother because he was blind to it, those kinds of things. At some point, she hung up."

"Do you think you two might have made up if Mrs. Rutherford hadn't died?" Blake asked.

"I don't know. I don't think so." Phyllis's voice hardened.

"And then you…saw the murderer the night Matilda was killed." I carefully brought the conversation back to the most important topic. "But you didn't tell the police?"

Phyllis was quiet for a moment. I already feared that I had sounded too accusatory and that she would retract her statement. Then she said, "At the time, I didn't know Matilda had been killed. I only put two and two together later. Besides, I feared the police wouldn't believe me. It would have been a fuss, my routine would have been disrupted, people would talk about me. I just didn't want to get into all of that for Matilda's sake." She sounded stubborn.

"Why wouldn't the police believe you?"

"Because"—Phyllis took another sip of the ridiculously sweet tea—"it was an alien."

I'd leaned forward in anticipation and just caught myself in time before I slid off the couch. "Umm, what?"

"It was an alien who killed Matilda."

I couldn't wipe my incredulity off my face in time, so Phyllis said defensively, "I know what I saw! I was in bed, and I got up on account of my bladder. Since I have to go a lot at night, I don't bother with the light. There's enough moonlight coming in through the bathroom window. When I looked outside, there was the alien, coming out of Matilda's back door. I thought I was dreaming. But when I heard Matilda got killed, I remembered. The timeline fits too. I'm telling you, it was an alien who murdered her."

"Of course, it is just…um…why would an alien kill Matilda Rutherford?"

"I thought you said aliens only exist on TV, Mom." Audrey looked a little scared.

"I've just never met anyone who has seen an alien with their own eyes. So let's keep an open mind, sweetie, and see what Mrs. Bishop has to say." Turning to Phyllis, I asked, "How did you know it was an alien?"

Our elderly neighbor blustered. "What do you mean? Everyone knows what an alien looks like. With this funny facial shape and the huge bug eyes."

"Of course. I see." I nudged Blake, who was sitting next to me. "Hey, Blake, why don't you get your sketchbook out and try to draw the alien Mrs. Bishop describes?"

"Like they do in crime series on TV?" Mrs. Bishop asked.

"Yes." I smiled. "I think that would really help. And we could give it to the police, if you decide to come forward officially."

"I don't know if I want to do that. I can see that you don't believe me when I say it was an alien. The police won't either, and I'll be the laughingstock of Fairwyck before long." She crossed her arms over her ample chest.

"Okay, maybe we won't go to the police. But you clearly thought you needed to unburden yourself. This is weighing on your conscience, because no matter how much you hated Matilda, letting someone know what you witnessed is the decent thing to do."

Phyllis considered this. Finally, she nodded.

Blake took the sketch pad and a pencil out of her bag and asked Mrs. Bishop more questions about the "alien." I obviously hoped that the image would show something different from an extraterrestrial creature. Maybe a man with a funny hat or something.

But when Blake was done, I had to admit that it really did look like an alien. Or a person with the head of a giant fly.

"That's exactly it!" Phyllis exclaimed. "This is exactly what it looked like. Crikey, you're good at drawing, child!"

Blake blushed. "I just drew the images that came to me. That's what I do. People often say that it's like I had a peek into their head when I draw something they describe."

I stared at my child. Could it be that they...but never mind that. I had something more important to consider right now. I'd been convinced that Phyllis Bishop murdered Matilda Rutherford. I'd come here thinking she was going to tell me that. I should have known that wasn't going to happen—surely, she wouldn't invite me and my children to afternoon tea for a murder confession!

Although...I had to question how sound of mind Phyllis currently was. She still seemed to think it was all right to talk about murder and seeing a killer in front of my kids. And what she'd confessed was a very unlikely story.

I certainly didn't believe in aliens, no matter how much I had widened my horizon of all things supernatural recently.

If Phyllis Bishop had wanted to throw us off her trail, why hadn't she just said she'd seen a man or a woman of generic description? Maybe because then there would be no excuse not to go to the police and tell them about it?

If that was the case, why had Phyllis bothered to make up the story just for us? She couldn't have known I was on to her.

I was absentmindedly nibbling a cookie while Blake was still drawing. After a while, Audrey put in, "Mom, are we staying much longer? I have a lot of homework, and you know I like to get it done before the weekend."

"No, umm, I guess not. You're right, we should go." I set my cup of tea down and stood. "Thank you for the invitation, Mrs. Bishop. It was nice to stop by, and I'm glad you confided in us. I'd go to the police if I were you. They might be skeptical, but they wouldn't broadcast it to the public. This is a murder investigation, and they would take everything seriously."

"Yes. Yes, you're right." Mrs. Bishop didn't get up from her armchair. She seemed withdrawn. "I'll think about it."

"Great. We'll see ourselves out. Thank you for the tea and cookies. Come on, kids."

We left through the front door but walked past the house through the garden and climbed over our fence, since it was so much quicker.

I didn't think Phyllis would mind in this instance—or even notice.

We didn't talk about what had happened at Mrs. Bishop's, but I could tell Audrey was upset. Maybe she was scared about the alien, but it could have also been the talk about murder. I decided it would be best to take her mind off things. "I know you wanted to do your homework, Audrey, but how about some TV? And we could have the ice cream now instead of after dinner?"

The kids were all for it. Audrey turned on the TV, and Blake finished whatever drawing she had started at our neighbor's.

When I brought over the bowls of ice cream, I got a good look at the drawing. It was a tarot card. I handed Audrey her bowl and put Blake's on the table.

"What are you drawing, Blake?"

"Oh, just something else I saw in Mrs. Bishop's head."

I nearly dropped my ice cream.

Blake was intensely focused on their picture. I didn't think they realized what they'd said. I gently took the pencil out of their hand to get their attention.

"Honey, I think we should talk."

CHAPTER TWENTY-ONE

Blake and I waited until Audrey went to bed that evening to talk about her gift.

They confessed that they regularly got very vivid impressions of images from other people and that drawing the images felt like channeling them through their hands onto the paper.

The tarot card I'd seen on the sketch pad and the sentence "forgive yourself or others for wrongdoings" had been plucked directly out of Phyllis's consciousness earlier.

"Why have you never told me about this before?" I asked.

Blake shrugged, turning red. "I didn't think people would like it. Thoughts are private. And until Aunt Gina told us about the abilities that run in our family, I'd never been sure that I actually saw what people think."

We spoke about the ethical ramifications of her abilities, but I wasn't worried that Blake would abuse their talent. They were a sensitive kid.

Plus, they reassured me they weren't getting these impressions from people all the time. The process of getting lost in drawing the image had something to do with it, so it pretty much only happened when they had a pencil and sketch pad in their hands.

Then we talked about the tarot card drawing in particular.

It made us think of Gina.

She read tarot cards, and even though Phyllis Bishop didn't strike me as the type who'd consult a medium, I could be wrong.

Did the tarot card have anything to do with the murder? And might Gina be connected to it?

I didn't say this to Blake, since I wanted to keep my suspicions about Gina and Emerald to myself. I was very much unsure about them, and I didn't want to poison my children's minds against our relatives.

But the next day was Saturday and my day off from my cleaning job. An ideal opportunity to invite ourselves over to Gina and Emerald's home for tea.

I didn't relish introducing my children to the nightmarish abode our relatives called home, but they would see it eventually, and this was as good a time as any.

I told Blake that I wanted to ask Gina about the meaning of the tarot card without revealing to her why, and thus breaking Phyllis's confidence, and we came up with a plan.

Walking to the Sacred Salmon Inn, I told my kids that the old building was a little spooky but that they shouldn't be scared. "Gina and Emerald have been living there for twenty years, so there's nothing to be worried about."

Still, Blake and Audrey looked like skittish kittens when we walked around the old inn, clearly sensing the haunted atmosphere.

When Gina and Emerald opened the door and greeted us, I asked them if we could spend our visit in the Victorian annex instead of the old taproom.

Emerald looked at her mother. "See, I told you, Mom.

The old inn isn't suitable for entertaining guests." She rolled her eyes when she said to me, "Mom just loves it. But I already set up tea and cake in one of the parlors. Follow me."

The parlor wasn't as haunting as the medieval pub, but it was still plenty nightmare-inducing. Our eyes were assaulted by a bright array of colors, bold patterns, lots of gold, and an immense amount of clutter.

I was more of a minimalist, preferring white or natural colors paired with wood, so this Victorian aesthetic wasn't my cup of tea. My brain felt overloaded with sensory data, and it took me a while to process the details.

The walls were red and turquoise, the velvet curtains purple. There were layered carpets with intricate patterns in all colors, and the room was crammed with antique furniture, paintings, and knickknacks. Everything, from the molding to the fabrics to the porcelain teacups, was trimmed with gold.

"So is this where you receive your clients, Gina?" I asked, as soon as I found words again.

"No, this is a private sitting room. There's a smaller parlor that is set up like a Victorian medium's space. A bit more atmospheric, you know?" Gina said cheerfully.

I raised my eyebrows. This parlor seemed plenty atmospheric to me, so I shuddered to think what the other room looked like.

My children seemed to have an entirely different opinion about this parlor, though.

"This is so cool," Audrey said enthusiastically, stroking the white-and-gold-patterned fabric of a chaise longue.

Blake asked if we could see the other room.

"Sure," Gina said.

"Let's have tea first, before it gets cold," Emerald said, pointing at the teapot and the etagere with cupcakes, petit fours, and finger sandwiches.

There was an array of furniture surrounding the table. Most were antique chairs with spindly legs that looked too delicate to support my weight. Gina had already taken a seat on the only solid-looking piece of furniture. I carefully sat down on the chaise longue and then noticed it was too low. I felt like a child playing tea party with grown-ups. Not exactly an excellent position to be in if one wanted to interrogate someone. My shady relatives were literally on higher ground than me, and I didn't like it.

Grumpy, I grabbed a cupcake and took a bite.

Blake, who'd wisely chosen one of the chairs and was thus on an equal footing with Gina and Emerald, took over. I smiled at her gratefully.

"I've been really into tarot cards lately," Blake mentioned. "You know, since your visit."

Audrey gave Blake a quizzical look but didn't contradict them. She'd stuffed a brownie bite into her mouth and gotten up to inspect the many knickknacks in the room.

"I think the illustrations on the cards are fascinating," Blake carried on.

"Do you have a tarot card deck, dear?" Gina asked. "I could lend you one."

"I ordered a deck online. I think it's the most common one. Smith-Waite?"

"Oh yes. I have others too. You can have a look, if you like, compare the images."

"I'd love that. I have so many questions. The meaning of the cards is all over the internet, of course, but there's also a lot of made-up stuff online, and since you're an expert, I was hoping I could ask you."

"I'd love to teach you about tarot cards." My great-aunt seemed delighted.

"Okay, great." Blake got out their sketch pad. "I like to draw the cards myself. Maybe I'm just imagining it, but I think it helps me connect with the imagery."

"Never second-guess yourself when it comes to your talents, child," Gina told her. "Trust your intuition."

Blake nodded. "These are the cards that spoke to me. Can you tell me more about them?"

They held up the image of a card called the Moon. On the top half, there was a large sun with a moon inside flanked by two towers—or standing stones? A small path in the middle led across a field to mountains in the image's background. There were also two dog-like animals, possibly wolves, looking up at the sun/moon. Right at the bottom of the card, there was a crustacean crawling out of the water.

"I'm not surprised this card struck you as important," Gina said, nodding sagely. "It signifies psychic abilities, secrets, and intuition. You're just discovering your own psychic abilities, as are your mother and your sister."

Blake's cheeks colored. "Well, to be honest, I drew this card with Mom in mind."

I looked at them in surprise. We'd decided they'd ask about three different cards, so it wouldn't be so obvious we wanted to know about the one in Phyllis's head. I'd just assumed Blake would choose the other two at random. I was thinking they hadn't been embellishing the truth much when they'd claimed an interest in tarot.

"Of course you did, dear. Like I said, Liv is currently discovering her own psychic abilities after suppressing them her whole life. On top of that, your mother is at the center of a murder investigation. The moon relates to our dreams, to our intuition, and also to our collective unconscious. It's all about the mystery, you see. The moon reflects light from the sun, which is why the card depicts the moon as being part of the sun. It can only partly illuminate the path, leaving a lot in shadows. Liv is navigating a situation with many unseen elements, the truth hidden in the dark. She knows the secrets are there, though, and she'll uncover them in due time."

I had goose bumps, and a shiver ran down my spine. I carefully put down the rest of my cupcake, having suddenly lost my appetite. How was my great-aunt aware of this? Did she know I was investigating the murder? Was she helping or warning me?

I suddenly had the dull feeling that this visit hadn't been a good idea. My relatives' behavior had been suspicious from the start. It had been weird that they hadn't introduced themselves earlier, only to barge into my home with an ominous warning supposedly gleaned from a tarot card reading.

I'd wondered why Ethel hadn't left the cottage to them —and why Gina and Emerald hadn't laid claim to the inheritance.

Blake had already moved on to the next page in her notebook, with the drawing of a blindfolded person clad in a long robe sitting on a stone bench against the backdrop of a lake. They were holding up two swords, crossing their arms in front of their chest, so the swords pointed in opposite directions.

"Two of Swords," Gina said. "It's about choices. There could be a conflict of ideas between people. The card could signify a negotiation or a truce."

"Really?" Blake looked a little disappointed. "I picked the card for myself, and I thought it looked really cool. The person is like a warrior, ready for combat, but perfectly serene and balanced."

Gina smiled and nodded. "If that's what the card signifies to you, then that's what it means. Interpreting a card is always personal, and you need to rely on your intuition when it comes to finding meaning."

If the entire visit hadn't unsettled me so much already, I might have rolled my eyes. Prior to moving back to Fairwyck, I would have taken this sort of wishy-washy interpretation as the typical drivel psychics employ to scam people.

But Blake looked at the drawing for a bit and nodded, smiling to themself. If Gina's explanation did something for them, I wasn't going to argue about it. It was Blake's card, after all.

Then Blake flipped a page again. They showed Gina the original drawing they'd made after speaking to Phyllis Bishop.

Gina furrowed her brows, and her eyes clouded over. Then she said in a rather flat tone of voice, "Forgive yourself or others for wrongdoings."

Blake's eyes widened, and they shot me a look.

I just sat there, stock-still, not moving a muscle. I was no longer just experiencing shivers down my spine. Now I was frozen with fear.

These were the exact words Blake had plucked out of Phyllis's head.

Gina was repeating them—had she told them to Phyllis Bishop before? Phyllis must have been her client. What did that mean? Was the card—and my great-aunt—somehow connected to "the alien," the person who'd killed Matilda Rutherford?

CHAPTER TWENTY-TWO

Gina cleared her throat. "I don't understand. The first card you showed me was for your mother. The next for yourself. You didn't pick this one for your sister, did you? I don't see a connection."

She looked over to Audrey, who was in the room's corner, playing with a cat I hadn't even noticed before. The cat's calico coat blended with the mix of colors and patterns on the carpet.

Blake turned red. "Um, no. This isn't a card I picked for Audrey. How did you know?"

"It's the Judgement card."

We'd already known this, because like with the Moon, it said Judgement at the bottom. The card was weird, with an angel blowing a trumpet in the clouds above and naked people stepping out of graves at the bottom.

"The card is about reviewing past choices," Gina explained. "I mean, technically, Audrey, like you two, is experiencing a rebirth, having to learn from the past, making choices about how to move on. But…" She cast a glance toward my youngest, who wasn't paying us any attention, too engrossed in the cat.

"It's not like Audrey had a choice in anything. She couldn't have acted differently or influenced the situation. We hope she'll learn something about what truly matters in life, but…" Gina shook her head. "It just doesn't seem like a card fitting for your little sister, Blake."

Blake looked at me, then at Gina. "No, actually, I drew the card with our neighbor in mind. Phyllis Bishop. We visited her yesterday."

Gina stared at them for a few seconds. "Ahh. That makes sense."

We waited, but she didn't elaborate. Gina must have thought that Blake had seen something or sensed something about Phyllis—which aligned with a card reading she'd recently done for her. But my great-aunt didn't explain this to us, or even tell us that Phyllis had been a client of hers.

Instead, she got up and changed the subject. "Do you want to see the other parlor and look at different tarot cards, Blake?" she asked with a beatific smile.

"Um…" Blake exchanged a look with me, and I gave a nod. "Sure. I'd love to."

"Do you want to come too, Liv?" Gina asked on her way out of the parlor.

"No, thanks. I'll finish my cupcake, and then we should go. I have to get ready for work."

I'd have plenty of time. But it was as good an excuse as any to get out of there. I just didn't know what to make of my relatives. I probably shouldn't let my kids spend too much time with them before I was sure I could trust them.

When Blake got back from the psychic parlor, I told a reluctant Audrey to say goodbye, and we left.

That night, I spent all of two hours behind the bar of the Owl and Oak, trying to focus on work while Jason shot me dirty looks the entire time. Out of the corner of my eye, I could see him having a chat with Ellie, and afterward, Ellie came over to tell me I could go home.

She didn't look me in the eye when she said it wasn't busy enough. I served the IPS guy with the aviator glasses the pint he'd ordered, then grabbed my things and left, holding my head up high until I was out the door.

Outside, my shoulders hunched, and I blinked away my tears of humiliation. We needed all the extra money I could earn. But Jason clearly didn't like me working at the pub for some reason. At least I'd be home with the kids that night. After the incident with the brick, I hated to leave them alone in the house. Blake and Audrey were still up, watching TV, and were pleased I could join them.

On Sunday, I was much too busy with work to even think about figuring out the identity of Matilda's murderer or pondering my relatives' involvement.

I wanted to reach out to Phyllis on Monday, hoping she'd told the police about what she'd witnessed—and maybe ask her about Gina. But then I got stuck dealing with the insane amount of life admin that comes with moving with children to another country and becoming a homeowner. I had put it off long enough. It took much longer than expected, but when I'd completed my tasks, I was in the mood for ticking more items off my to-do list.

Blake and Audrey had gotten started on sorting Ethel's old clothes yesterday, and the bags were sitting next to the front door. I didn't know when I'd next have a chance to drive to the charity shop in Cirencester, so I decided to take care of that too. Driving back, I was just in time to pick up the kids from school. They both had tests the next day I helped them study for.

After dinner, I slowed down enough to notice that my day off had passed me by without making any headway with the investigation, but by the time I thought about calling Phyllis, I saw all the lights were out in her cottage. She'd probably turned in early.

From the moment I put my head on the pillow, my worry spiral started up again. I was overwhelmed with everything, and I couldn't really make finding Matilda's killer a priority, even though Phyllis had given me a good lead—well, *a* lead.

Would this ever get resolved, and could I move on from it soon? At some point, I fell into an uneasy sleep, but after tossing and turning in the early morning hours, I finally gave up. I embraced getting a head start on the day, got dressed, and went downstairs. It was Tuesday, which meant I had a long workday ahead of me.

I considered preparing a casserole for dinner that I could just pop into the oven later. Checking the pantry and fridge, I was pleased to find all the ingredients. The audacious thought that today might finally turn out to be a good day crossed my mind…and that's when I saw I was out of coffee.

I wouldn't be able to handle the day without coffee. I already felt my eyelids drooping. But then I pulled myself together. Fighting off the symptoms of serious caffeine withdrawal, I managed to make lunches and put the casserole together.

A glance at the clock told me it was a few minutes before the village shop opened. If I hurried, I could get coffee and fresh croissants just in time for breakfast.

I ran upstairs to wake the kids and tell them about my errand. Then I put on a cardigan and ran out of the house.

Halfway down the road, I heard someone call my name. Looking over my shoulder, I spotted Phyllis Bishop huffing and puffing behind me.

I slowed down a little. "Phyllis, hi! I'm in a bit of a rush to get to the shop before work, I'm afraid."

Phyllis, cheeks flushed and gray curls in disarray, caught up with me. "I'm off to the shop too," she said, lifting her basket, "but I also wanted to talk to you. I was going to stop by your house before doing my weekly shopping, but then I saw you…" Phyllis took a few wheezing breaths. "You're so fast."

"Sorry," I grimaced, sneaking a peek at my wristwatch. "I'm out of coffee, and I really wanted to make some before setting off to work. I've been meaning to talk to you too. Let's walk to the shop together, then we can chat."

"Umm, okay…" Phyllis tried her best to keep up. "So I understand now what I saw the other night."

My head whipped in her direction. "You mean the night Matilda, um…"

"Was killed, yes." Phyllis seemed impatient.

"The alien?"

"It wasn't an alien. How silly of me." My elderly neighbor shook her head in disgust. "Maybe it's time for me to admit that my eyesight isn't as good as it used to be. Had twenty-twenty vision, once upon a time."

We had arrived at the shop, and I pushed the door open. Phyllis tried to stop me. "Wait a minute, this is important."

"Sorry, please keep talking. I just really need to get my coffee." I linked arms with her, helping her up the steps and into the shop.

Phyllis Bishop took a deep breath, then said, "So I know it wasn't an alien. Simple mistake to make, you'll think, when I tell you what I really saw that Saturday night outside Matilda's cottage. I know who the murderer is now!"

I stood there, staring at her intently, having all but forgotten about my errand.

But Phyllis suddenly stopped talking, looking around

self-consciously. In a quieter voice, she continued, "I can't tell you here. Let's talk in private. Can you come by later?"

A little exasperated, I looked at my watch again. I really wanted to know now. But it wasn't possible. "Yes, I can visit after work. I'm working late today, so it'll probably be after dinner, actually."

Phyllis Bishop nodded. "Good. I'll explain everything then."

"Okay." Flustered, I grabbed a bag of coffee and haphazardly threw fresh croissants into a bag.

I hardly looked Michelle in the eyes when I paid, and then I dropped my coins on the floor. "Shoot."

"Are you okay?" she asked with concern.

"Yes, sorry." I forced a smile, chucking the coins I'd picked up onto the counter. "Just in a hurry. Keep the change."

Turning around to Phyllis, who was doing her shopping in a much more leisurely manner, I shouted, "See you tonight."

Then I rushed out of the shop and back home again.

I made a thermos full of coffee, pushed breakfast on the kids, and then had to take my croissant to go as I hurried to work.

It was a full day without much of a break, but I didn't mind. I could listen to music and found my cleaning chores actually quite meditative. They kept me occupied so that my thoughts couldn't spiral again.

At the end of the long workday, I was pooped, though. Having prepped the casserole, I could at least take a quick break with a cup of tea, Ethel the cat on my lap, waiting for dinner to heat in the oven.

We had a nice meal, even though Audrey was unusually quiet. When my daughter was overly perky, it usually meant she felt the opposite inside, so I figured I'd let her work out whatever preoccupied her. I thought it was a good sign to see her more contemplative. We talked about school and how Blake was handling things, and for the first time since moving here, I felt optimistic.

I should have known that wasn't going to last long.

Stepping over the fence into Phyllis Bishop's garden, I almost dropped the carton with the leftover Cherry Garcia ice cream we'd had for dessert, and which was supposed to be my apology gift for leaving it so late to come over.

I felt like I was hit by a wall of…something dark. As if there was a gray cloud hanging over Phyllis's property.

Explaining away my intuition had been my MO my entire life, and it was a hard habit to drop. I told myself I was being silly.

Maybe it felt dark because there was no light on in any of the windows. I checked my wristwatch. It wasn't eight o'clock yet. Surely Phyllis didn't go to bed that early, did she? Plus, she was expecting me.

Dread spread through my insides as I knocked on the back door and Phyllis didn't answer. I went around to the front of the house to ring the doorbell a couple of times. Nobody opened up.

My old self came up with a bunch of explanations. Phyllis could've forgotten about our chat. She had a reputation as a loner, but she might be out and about, partaking in some sort of leisure activity. Knitting maybe? Or aerobics? I scrunched up my nose. Imagining Phyllis in spandex seemed incongruent. And she really wasn't sociable.

Even if any of those explanations had made sense to me, I had a hunch that something was wrong. I'd ignored these gut feelings all my life, and others, like Jamie Rees, might not put stock in them either. But I was learning to trust them.

So I traced my steps back to the kitchen door and pounded my fists against it. Only that didn't help either. It just hurt my knuckles. I yowled with pain. The noise was echoed by a meow, and I looked down to see Ethel the cat.

"Phyllis doesn't like it if you visit, but it looks as if she's not home," I said, frustrated enough to tell my woes to the cat again. "She wanted to tell me something important about Matilda's murder. It's my fault. I should've gotten here sooner." I raked a hand through my hair, feeling like a fool.

As if the cat could help me.

It turned out she could.

Ethel kept pawing against a planter until I got the hint. I looked underneath and—lo and behold—there was the key to the back door.

"How did you know?" I asked Ethel. "Never mind. I could kiss you!"

The cat looked suitably disgusted, and I straightened to unlock the door.

"Phyllis?" I called into the dark house, my feeling of triumph quickly displaced by a sense of foreboding.

"It's me, Liv. You asked me to come over, remember?"

No answer.

"I'm worried, so I'm coming in!"

I slowly walked into the kitchen. It was eerily quiet. An open pack of cookies and a teapot were sitting on the kitchen counter. I put a finger against the flower-painted ceramic pot. Stone cold.

With shaky legs, I crossed the kitchen to the hallway. "Phyllis?" I croaked.

I went into the living room. It was dark, but I could still see the outline of the furniture and even made out the cup of tea on the couch table.

The high-backed armchair Phyllis had been sitting in when we had visited her the other day had its back turned to me. I couldn't be sure, but somehow I knew someone was sitting in the chair.

Holding my breath, I gingerly stepped toward and then around it.

"Phyllis?"

My neighbor was right there.

"Phyllis!"

But in a way, she wasn't there anymore.

I dropped the container with ice cream I'd been holding on to this entire time.

Red-stained melted goo spilled onto my Birkenstock-clad feet.

Instinctively, I backed away until I hit the sideboard. Out of the corner of my eye, I spotted Phyllis's telephone in its charging station.

Unable to take my eyes off my neighbor, I fumbled a little until I successfully grabbed it.

I couldn't even remember the emergency phone number for the UK, only kept thinking it wasn't 911. The only phone number that popped into my head was my own landline, which I'd had to write down a few times yesterday when filling out a bunch of forms.

Blake picked up. I tried to keep my voice even. "Honey, please get my cell. It's on the kitchen counter." When they'd located it, I told them my pin and asked them to look for Jamie Rees in my contact list. "I need you to call him, Bianca."

Despite my best effort to sound calm, Blake must have realized something was wrong because they didn't correct me. In my state of emotional turmoil, I'd forgotten about the name change.

"What is it, Mom? Should I come over to Mrs. Bishop's and bring you the phone?"

"No!" I said sharply. "Don't come over. Call Jamie Rees and tell him to get to Phyllis Bishop's house as soon as he can. Something terrible has happened."

CHAPTER TWENTY-THREE

It felt like an eternity until Jamie Rees arrived.

I was torn between not being able to take my eyes off my dead neighbor and worrying about my children. A killer was on the loose. I wanted to run back home to protect them. But I also had to stay here. I couldn't leave the scene of a murder, not after the police were already suspicious of me. I had to do everything by the book.

Contaminating the crime scene with ice cream was already an inauspicious start.

Luckily, I had Ethel by my side. The cat had followed me into the house and was trying her best to get rid of the mess by lapping it up furiously.

"It doesn't matter, Ethel," I said, half crying, half laughing. "The ice cream is the least of my worries. I'll have to explain why I entered a murdered woman's house —and how."

The lights turned on and I screamed.

Ethel rounded her back and hissed, then shot off into a dark corner.

But it was only DS Rees.

"Liv? Is everything okay?"

I gave a hollow laugh. "No. It's Phyllis Bishop. She's dead."

In the glaring light, it was more than obvious. Phyllis had probably died hours ago, so I couldn't have saved her, even if I'd arrived an hour earlier. Her face was unnaturally pale, with a waxen sheen. Her eyes were open and staring.

Jamie came closer. He stopped next to me, most likely so as not to disturb the scene of the crime. "Looks like she dropped something." He pointed at the ice cream container and the stain on the floor. "Maybe she doubled over in pain, dropped this, and sank into the chair."

There *was* an expression of agony on the frozen mask that was Phyllis's face.

"No, that was me."

Jamie's head spun around. "What? What do you mean?" He stepped away from me.

"The ice cream. I brought it over. I dropped it when I saw her. God, what did you think I meant?"

"Nothing," he mumbled.

But my shoulders hunched. I knew what he'd meant. DI Farrow had gotten to him.

Then I spotted a small bottle with a pharmacy label on the coffee table next to the half-empty cup of tea.

"Hang on," I said, taking a step toward it.

"Stop, Liv!" Jamie got his phone out. "I need you to stay exactly where you are. I'm calling the crime scene unit right now."

I stopped in my tracks, but I leaned forward and squinted to read the label. "Propranolol," I read out loud. "It must be the beta blocker Phyllis took because of her high blood pressure. Do you think that could have caused this?"

I said it, but I couldn't quite believe it. I hadn't considered anything but murder.

"Then it could be an accident. But it's best to treat it as a suspicious death," Jamie said. "We're going to do everything by the book."

I shook my head. "I just don't believe it was accidental. Phyllis wanted to tell me something tonight, Jamie. She knew who Matilda's murderer was."

Jamie narrowed his eyes. "Didn't you try to convince me just the other day that *Phyllis* murdered Matilda?"

"Yes," I said impatiently. "But since then, new information has come to light, and—"

"Didn't I ask you to stay out of this investigation and let the police handle it?" Jamie said sternly.

I sighed. "But listen. Phyllis first thought the murderer was an alien, and then she told me—"

"Enough," Jamie cut me off. "Enough with your fantasy and science fiction stuff. This is real, Liv. An actual, real-life dead person. I don't know what's wrong with you, but there are people in charge who take this seriously. You're not qualified, and frankly, I'm questioning if you're even of sound enough mind to figure that out. Let me call it in so the police can handle it."

I turned bright red. His words had cut deep. I was equally mortified and offended.

When he got off the phone, he said to me, "Look, sorry to be harsh. But this is serious, Liv. You're at a crime scene again. I'd advise you to say as little as possible, stick to the facts, and not mention fantastic and wild theories. You're lucky Farrow is out of town today. He'd arrest you on the spot."

Tears shot into my eyes as I thought about my kids.

"Do I have to stay, or can I go over to my house?" I whispered, not looking him in the eyes.

"Actually, it might be best for you to go home and let me handle everything with the coroner and the crime scene team by myself. We'll go over your official statement tomorrow."

I just nodded and turned to leave.

"Wait… Maybe you should wait until someone gets here so I can walk you home. It's dark, and if there's really a murderer running around…" Jamie looked skeptically at Phyllis.

"Make up your mind," I said, a little too sarcastically. "I'm either the suspect who kills off old ladies, or I'm in danger."

There was hurt in Jamie's brown eyes. "I don't think you're the murderer. Really, I just—"

I held up my hand, suddenly completely exhausted. "It's okay. I just want to get home and be with my children. It's a quick walk across the back gardens. I'll be fine."

Ethel shot past us like a ginger lightning bolt. "My cat will look out for me."

Jamie sighed. "I really need to stay here, so okay… Give me a quick call when you arrive home, though."

"All right." I gave a last glance over my shoulder in Phyllis's direction, but I could only see the back of the armchair.

I couldn't help but wonder if my murdered neighbor was still here in spirit. Obviously, I hadn't brought my camera. Not even my cell phone. If I had the opportunity to take pictures, maybe Phyllis could give me a message, tell me what happened.

I thought about quickly grabbing my Nikon and rushing back over, taking a few snaps before the coroner or anyone else got here…

But no. Jamie wouldn't let me. He'd made it abundantly clear that he didn't believe in my ability, or anything I said, really.

And I probably couldn't come back to Phyllis's cottage either. Farrow might be off tonight, but as soon as the DI found out about this, he'd watch me like a hawk.

I slunk off, disappointed I'd wasted the opportunity. I should have gone home, gotten my camera, and taken a few photos before DS Rees got there. My gift and how it could help hadn't even entered my mind because I'd been in too much shock from finding Phyllis dead.

Jamie was right about one thing. I wasn't the right person to solve this, or any other case of suspicious death. I made a terrible detective, and I should leave it to the professionals.

Yes, getting Matilda's—and now Phyllis's—killer caught was a priority for me, but it seemed as if I was just making things worse for myself by trying to do it on my own.

I crossed the kitchen to the back door. Jamie must have come in this way, since I'd left the back door open, and he had turned on the light. Now I noticed something else on the kitchen counter, next to the teapot and the cookies.

It was a magazine. One of those marketed to stay-at-home ladies, with gossip about the royal family, recipes, articles about personal tragedies, diet and cleaning tips, and whatever else a homemaker might find interesting. The magazine also featured a lot of full-page ads that looked like articles, selling diet pills and hemorrhoid cream.

Why this magazine had a picture of a gas mask in it wasn't entirely clear to me, since it didn't seem to fit the demographic, but apparently there was one.

Phyllis had ripped it out.

I looked around to make sure Jamie couldn't see me from the living room before I grabbed the piece of paper and stuck it in my pocket.

The gas mask looked like the face of the "alien" Blake had drawn from the image in Phyllis's head.

And I suddenly had an inkling of what Phyllis had wanted to tell me.

She hadn't seen an alien outside Matilda's house that Saturday night.

She'd seen an actual person with a gas mask on.

CHAPTER TWENTY-FOUR

The next day, I was so nervous that I didn't remember doing any of my cleaning tasks afterward. I could only hope I hadn't done a subpar job and that I wouldn't get fired as a result. I always had my phone on me, expecting to hear from the police, but it didn't ring. In the late afternoon, just as I was ruining dinner by burning sausages and letting pots boil over, there was the dreaded knock on the door.

I immediately dropped the oven tray I was holding, leaving frozen hash browns to skid across the kitchen linoleum tiles.

It was Jamie Rees, come to take my statement. My greeting would have been equally as cool as his if I hadn't been occupied with picking hash browns off the floor.

And Jamie quickly became distracted from playing the role of serious and proper police officer. "What's that smell?"

I pointed at the charred sausages. "Can we get this done and over with? As you can see, I have to call the pizza delivery service in order to get dinner on the table today."

"There's no pizza delivery service in Fairwyck," Jamie said deadpan.

"Of course not." Defeated, I sank into a kitchen chair. "Do me a favor and open the top cabinet above the stove, would you?"

I'd considered dating Jamie Rees. Maybe, eventually, sometime in the future. But after the way he'd spoken to me yesterday, it didn't really matter what he thought of me as I demolished my secret stash of M&Ms. "Pass me the yellow bag, please."

Jamie did as asked, raising an eyebrow. But the corners of his mouth were raised slightly.

As I popped the delicious chocolate-covered peanuts into my mouth, Jamie opened more cupboards and pulled out ingredients like pasta and olive oil.

I asked, "What are you doing?" but I didn't stop him when he got more items out of the fridge.

"I brought over a statement I typed up, based on what you said yesterday," he told me as he started chopping things. "You need to sign it."

"Doesn't it work the other way around? I give you a statement, and—"

"I wanted to save you the trip to the station, and also, Liv…" He put the knife down and turned around, giving me a serious look. "Farrow is still out of town. I had to update him on the phone. But he'll be back tomorrow, and he'll ask you to come in for questioning. He's convinced you're responsible, for both Matilda's and Phyllis's deaths."

I frowned. "From some of the things you said yesterday, I thought you were coming around to that theory too." I lined up a few M&Ms on the table, sorting them according to color, just so I wouldn't have to look him in the eye.

"Liv." His tone softened. "I'm sorry for the way I spoke to you. I don't believe you're a murderer. I just don't know what to make of the stuff you're telling me half the time. You are, strangely, always at the center of things, in the wrong place at the wrong time, and I just think you need to take yourself out of the investigation as much as possible."

I looked up as anger boiled up inside of me again. "Well, that's hard to do if the chief investigating officer thinks I'm the prime suspect, isn't it?"

Jamie sighed and turned around, busying himself with cooking. "Yes, I get that. Which is why I tried to craft your statement in a way that makes you seem as uninvolved in Phyllis's death as possible."

"Oh," I grumbled, popping a brown M&M into my mouth. "Thanks."

Jamie filled a pot with water and put it on the stove to boil. "But I've got to tell you, there's evidence that makes you a solid suspect in Farrow's eyes, so—"

I almost choked on my chocolate-covered peanut. "What evidence?"

"Our theory is that Matilda's killer mixed bleach and ammonia, creating a fatal gas in Matilda's kitchen. It's possible the murderer thought it would look like a fatal asthma attack and Matilda's death would be treated like an accident. You're working for a cleaning company, and you got caught taking cleaning products from the scene of the crime."

"I brought my own cleaning products, because there weren't any in the house to do my job," I cried. "And I hope it has by now been established that my boss sent me to Matilda's cottage. Matilda made her own organic cleaning products because she was sensitive to chemical ones. I found a bunch of empty bottles under her sink—those were most likely the ones the killer used."

"Yes, we secured those, but—"

"They weren't mine. I brought mine and forgot them, which is why I came back that night Tracy caught me, to pick them up." I was so worked up by now that my voice got screechy.

"The gas mask!" I exclaimed. "I told you Phyllis Bishop had confided in me and my kids that she'd seen the killer. Phyllis thought it was an alien. Of course, we didn't believe her. Turns out, it was a gas mask."

My loud voice must have alerted my children, because they were coming down the stairs. "Mom?" Blake asked, concerned. "Is everything all right?"

"Yes," I said, forcing myself to calm down. "Jamie Rees came over to talk about last night. And to cook, apparently."

Jamie had put spaghetti into the pot of boiling water and was now getting out a frying pan. "Hi Blake, hi Audrey." He smiled at them.

"Talk about what happened to Mrs. Bishop, you mean?" Audrey frowned.

I nodded.

"Do the police know details yet?" Blake asked.

"No," I said, suddenly thinking of something. "Hey, can you get your sketch pad and show DS Rees the drawing of the gas mask?"

I explained to Jamie about nearsighted Phyllis's alien theory. "It really looks like an alien, but I think it's a gas mask. Phyllis must have realized it too, because she spoke to me early yesterday morning, in the village shop, telling me she now understood who the murderer was. What if someone overheard it? Michelle, for sure, and she's the biggest gossip. Don't you think it's possible Matilda's murderer wanted to silence Phyllis?"

Blake was back and showed the drawing to Jamie.

"Hmm," he said with knitted brows. "We're still not sure if Phyllis simply died of an accidental beta-blocker overdose, but…" He looked at me with his chocolate-brown eyes. "I'm taking your theory seriously, Liv. I'll tell Farrow about it."

I gave him a sad smile. "But you can't take everything I say seriously, can you? Like my…ESP." I couldn't think of a better word for my ability to photograph ghosts.

Jamie didn't get a chance to answer because at that moment I noticed my children were sitting at the kitchen table, watching and listening—and eating my M&Ms.

"Hey!" I said, snatching the bag away but leaving the row on the table. "You're spoiling your appetite. Jamie is making…?" I looked at him.

"Spaghetti aglio e olio. With olives. I hope everyone likes olives?"

Audrey scrunched her nose. "Can I have just spaghetti with ketchup?"

Jamie shuddered at the thought but complied, and stayed for dinner, no less. I signed his statement, and after he left, I felt a little more hopeful that the police would finally see reason, clear me as a suspect, and find the real killer.

My hopes were dashed the next morning when DI Farrow called at the crack of dawn to ask me to come to the station first thing.

I wasn't too pleased about the rude awakening, but I hoped we could get the questioning over and done with before I had to be at work that morning.

I woke my children, told them where I was going, and had Blake promise me they'd have breakfast and get to the school bus on time.

As soon as DI Farrow sat down opposite me in that small, windowless room in the police station, only furnished with a table and a couple of chairs, I knew he wouldn't let me off the hook as easily as I'd dared to hope after my conversation with Jamie last night.

Farrow wasn't disputing my theory at all.

He simply believed that *I* had been the gas mask–wearing killer.

That Phyllis Bishop had realized that *I* was the murderer she'd mistaken for an alien.

And that *I* was the one who'd silenced Phyllis before she could go to the police with that information.

Our conversation was going around in circles, with me stressing that I had an alibi for Matilda's murder and Farrow explaining it away with ridiculous arguments. He kept harping on about my criminal past, even though I insisted the FBI had cleared me of being in cahoots with my husband, and he seemed to have an unhealthy obsession with my mother.

After I'd looked at my wristwatch a thousand times, I said in exasperation, "Look, I don't know what you think we'll accomplish by asking the same questions repeatedly, but if I'll be here much longer, I'm going to have to call my boss and let her know that I'll be late for work. I really don't want to do that. So level with me here. I'll do anything to convince you. What do you need from me? Fingerprints? DNA?"

Farrow leaned back and twirled his mustache. "We don't need any of that. We know you were at the scenes of the crimes because you were caught there."

Jamie, who'd been mainly silent during the interrogation, looked like he could no longer hold back. "Sir. To be fair, Ms. Grantham wasn't caught at Phyllis Bishop's house. She called me herself after finding Phyllis dead in her living room, so…"

Farrow turned bright red. "Rees. A word outside, if you will."

The two police officers stepped out of the interrogation room, leaving me to check my watch again. I'd rather not tell Judith I couldn't come in to work because the police were questioning me for murder. But it looked as if I needed to do just that.

The argument outside grew louder, and I could make out Farrow's booming voice. "Maybe she offed the old bird, then hightailed it to work. It's the perfect crime. You're blinded by her charm and good looks, Rees, and I have half a mind to suspend you."

My heart sank. Jamie Rees wasn't perfect, and he'd said some things to me that were hard to get over, but I couldn't deny that he'd been a good friend to me, looking out for me as much as he could. He'd even cooked dinner for me and the kids, for Pete's sake! He was a good guy, and I didn't want him to lose his job over this.

I got up and opened the door.

The two police officers looked at me, dumbfounded.

DI Farrow's face was as red as a tomato. "What are you doing? Sit back down. This interview isn't over."

"This is ridiculous. If you think you have grounds to charge me, please do. I'll get a lawyer, and I hope he'll be able to counter your unfounded allegations."

I tried to sound calm and confident, even though I was shaking in my sneakers at the thought of a) being arrested and leaving my kids to fend for themselves, and b) having to pay a lawyer with money I didn't have.

"Right now, I need to go to work, so…"

"I will arrest you, Mrs. Grantham, believe you me!" Farrow came toward me, and I backed into the room.

At that moment, a uniformed officer arrived and interrupted Farrow. "Sir, you'll want to see this."

He tried to pass the DI a piece of paper, but Farrow barked, "Not now!"

The officer gave the paper to Jamie.

Farrow got out his handcuffs. His beady eyes glinted as he said, "Liv Grantham, I'm—"

"Farrow!" Jamie called out. "This is the coroner's report."

The DI stopped in his tracks and turned to look at Jamie.

"He ruled Phyllis Bishop's death an accidental overdose."

Farrow's mustache trembled with indignity. "Give me that." He snatched the paper from Jamie's hands.

I grabbed my bag and jacket and swooshed past them. "Sooo… No murder I can be arrested for then?"

Farrow, his eyes still on the paper, grumbled, "Looks like it."

"All right, I really have to go to work. Bye-bye."

Farrow didn't stop me, but his face looked like thunder. I had a knot in my stomach when I left the station, distinctly feeling his hateful glare in my back. I'd set out to make friends in Fairwyck, but it looked as if I'd only managed to make enemies.

CHAPTER TWENTY-FIVE

That night, I spent an hour researching how much a lawyer costs before giving in to my drooping eyelids around eight thirty because of total exhaustion.

After sleeping like a log, I woke up oddly refreshed the next morning. I was still terrified about getting arrested and not knowing what would happen to my kids in that event. But with a rested body and mind, it was easier to think clearly.

The coroner had ruled Phyllis Bishop's death accidental, but I didn't believe it. The murderer had just been very clever. They'd tried to disguise Matilda's death as an accident and hadn't gotten away with it. With Phyllis, they'd just done a better job.

In both cases, the killer had known about the victim's medical condition. Matilda's asthma probably hadn't been that much of a secret.

Thanks to village-shop gossip Michelle, it could very well be that just as many people knew about Phyllis's heart condition. But in order to get away with making the beta-blocker overdose seem accidental, the murderer would have needed to be familiar with the type and dose of medication.

Phyllis had been famous for keeping people at arm's length. There wouldn't have been many people with that knowledge—or the opportunity to doctor Phyllis's bottle of propranolol.

I knew of one person who might have had access to Phyllis: my great-aunt Gina. Conveniently, their client-psychic relationship appeared to have been a secret. I guessed Phyllis had probably been embarrassed about consulting Gina, and Gina hadn't confirmed that the tarot card Blake had shown her had been the same as one in her most recent reading for Phyllis Bishop.

Of course, this theory revolved around a lot of guess-work. It could all be in my head, and Gina had merely picked up on Blake's impression of the card or cited the card's general meaning—and it had been coincidental that the wording had been the same.

Except…I had suspected my relatives from the beginning. There were many reasons their behavior had rubbed me the wrong way. I had to admit that I sort of…liked them, though. Yes, they scared me, and I didn't know what to make of them, but it was also thrilling to have relatives in Fairwyck. Other Seven women with paranormal abilities who might help me understand my own.

Also, why would Gina and Emerald want to kill Matilda Rutherford?

After finishing work on Friday afternoon, I checked the library hours and saw that I had half an hour left to catch Emerald at work.

The library was in a honey-colored cottage adjacent to the church. I assumed it had belonged to the church at one point in time, probably as accommodation for the reverend.

When I asked Emerald about it, she said that I was

spot on. The library was run by the council on a rather small budget, and the church had generously donated the space to house it.

The entire ground floor had been converted into a more or less open-plan space with columns supporting the ceiling. It was dedicated to children's and YA books. "But we also hold events and group meetings here," Emerald told me. "There's enough room for a few rows or a circle of chairs."

Emerald gave me a quick tour of the upstairs rooms, where adult fiction and nonfiction were housed. Then she made me a cup of coffee in the kitchen, and we went to the reception desk, where Emerald issued me a library card.

Once that was taken care of, Emerald asked me how I was doing. "I heard about Phyllis Bishop. You must be a little freaked out. Two of your neighbors passing away within weeks of you moving here."

When she saw my face, she stopped talking and put her hand over her mouth. "Oh, I'm sorry. I didn't mean to imply…"

"No, it's okay." I gave her a weak smile. "You aren't the only one who thinks that's rather suspicious."

I looked around, but there weren't any other patrons—the library was about to close. If I wanted to learn something from Emerald about her and her mother's potential involvement, I had to give her something first.

"DI Farrow is dangerously close to arresting me. I have an alibi for Matilda's murder, and Phyllis Bishop's death was ruled accidental, but still. He's been set to arrest me from the beginning, and he's like a dog with a bone."

"Oh, I'm so sorry. Well, you're innocent, and he'll have to come to that conclusion eventually. Don't let him rattle you."

"Hmm." Emerald sounded so genuine, as if she really

was concerned about me. I didn't know what else to say, and the silence stretched for a good long minute.

Suddenly, Emerald's eyes glowed, making them appear much greener. She had a funny expression on her face, as if she'd heard something…a beautiful song or church bells or something.

"Excuse me," she mumbled, and walked from behind the reception desk to the stairs.

I followed her. "Is everything all right?" I asked, but she didn't answer.

In sleepwalker-like fashion, she glided up the stairs to a room with a sign above the door that said NONFICTION: GARDENING. NATURE. OUTDOORS. HOUSE & HOME. ARCHITECTURE. ANTIQUES & COLLECTIBLES.

She walked straight up to a book and pulled it out. I looked over her shoulder as she leafed through it. Or, more accurately, I peeked around her, over her elbow, because she was quite a bit taller than me.

Emerald was looking at a book about landscaping. "Garden ponds, garden ponds," she repeated to herself. "Oh, right," she exclaimed, and slapped her palm against her forehead.

Emerald put the book back into its slot on the shelf while I looked at her askance.

"What just happened?" I asked.

My cousin turned to me and smiled. "Didn't I tell you that books talk to me?"

"Hmm, yes? So the book about garden ponds…just called you up here…to have a chat?"

"Kind of. Listen. Judith Winters wants to rent out all three cottages, merge the gardens, and put a pond in the middle."

"I beg your pardon?"

"Ah, from the beginning, sorry!" Emerald hit her forehead again. "Did you know that Judith Winters was Phyllis Bishop's only living relative?"

"My boss Judith Winters?"

"Yes. They weren't close, but they didn't exactly hate each other either. Phyllis sort of respected Judith for running a successful business as a single woman, I guess. Anyway, Judith knew Phyllis intended to bequeath her the cottage. Tracy Martens also knew she'd inherit Matilda's cottage and wanted to list it with Judith's agency. Judith said that the three cottages would be ideal as a high-end rental property for larger parties like family get-togethers, luxury hen-dos, that sort of thing."

"Hen dos?"

"What we call bachelorette parties over here. Anyway, she wanted to tie the properties together by joining up the gardens and installing a pond in the middle."

I shook my head in confusion. "How do you know this?"

"Book club. Monday nights at the library. I run it. Judith and Tracy both attend it." She pushed her glasses up her nose.

"Ah."

"I wanted to invite you, but I figured you have too much going on."

"I love reading, so I'd love to come." Although it might be awkward with my boss there—and the lady who thought I'd broken into her late aunt's home to steal jewelry. "Once things have calmed down a bit."

Emerald nodded. "Sure."

"But…back up a bit, okay? You said *three* cottages. Judith wants Phyllis's and Matilda's cottages in her portfolio, but also Ethel's? Am I understanding you correctly?"

"Yes. That was her plan."

"Judith never said anything to me. About renting out my home or wanting to buy it…"

Emerald drew her brows together. "That's odd. I know when Aunt Ethel was ill, Judith approached her a couple of times. But…" She tilted her head. "Now that I think about it, I remember Judith said she couldn't rent the cottage as is. Not for her high-end property plan. It would need substantial renovations. It wouldn't have been worth the investment if she'd had to buy the property and put in lots of money for the renovation too. And Aunt Ethel didn't have the money or energy to do it herself. At least that's what she said. She probably wouldn't have sold it, anyway. She was really attached to her home. It had belonged to her mother, and her grandmother before that."

"Oh. I didn't know that." Her bequeathing me the cottage suddenly held much more meaning than just giving me and my children a roof over our heads. "Shouldn't she have left it to you, then? You are her niece. I'm a more distant relative."

Emerald laughed as if I'd made a joke. "Goddess, no, that was never in the cards. You were always meant to have it—you were her goddaughter."

"What?" I had known it somewhere in the distant memory of my childhood, but I'd repressed the fact that Ethel and I had once shared a special bond—much like I'd repressed so many other things. I suddenly felt devastated that I'd missed out on having a relationship with her when she'd been alive.

Emerald studied my face. "Come back downstairs with me. I've got something to cheer you up."

Weighed down by sadness, I followed Emerald into her office.

She pulled open a drawer. "I've got a secret pick-me-up here somewhere."

I held up a hand. "I'm not much of a drinker. A glass of wine now and then, but anything with more—"

I stopped talking when I saw the yellow bag Emerald held out to me. "M&Ms?" I screeched. "Are you joking?"

Emerald's forehead creased. "Why, do you not like them? They always make me feel better, and I thought everyone likes chocolate, so…"

"No, they're also *my* special treat. I can't believe we have that in common. That's so odd…" I narrowed my eyes. "Hang on. Did your mother get a psychic vision about this? Told you this would be a good way to bond with me? Did a book tell you this is my ultimate comfort food?"

"Noooo." Emerald's eyes widened. "I love them. I swear."

I relaxed. My cousin seemed genuine. And we *were* related. So I chose to see it as a sign from the universe that I could trust Emerald.

Although if she'd told me a bunch of lies, her killing Matilda and then Phyllis would make perfect sense. If she thought she was Ethel's rightful heir and could somehow lay claim to my home once I was behind bars or driven out of Fairwyck, she'd stand to gain once Judith Winters put her three-cottage-and-a-pond plan into action. If Emerald…

No. I stopped my thoughts from veering in that direction.

I didn't want to believe Emerald, my new M&M buddy, was capable of such horrible crimes.

I'd rather focus on my new prime suspect.

Judith Winters.

Judith had never asked me to sell my home to her, but she might have been biding her time. Was Judith behind the brick attack? Had she sent me to Matilda's cottage that Monday on purpose, so the police would catch me there? Driving me out of Fairwyck or getting me arrested would be in her favor if she wanted me to panic-sell the cottage for a cheap price.

As Phyllis's only living relative, Judith would have been in a perfect position to know about the old woman's medication, and get access to it too.

It seemed insane to destroy so many lives for a business opportunity. But Judith came across as cold and calculating.

"Emerald, how does it work exactly, the books talking to you?" I asked, lost in thought. "I mean, why do books tell you what they tell you?"

"Because they want me to know something," Emerald said in a very matter-of-fact way.

"Okay, so do you think the book upstairs telling you about the garden pond, leading you to think about Judith's plan… Do you think it's significant?"

"You mean, do I think Judith has something to do with the deaths?" Emerald shrugged. "I can't say for sure. Her plan with the pond is significant somehow."

"Hmm." I popped one last M&M into my mouth. "Thanks. I've got to go. The kids are probably wondering where I am."

"Okay. I've got to lock up, anyway. Thanks for stopping by!"

Emerald walked me out. On the doorstep, a thought occurred to me, and an icy shudder ran down my spine.

I turned around. "Emerald, there's no doubt that Aunt Ethel died of natural causes, is there?"

Emerald's eyes widened behind her glasses. "She had cancer for many years. She was in remission, but then it came back, and it got her in the end."

"Of course." I forced a smile. "Have a nice evening."
"You too. Bye."
I felt numb all the way home.
Three old friends living next door to each other. All

dying within the space of a few months. One of them had been murdered for sure. It seemed like too much of a coincidence to me that the other two would have died of natural causes.

And there was someone with a plan for their houses: Judith Winters.

It made my boss a suspect, but I couldn't disregard the fact that there were also others who'd benefit if that plan came to fruition. My cousin Emerald might be among them, even if I didn't want her to be involved in this.

I parked the car in front of our house.

When I walked in, my kids were sitting at the kitchen table doing homework.

I smiled at them, but my smile froze when my gaze was drawn to the boarded-up window in the living room.

Whether Ethel's death had been helped along in the final stages of her illness or not—if there was something to my theory, and the deaths of our neighbors had to do with the three-cottages-and-a-pond rental plan, whoever wanted to make sure that it would come to fruition only had one more stumbling block to clear.

Me and my family.

CHAPTER TWENTY-SIX

I rushed to make a quick dinner of quesadillas with peppers and mushrooms before I had to get changed for my shift at the pub.

I'd just flipped the last tortilla with cheese and vegetable filling when my cell phone rang. It was Ellie.

"Hi!" I answered, phone between shoulder and chin, pan in the other.

"Liv? Um…hi. We don't need you to come in today, I'm afraid." Ellie sounded funny—not her usual cheerful self.

I put the pan down and turned the heat off.

"What's the matter?"

"Nothing. It's just that… Jason's working."

"Oh." It seemed as if there was more to the story, but I wasn't sure if I wanted to know—in case Ellie thought I wasn't doing a good enough job and was trying to let me down easy.

But I had made no big mistakes, Ellie had told me I was getting the hang of things, and I'd gotten decent tips. I could really do with the extra money since I had to pay for the new window—and maybe a lawyer.

"Are you sure? I wouldn't mind coming in just for a few hours."

"No, that's okay. Sorry."

"Okay, then I'll see you next—"

But Ellie had already hung up. Irritated, I looked at the phone.

"What's up, Mom?" Audrey asked. She'd fed Ethel and was now playing with her in the kitchen.

"Looks like I've got the night off." I put on a smile, but it turned genuine when I saw Audrey's face.

"Awesome. I don't like it when you're gone in the evenings."

Cue mom guilt. Of course my kids were scared to be on their own, especially after the incident with the brick. I had to make a living, but still. I decided to make the most of the fact that I could stay in with the children tonight.

"Hey, I still haven't gone through all of Ethel's stuff in the living room. Maybe we can check out the cabinet next to the bookshelf. I think I saw some board games in there."

Audrey crinkled her nose. "Old board games smell."

I had to laugh. "If it's Scrabble tiles or checkers or something, we can clean them. Get Blake. Dinner is ready."

I put the last quesadilla on a plate and got out the stack I had warming in the oven.

During dinner, I asked about school. "In the beginning, you weren't that thrilled about going to an all-girls school. Do you still feel that way? We can look for another school that suits you better for next year, if you like."

"Actually, it's fine." Blake looked up from their plate. "There are others who don't like to dress in girly clothes."

"Oh, right, your principal mentioned something like that. She said you're a role model."

Blake's cheeks turned red. "Maybe. But not on purpose."

"I know." I smiled at them. "Those are the best role models. Just stay true to who you are, and don't put your light under a bushel. Don't worry about what others think."

They shrugged and stuffed a gigantic piece of quesadilla into their mouth.

"So what about the uniform? Sounds like it bothers you to have to wear a skirt, right?"

"Yeah, I've got good news about that." Blake's face lit up. "A few friends and I led a campaign to introduce pants as part of the school uniform. Or trousers, as they're called here." They laughed at the word they'd pronounced with an over-the-top British accent. "I mean, most schools already allow girls to wear them, so it's not a big deal."

"I think it is. It's great that you're doing this."

"I want to wear a skirt," Audrey chimed in.

"And you can," I said, just glad Audrey had said nothing about changing schools either. She hadn't made any friends, as far as I knew.

Following an impulse, I grabbed my phone to look up extracurricular activities in the area for kids her age.

When I came across a children's theater group in Meckham, which was the next village, I knew I'd found the right thing for Audrey. Her eyes lit up when I told her about it. "They meet on Sunday afternoons. Maybe you could check it out tomorrow?"

She just nodded, but her eyes shone.

I called the number listed on the website for the person in charge of the group. "It's all set," I said, after I'd hung up.

Audrey seemed pleased, but then something shifted in her expression.

"What is it?" I asked. "It's normal to be nervous."

"That's not it," Audrey said. "Just… It's going to cost money to join this group, won't it? Can we afford it?"

My heart broke a little. Sure, I'd wished Audrey would be less materialistic and have a better concept of what it meant to live frugally. I'd blamed myself for raising an entitled child in the wrong environment. Moving to England had changed my outlook—and now I could see that it had already changed Audrey too.

I smiled at her. "Thanks for taking that into consideration. But it's important to have friends, and I want you to do what you love. If you're enjoying yourself tomorrow and decide you want to join the group permanently, we'll budget for it."

I spun around and pointed at the living room. "That reminds me. I've been wanting to go through the books and everything in the living room to see if there are things we could sell." I passed my phone to Blake. "I already downloaded a resale app for books, DVDs, and games. Why don't you and Audrey get started on the bookshelf while I clean up the kitchen and make us hot chocolate with marshmallows for dessert? I think you just need to scan the barcode, and the app tells you how much money they'd buy it for. If it sounds good, you can put it in the cart. Postage is free, so every cent counts."

The kids got busy in the living room getting books off the shelf.

By the time I joined them, bringing over our hot chocolates, the bookshelf was almost empty. The books were neatly stacked in front of the shelf. Only the bottom row of time-traveling romance novels was still where it had been.

I carefully blew on the surface of my cocoa. "How much have we made so far?"

"Three thousand five hundred," Audrey said.

"Phhhh…" Mini marshmallows flew from my cup. "What?" I put the mug down on the table to pick up the marshmallows.

Audrey repeated the figure.

"Are you joking?" I went over to the kitchen to throw away the dirty marshmallows and got the bag from the counter to replace them.

"No, it's true," Blake confirmed.

"Show me," I said, still skeptical.

Blake passed me the phone. The cart in the app I'd downloaded showed just under two hundred pounds. More than I'd expected, but nowhere close to the amount my kids had cited.

I looked up with raised eyebrows.

Blake and Audrey exchanged a glance.

"Um, this service only buys newer books, so that's all we got on there. But I also set up an account with this rare-books resale site. Here, let me show you…" Blake took the phone and opened the browser. "Aunt Ethel had some first editions and other valuable books, so that's where most of the money comes from."

"That's amazing." I furrowed my brows. "But how did you know? And how did you know about the site?"

Blake's eyes went to Audrey. My youngest was suspiciously quiet, hiding her face behind her mug.

"Audrey? How would you know anything about smelly old books?"

She mumbled something.

"What?"

"Aunt Ethel," Blake repeated. "She told Audrey about the site. And she let us know which books are valuable."

I shook my head in confusion. "But Ethel is…ohh! The cat?"

My eyes searched the room for the orange feline. She lay with her head on her front paws next to Audrey's armchair. Ethel was asleep, her tail twitching—maybe she was dreaming about chasing a mouse.

Or about making a mint with rare books, apparently.

"Audrey…," I said slowly. "How did the cat tell you about a website?"

Audrey looked down at her cocoa. She had a chocolate-milk mustache, and her blond curls were falling into her face.

She looked so cute. Audrey often acted like a teen, so it was easy to forget that she was only nine years old.

"It's okay. You're not going to get in trouble. You can tell me anything. You know that, right?"

"It's not about getting into trouble," Audrey said quietly without looking up. "It's just… I didn't think you'd believe me."

I cleared my throat. "Is this about your supernatural ability? The one that Gina mentioned?"

Audrey gave a slight nod.

"Umm, I think it's because of the way you reacted when Gina and Emerald came here the first time," Blake explained. "You threw them out, remember, because you didn't believe them?"

"Oh!"

"But I told Audrey you know these abilities exist."

"Yes," I hurried to say. "I talked to Blake about theirs. And it's not like I don't believe in Gina and Emerald's gifts either. I was so dismissive because of the way they'd barged in here and scared us with the tarot card warning."

Audrey looked unsure. "So if I told you I can talk to cats, you wouldn't tell me it's just my imagination?"

I thought for a moment. "I wouldn't. From my own experience, I know what it's like to be told one is just imagining things."

Audrey looked at me with big eyes.

"I never really told you about my own abilities. It's scary. It scared me when I was a little girl, not much younger than you, Audrey. Because it meant that ghosts are real and that they're all around us. I haven't been open with you about it because I don't want to give you nightmares. But I think now the time has come."

I explained to my children what I could see through a camera lens.

"Wow, that's amazing," Audrey breathed after I'd finished.

"I don't know. It's not really a useful talent to have," I was speaking from the heart. It made me realize how frustrated I had been. "I wish I could do more with it, you know? Help figure out what happened to our neighbors."

"Maybe you're supposed to help them cross over, like they do with ghosts on TV?" Blake suggested.

I shrugged. "How? I can only see them through the camera."

"If you can see them, you can communicate with them."

"Yeah, Mom," Audrey put in, as if it made perfect sense. "If you weren't able to see them through the camera, you wouldn't know they aren't at peace."

"Hmm. Your talents are so much cooler, though." I turned to Blake. "Drawing what's in people's heads. Talking to cats." I spoke to Audrey in a casual manner, hoping not to spook her. I really wanted to know more about her ability. "Have you always known you could do that?"

My youngest shook her head. "Only since we moved here. I kept hearing a voice…thoughts that weren't my own. At first, I thought it had to be the TV or the cell phone or something. And then Gina and Emerald said that thing about talking to animals. And I got it." Her gaze went to the sleeping cat on the floor next to her.

"She was Great-Aunt Ethel. I tried to communicate with her, and suddenly it was really easy. We can talk to each other in our heads. She's cool."

I didn't know what to say. Part of me didn't want to

believe that my daughter had telepathic conversations with the cat. I should be worried, probably get her to a psychiatrist. But there was something deep inside me, some primal wisdom, that told me she was telling the truth.

"So…just to make sure I'm getting this right. Ethel the cat is really my departed Great-Aunt Ethel?"

"Of course," Audrey said.

I blinked. *Of course.*

Something occurred to me. "Hey, honey. When we were at Gina and Emerald's the other day, did you talk to their cat too?"

Audrey nodded.

I leaned forward, grabbing some mini marshmallows from the bag and stuffing them into my mouth. That cat probably had rather interesting tales to tell, living in the haunted house with my kooky relatives. "What did you talk about?"

"We both thought cucumber sandwiches are dull. Beltane—that's the cat's name—agreed that putting them next to cake didn't do them any favors either. We thought it made no sense that people kept serving them as part of an afternoon tea. Beltane said it was a thing they do in England."

"Ah," I said, leaning back, a little deflated, as Audrey prattled on about the cat's culinary preferences. "Oh, she also said something about you."

"About me?"

"Yes, um…" Audrey's smooth forehead crinkled. "That Gina and Emerald think you can figure out what happened to our neighbor. That they believe in you."

I almost choked on a marshmallow. "Really?"

Audrey nodded, then yawned.

I looked at the time. "I think it's time for you to go to bed, sweetie."

"Mom!"

"You can finish your hot chocolate and watch one episode of that ballet school series you like so much. But then it's time to brush your teeth and change into your PJs."

"Okay."

I double checked what Blake and Audrey had done with the books, agreed to the sale in the app, and sorted the volumes so I could pack them up tomorrow.

Audrey didn't argue again about bedtime when I switched off the TV. Blake also decided to go to bed.

"I'll be up a little later to say goodnight," I said.

Audrey turned around on the stairs.

"Oh, Mom?"

I was on my way to the kitchen with the mugs in my hand. "Yes?"

"Ethel wanted me to tell you something, but since you didn't know I could talk to her, I sort of forgot."

"That's okay. What did she want me to know?"

"I was meant to tell you that you can trust Gina and Emerald. They're good people."

"Oh." I was relieved to strike my relatives off my suspect list.

If Ethel had been the first of the three friends to die by someone else's hands, Gina and Emerald would have had the means. They had been closest to her. But Ethel would know that. If my great-aunt had been killed, she'd surely pass on that message to me.

I had so many questions for Audrey, or, better said, for Ethel.

What else did the cat, formerly my great-aunt, know? Maybe something about the murders?

But I didn't want to overwhelm my daughter, who looked tired.

I'd have to broach that subject another day.

"Thanks, Audrey. Get ready for bed. I'll be up soon."

I rinsed the mugs, then took one of the romance novels from the bottom shelf. I decided to snuggle up in bed and read.

My eyes fell on the sleeping cat next to the armchair.

I returned to the kitchen to grab my Nikon. I tip-toed back to the armchair, lifted the camera, and took a picture. There was a flash, but it didn't wake the cat.

My heart was racing, and my breath was fast with anticipation when I looked at the display and zoomed in on the picture I'd just taken.

There was a ginger feline rolled up on the floor.

No, wait, it was a woman with ginger hair and a Mallen streak.

A cat again.

I tilted the camera this way and that, and the image kept changing from one to the other, like with lenticular prints, or "wiggle pictures," as we used to call them as kids.

I couldn't wait to print out this photo to see what it would look like.

I carefully crept close to the cat. It looked asleep, but it moved its ears when I whispered, "Hey, Ethel. I'm so glad you're still here."

A few tears escaped my eyes as I put the camera away and gave Ethel one last glance before going upstairs.

I'd missed out on having a relationship with my great-aunt—my godmother—while she was still alive. My mother might have been to blame, but I'd had a part in it too. And I didn't know how hard Ethel had tried to overrule my mom's wishes.

It didn't matter.

My heart was filled with gratitude that we had something like a second chance now.

CHAPTER TWENTY-SEVEN

The next day, it was cleaning work as usual. During my break, I drove Audrey over to Meckham, which was a little larger than the village of Fairwyck. It was where her theater group meeting took place—and the WLA office happened to be there too.

It was a Sunday, so there wasn't a guarantee that Judith would be in, but she was a workaholic, and weekends were the busiest days in her business, so I took my chances.

The office was locked, but the light was on, so I knocked.

Judith Winters opened the door and raised her perfectly shaped eyebrows at me.

"Liv! Is everything okay? Is there a problem with a rental property?"

"Um, no, not at all. I'm on my break, actually. I dropped off my daughter for a theater group meeting, and I'm heading over to grab lunch at the café next door. I figured you might be working and wondered if you wanted to join me."

It sounded like a perfectly good excuse, but I wasn't

that great an actor. Judith looked me up and down, clearly figuring out I had an ulterior motive.

"All right. Let me grab my bag."

My boss reappeared seconds later with a Gucci Jackie bag in mint green, which I remembered had been the most fashionable color a couple of seasons ago, when that kind of thing had still been important in my life.

It was bold, but a great accessory to her coral jacket over a figure-hugging black dress. I couldn't help but admire Judith's style, even though I'd never dress like that. I was well endowed in the boob department myself, especially since I'd put on weight in the last couple of years. But I wasn't comfortable showing so much of my cleavage, feeling as if I was trying too hard to be sexy.

Kudos to Judith for not worrying about anything like that. But then, she had a narrow waist, flat stomach, and toned long legs as well as the big boobs, so she could definitely pull off what I'd termed the Anna-Nicole-Smith look.

Judith looked a little like the infamous model in her good years, but a tad more classy, despite the caterpillar-like fake eyelashes and red lips. She had her bleached-blond locks piled on her head in a casual up-do. In fact, her hairstyle wasn't dissimilar to what I'd tried with my dark tresses this morning, but on me, it looked like a messy bun.

Add to that my grubby jeans and ratty old P!nk T-shirt, and I felt distinctly mousy next to my boss when we walked into the café.

Heads turned. Everyone seemed to know Judith. The upside was that we were served almost as soon as we sat down at one of the tables in the back. Judith had her usual —a bagel-salad combo—and persuaded me to order the same.

The server came right back over with our drinks. I

checked my watch. There was still half an hour left of my lunch break. I hadn't exactly rehearsed what I wanted to say, so I fumbled for words.

"Um… First of all, I wanted to express my condolences. I only learned yesterday that Phyllis Bishop was a relative of yours. I'm so sorry for your loss."

"Thanks. We weren't that close. She was an older cousin of my mother's, and we barely had contact with that side of the family. And Phyllis, she…well, she liked to keep to herself. She wasn't the easiest person to get along with. Of course, it's still sad that she passed before her time. Did you get to know her?"

Judith's dark-blue eyes bored into mine.

"We exchanged a few words. Like you said, she wasn't particularly sociable. Didn't like my cat coming over into her garden, so we had words about that." I laughed nervously. "Still, like you said, it's so sad. Especially since her death could have been avoided had she taken her medication properly."

Judith didn't comment on that, so I bravely carried on with my line of questioning.

"You're inheriting Phyllis's home, I heard? Are you planning on renting it out?"

Judith narrowed her eyes. "You certainly seem to hear a lot of things."

"Um, yes." My cheeks flamed, and I took a sip of my lemonade. "If you move in, we'd be neighbors, so I thought I'd ask."

Judith's face relaxed. She laughed. "Oh, now I get it. You're worried about living next door to your boss."

"No!" I was mortified. I hadn't thought about that at all.

"Relax. I own a lovely modern four-bedroom with a heated pool. I'm not planning on moving next door to you."

"Oh. Well, yes, someone told me you wanted to join the gardens behind Matilda Rutherford's and Phyllis Bishop's cottages, install a pond, make it a high-end rental property for groups?"

The food came, and Judith didn't answer right away. She took a few bites of her bagel, observing me from under her thick black lashes.

I felt too self-conscious to eat and just picked at my avocado salad.

Judith sipped her sparkling water and then said, "Yes, I've been toying with that plan. It would be nice to have a cluster of properties that can be rented out separately but also together. With larger family get-togethers, people aren't often happy about staying in one large house—it can get too crowded, heightening tension. Three separate cottages, with a larger communal space in the middle, maybe a partly covered outdoor dining area, would be an ideal setup. And a pond would really tie it all together."

"Three cottages…that sounds as if you'd be interested in renting out my home as well."

Judith tilted her head. "Is that why you wanted to talk to me? Are you interested in listing your home with WLA? I thought you had nowhere else to go. Are you planning on leaving Fairwyck?"

I took a big bite of my bagel so I had a moment to think about my answer.

"It's just hypothetical," I finally said. "You're right. We don't really have anywhere else to go. But it sounds like a great opportunity, and as you know, I'm trying hard to improve our financial situation."

Again, Judith's face softened, and she looked at me with what seemed like genuine empathy. "I know."

She sighed. "Let me level with you. I talked to your great-aunt Ethel about my idea. But her cottage needs a ton of renovations."

"Ugh. Don't I know it." I felt more on an even keel with Judith now. I took another bite of my bagel with hummus and roasted veggies. It really was delicious.

"What I'm envisioning is more of an upscale deal. Phyllis's home is in great shape. We need to change the interior design, but that's cosmetic. Matilda Rutherford's cottage is not quite in the same league. The owner will have to do something about the roof soon, but as you might know, Tracy Martens's father owns a roofing company. The cottage still looks good, though, because Matilda really had an eye for that kind of thing and did the best with what she had. Ethel's is the smallest of the three cottages, and it needs…well, everything. It needs a new roof, new windows, a kitchen remodel. We can definitely strip it down to a rustic look—that's actually in right now—but it can't look old-fashioned or run-down. It needs to give off luxury vibes, if you know what I mean?"

I just nodded. Judith was clearly in her element.

"Ethel couldn't afford such substantial renovations," she carried on. "When she got really sick, I didn't pester her anymore. I knew she needed all her savings for the treatments that weren't covered by the NHS plan. When you moved in, I knew you couldn't afford a complete remodel either."

I swallowed my forkful of salad. "So are you still going ahead with your plan, now that you have the two other properties? Take down the fence separating Matilda's and Phyllis's gardens and install a pond and all that?"

Judith shrugged. "We'll see. Phyllis just passed. It's too early to think about."

I turned somber. "Of course. I'm sorry."

"But don't worry, I'll let you know well in advance if you can expect construction in your back yard."

"Okay, thanks."

We finished our lunch in silence, and I was getting

antsy. I hadn't really gleaned any new information, and it was hard to get a read on Judith Winters.

It seemed as if there were two sides to her. On the one hand, she could appear cool. A shrewd, confident businesswoman who wouldn't let anyone stand in her way. But she clearly also had a softer side, showing an understanding of other people's money worries.

Judith didn't seem too bothered about not adding my home to her list. She'd had an idea how to market the three rental properties, but she didn't seem too stuck on it. She certainly didn't seem so fixated that she would murder for it.

It also didn't look as if she needed her plan to work out soon for financial reasons. By all appearances, her business was doing very well.

But I knew appearances could be deceiving.

Judith could just be great at hiding her emotions. And you had to be very cool and calculating to pull off serial murders of little old ladies.

From what I'd learned yesterday, it didn't seem likely that my great-aunt Ethel had been murdered, and, apparently, Gina and Emerald were off my suspect list.

But maybe her death had gotten the ball rolling for Judith. Ethel had never wanted to sell, and she hadn't had the money to renovate her home, anyway. There would have been a better chance that Ethel's heir might sell off the property cheaply, or even have the means to get the cottage ready for high-end renters. It sounded like an excellent business opportunity, after all.

Then I'd turned up with my family, and Judith might have figured she'd kill two birds with one stone. Get rid of Matilda Rutherford, knowing the old lady would bequeath her home to her niece, Tracy, whose intention was to list the cottage with Judith's agency. And spook the new owner of Ethel's cottage by sending me to the crime scene and arranging for me to get caught there. DI Farrow had already had a preconceived opinion of me when he'd found me there. I'd thought he'd held a grudge against my mother, but had Judith poisoned him further against me? The "criminals get out" message on the brick through my window fit with that bullying tactic too.

Maybe Judith wouldn't have been in a hurry to get rid of her relative if she hadn't caught wind of what Phyllis had wanted to tell me. In the village shop, Phyllis had said that she'd understood who she'd seen the night of Matilda's murder—not an alien—which could be construed as a person familiar to her. Maybe Judith figured Phyllis had recognized her.

It all sort of made sense, especially when I couldn't think of anyone else with a motive—but I had trouble imagining Judith donning a gas mask and doing the dirty deed with the cleaning chemicals. It would seriously mess with her hair and makeup.

I also couldn't picture her in our sheep-dung-filled garden, setting down her Jackie bag to throw a brick through our window.

I was very much on the fence about whether I could believe Judith was the murderer. We were almost finished with lunch, and I didn't know when I'd have another opportunity to talk to her about this again. So I desperately blurted out, "I just hope there won't be any more deaths in the near future. Matilda's death was so shocking too. I had no idea what had happened. I wasn't even there when Matilda died. Next door, I mean. I was at the pub, working. I help out at the weekends, you see," I babbled on. "It's always so strange to think about what you were doing when someone died, isn't it?"

Judith's red lips twisted. "Is it?"

"Yeah. What were you doing that Saturday night? Did

the police ask you about an alibi?" I drained my glass of lemonade.

"Well, if the *police* would ask me for an alibi, I might or might not be able to give them one. They haven't because—why would they? It sure sounds to me ask if *you're* asking, though."

"Oh god, no, of course not. I was just wondering…" I trailed off.

"Hmm." Judith put money on the table and grabbed her Gucci bag. "This has been interesting. I think it's high time for you to get back to work, don't you?"

I scrambled to get my wallet out of my purse. "Oh, yes, yes."

Judith gave me a curt nod. Then she turned around. "Can I give you a little piece of advice?"

"Of course."

"It seems to me you have a lot on your plate, trying to provide for your family. Getting back on your feet. I believe in giving underdogs a chance, especially women who have been screwed by their husbands. That's why I gave you a job, even though you had no experience or references. Why not focus on that second chance, and, you know, stick to *your* business instead of running around taking part in gossip and interrogating random people like a bad amateur detective?"

I just stared at her like a moron, unable to come up with an answer.

Judith gave me a saccharine smile and left.

The server came with the bill, and I was digging coins out of my wallet, trying to make up the rest of what I owed for lunch, while trying to blink away my tears.

I should have said that it *was* my business to figure out who Matilda's killer was because DI Farrow was convinced that person was me. But mentioning my troubles with the police wouldn't have been a smart idea either, if I wanted to keep my job.

And it seemed as if I was treading on very thin ice there. I really needed to stay employed—how else was I going to make a living? Judith was right. She'd thrown me a lifeline with this job. My pub job seemed to be a bust. Chances were slim someone else would hire me in a pinch, especially if Judith sacked me.

I had gone about this all wrong. I shouldn't have questioned Judith in the first place. Even if she was somehow in involved in all this—I couldn't pursue that avenue any further.

My boss's advice had clearly been a warning.

I needed to keep my head down if I wanted to keep my job.

CHAPTER TWENTY-EIGHT

I tried to tell myself that I worried too much. If I continued to do a good job as a cleaner for Judith's company, she wouldn't sack me, would she?

My fears were confirmed that evening after dinner, however, when I got a message from Judith. She informed me she had given me the next morning off. In the afternoon, Esme would supervise me. I groaned. It looked as if I was back on trial.

Panicking about our financial situation, I spent Monday morning sorting out the rare books sales. After I mailed the packages at the shop, I thought of another way to ease my worries about becoming destitute.

I headed to the pub to speak to Ellie. I wanted to clear the air—for whatever reason it needed clearing… I didn't know, but I was ready to face it head on. Securing my weekend shifts at the pub seemed like a good idea, in case I never made it into Judith's good graces again.

I psyched myself up for the talk, but when I got to the Owl and Oak, my enthusiasm dampened. A sign on the door informed me that the pub was closed on Mondays.

I was about to turn around when I saw the lights were

on. I called Ellie, on the off chance that she was inside. She didn't pick up, but I heard a ringing phone inside. The window next to the door was partially open.

"Ellie?" I shouted. "Ellie, are you in there?"

I pressed the call button again, and it definitely rang inside. "Hey, Ellie, I can hear your phone. Can you let me in?"

"Go away!" The voice could have been Ellie's, although it didn't sound like my usually softspoken friend.

"Ellie, it's me, Liv. I need to speak to you."

A few seconds later, the front door to the pub was pushed open. I hurried there from the window, making it through the door before it shut again.

"Ellie?"

My boss was staggering to the bar. She dragged herself back onto the bar stool where she must have been sitting—for a while, judging by the half-empty bottle of whiskey in front of her.

I went over and sat on the bar stool next to her.

"Are you all right?" I asked, examining Ellie's face with concern.

She didn't look good. Her face was swollen and her eyes puffy, as if she'd been crying. She also appeared to be completely wasted.

My eyes went to the whiskey bottle. During one of my shifts, Ellie had told me she didn't drink. I assumed this wasn't how she usually spent her days off.

Something must have happened.

"Did Jason—"

"I'm sooo sorry, Liv," Ellie slurred. "I'm gonna have to let you go."

"What?"

"Fire you. I have to fire you. I don't want to, but Jason is making me. So there you go." She poured another shot, although most of it spilled on the bar.

I touched her hand to prevent her from downing it.

"Ellie, I think you've had enough. What is this about? I understand if you have to let me go." I didn't understand at all, but this wasn't the time to argue about it. "It's not the end of the world. No reason for…" I looked at the shot. "This."

Ellie tried to swat my hand away but missed it. "You don't understand. It's bad. It's so bad. I love my husband, but after what he did…" She shook her head, spilling most of the remainder of her whiskey. When she tipped back the shot, there was hardly anything left in the glass, so I let her.

I was distracted by her words, anyway. "What do you mean? What has Jason done? Has he done something to you?" I inspected the skin that was visible for bruises but didn't see any. The couple of times we'd met, I'd never seen anything like that either.

"No, no, no." She shook her head again. "Not to me. To you." She bent forward to touch my arm and almost slid off the stool.

I steadied her.

"What did he do to me? Get me sacked? Yes, it sucks. As you know, I really need the money. But it's okay, really. I have another job."

At least I hoped I would. I'd come here to get more shifts at the pub, and it was terrible timing to lose the gig completely. But right now, the priority was to calm Ellie, get her to stop drinking.

"If it were only that," Ellie said, tears welling up in her eyes. "He hates you, Liv. He wants you gone. And what he's done, to get you into trouble, to make you leave..." She was sobbing now and even harder to understand.

I thought she said, "You don't deserve any of this. Being framed for murder. And your poor children, putting them in danger… He was bullied as a child. That's why he's like that now. Bullying others, wanting to be in control. He's always been good to me. I always held on to the fact that there was a scared, vulnerable little boy inside him. A good person. But I can't believe in that anymore. He's gotten worse and worse. And now he's done unspeakable, horrible things…"

"Hold on, Ellie," I said. "What are you talking about? What has he done?"

But she was crying hard now, in an awful state, and not able to answer me. I put my arm around her, just trying to calm her down.

It took me ages to get her to stop crying. I didn't dare ask her any more questions for fear of setting her off again.

"Let's sit down over here, where you can be a little more comfortable." I led Ellie to one of the booths, then got her a glass of water and a packet of chips from behind the bar.

My gaze fell upon the big clock above the door, and I sucked in a breath when I saw what time it was already.

I was cutting it close to get to work. There was no way I could be late to my new trial shift. That would give Judith an actual reason to let me go.

On the other hand, I couldn't leave Ellie by herself.

After pressing the glass of water into Ellie's shaking hand and ripping open the packet of chips, I pulled out my phone. Who could I call?

I knew Jason hated Gina and Emerald as much as me, so if he turned up here and saw his wife with them, it could really set him off.

Jamie Rees was a possibility, but if Jason had done something criminal, Ellie might freak out if the police turned up here.

I didn't know what to do, but I was running out of time, so in my desperation, I called Esme. My colleague had sent me a message earlier, letting me know which rental property to meet at.

"Hey, I'm so sorry, but I'm afraid I'm going to be late."

Esme took a moment to answer. She seemed baffled by my behavior, since she knew how important this job was to me. "Is it an emergency? Something with your kids?"

"Kind of. But nothing to do with my children." I sighed, looking at Ellie. Moving away from the table, I whispered. "I'm at the Owl and Oak. It's usually closed on Mondays, but I really needed to talk to Ellie Bullwart, the owner."

"I know Ellie." Esme sounded cautious, clearly waiting for a good enough explanation.

"She was getting smashed—and as you might know, Ellie doesn't drink. Something happened with her husband, I think. She broke down crying. I took me ages to calm her down. Ellie said some stuff I can't really make heads or tails of, but she sounded afraid of her husband. I don't want to leave her alone here, like this, in this state, you know? I don't know who to call or what to do…"

Esme said, "I know who to call. Once she gets there, you can come to work, okay?"

I breathed a sigh of relief. "Okay, thank you!"

I went back to Ellie and made sure she ate all the chips. Then I found the coffee machine behind the bar, worked out how to operate it, and made a triple espresso.

I brought it over to the table, together with a handful of sugar and cream packets.

"Here, drink this."

Ellie just nodded. She was really pale, but at least she'd stopped crying.

I desperately wanted to ask her more about what she'd said earlier. It sounded as if Jason was responsible for something to do with my situation. Throwing the brick?

Maybe even the murders? But why? Just because he hated me and wanted me gone? Because he wanted to frame me?

Who would kill for that? It didn't make a lot of sense. But I'd have to wait to ask my questions another time, when Ellie was herself again.

So I was biting my nails, waiting for the person to arrive who could look after my friend.

When the pub door opened and I saw who it was, I nearly bit my fingertip bloody.

It was Judith.

CHAPTER TWENTY-NINE

I jumped up.

"Judith? What are you doing here?" I rushed over to her.

My boss stayed cool and collected, her face giving nothing away. "Esme called me."

"Oh."

Judith lowered her voice. "I understand Ellie isn't doing so well."

I just nodded. I was thoroughly confused and also a little scared.

I didn't know what to think anymore.

Since my conversation with Judith yesterday, I'd been mulling over the possibility that my employer was a murderer who had framed me. Somehow I couldn't imagine it, but she had motive and opportunity—and looking back, she'd overreacted when I'd asked her for an alibi for the Saturday night of Matilda's murder.

Why warn me and tell me to mind my own business? So what if I wanted to figure out what had happened to my neighbor? I could have given her a legitimate reason for it too, if she'd given me half a chance.

Why not just tell me where she'd been during the night in question? It seemed as if Judith definitely had something to hide.

Now Ellie had blurted out stuff that made me believe Jason had something to do with it. He certainly seemed like the type of person who could have done that sort of thing—especially the brick throwing. But what was his connection to Matilda and Phyllis? How would he have known about Matilda's high sensitivity to cleaning chemicals and Phyllis's medication?

Could he have been a hired hand, someone whose hatred for outsiders would have gladly made him accept his role as goon? For whom—Judith Winters?

And now Esme had called Judith, of all people, to look after Ellie.

It didn't seem like the best scenario here, especially if Judith was in cahoots with the husband Ellie was so afraid of.

While I was still standing there, frozen with indecision, all those thoughts zooming around in my head, Judith had gone over to Ellie. They were talking in quiet tones, and Ellie seemed happy to see Judith. She certainly wasn't afraid of her. When Judith looked at me and said, "It's all right, Liv. You can start your shift," I couldn't contradict her.

If I was completely off base with my crazy suspicions, I'd *really* shoot myself in the foot by refusing to go to work when my boss flat out told me to.

Clearing my throat, I looked at Ellie. "You okay?" I asked.

Ellie gave a sad smile. "I know Judith can help me." She grimaced. "Sorry about laying everything on you earlier. I'm not even sure what I said. I was so out of it. Hopefully, I didn't freak you out."

"Um, it's all right. Let's talk later. Feel better, okay? I

have to go to work now." I nodded in Judith's direction and then left the pub.

I could barely focus on the traffic as I made my way to the rental property I was cleaning with Esme. By the time I parked my car in front of the cottage, I was a nervous wreck. How was I supposed to do my very best work as a cleaner today? Suddenly, it was all too much. I burst into tears.

The sound of the passenger door opening made me start. But it was only Esme. Her black braids with colorful beads spilled over her shoulder when she leaned forward. "Hey. I saw you drive up a few minutes ago. Is everything okay?"

When she saw me spilling fresh tears, she slipped into the passenger seat.

"Is this about Judith extending your trial period? She didn't say anything, but she doesn't normally do that. Nobody has complained about your cleaning, so I wondered what the reason was. Did you piss her off somehow?"

I shook my head, not sure how I could explain everything to Esme. I had to say something, though.

"The police have me down as a suspect in Matilda Rutherford's murder. They think I killed Phyllis too. I just seem to be in the wrong place at the wrong time again and again. This was supposed to be a second chance for the children and me, a new start. Now things are going from bad to worse. I'm trying to figure out who the killer really is, so we can truly move on. I'm asking people for alibis to rule them out, and as much as I hate the idea, and don't even really think it's true…" I took a deep breath, then said it anyway, even though I wasn't sure it was wise. "Judith has a motive. I had to ask her. But it was tactless, I get it. She was pissed off. And you know how much I need this job."

Esme stayed quiet for a few seconds. "I understand. I know what it's like to be down on your luck and trying to make it as a single mom without money. It feels like the entire world is against you. Sometimes, nobody wants to give you a break. It's hard."

I nodded, wiping my tears away. I felt silly. Esme had reminded me I wasn't the only one struggling.

"But you've got to start trusting people who are lending a helping hand," Esme said in a much sterner voice. "Like I said, I absolutely empathize with getting royally screwed by the person who should have had your back. It's difficult not to be distrustful of everyone in life right now."

I looked at my colleague in surprise. Was this what was going on here? Had Steven turned me into some bitter lady who could only see the bad in people, expecting the worst of everyone? I certainly didn't see myself as someone like that. But maybe it was a reaction to people treating me unfairly—to life treating me unfairly. DI Farrow and his ridiculous allegations certainly didn't help.

"But one thing I learned is that there's no way we can make it on our own," Esme continued. "We need help."

"Ugh. My so-called best friend from home already wanted to set me up with some widower, but I'm not ready or willing—"

"I'm not talking about a husband." Esme waved it off. "I'm talking about friends. Girlfriends. Sisterhood. You know. We need to rely on each other. We can't go around all distrustful, accusing each other of murder."

"I don't *want* to do that," I said, now a little exasperated. "Don't you think I'm incredibly grateful to Judith for giving me a job? I hate that she's on my suspect list. I would have loved to clear her. *That's* why I asked about the alibi."

Esme thought for a second. Then she nodded. "Listen. For what it's worth, I'd walk through fire for Judith

Winters. She's a good person. One of the warmest people I know."

I couldn't hide my surprise. "Warm" wasn't an adjective I'd associate with Judith.

Esme had to laugh when she saw my face. "She comes across as this hard-ass, business-savvy bitch, I know. But it's a persona. It's served her well. Judith had a poor upbringing. She grew up with a physically abusive father. Her mom couldn't leave him because she had no means of supporting herself and her children."

I put my hand over my mouth. "Oh no, that's horrible."

Esme nodded.

"Judith left school early to work as a cleaner. She went to night school and completed a business degree, all while supporting her mother and younger siblings who had escaped the abusive father. She worked at the letting agency and then took it over. Judith could have made money in a lot of different ways. I mean, look at her. She definitely got some offers from sugar daddies and escort agencies. But Judith has a moral code. Oh, she loves money, don't get me wrong. She likes to enjoy the finer things in life. Money is like a security blanket for her. But she wants to earn it herself—fair and square."

I didn't quite know what to say. "Wow, you make one hell of a character witness. But…how do you know for sure? Did she tell you all that? People can come up with the most convincing stories. It doesn't mean it's true." I held up a hand. "I'm not saying you've got Judith pegged completely wrong. Maybe you're right. God, I hope you're right. But theoretically, it's possible she pulled the wool over your eyes."

Esme put an arm around my shoulders. "Oh, honey. Your husband really did a number on you, didn't he?"

I sank deeper into my seat, fighting off the tears again.

Looking up at Esme, I said, "Do you think what he did messed me up so much that I can't read people anymore?"

Esme shrugged. "It's not a surprise you're doubting yourself. I'm only guessing, but if you're anything like me, you had known for a while that you couldn't trust him, long before he pulled this shit on you, right?"

I nodded.

"So you aren't bad at reading people. You were wrong about your husband. He's one arsehole. Don't let it stop you from trusting again. That would be a mistake. Then he really would have screwed you up. Don't give him that power."

I took a deep breath. "All right. Thanks." I looked at the clock on the dashboard. "Oh my god. We really should get started."

Esme nodded but didn't make a move to get out of the car. She took a scrunchie from her wrist and gathered her braids in a high ponytail. Then she said, "Maybe don't tell Judith I blabbed about her background. I only told you so you could take her off your suspect list. Understandably, she's not that keen on people knowing she has a heart of gold. Bad for business, I guess."

"Of course. I won't say anything."

"That's also the reason she got angry about being interrogated about her alibi. She has one. I know, because I saw her there."

I sat ramrod straight. "What? What's her alibi?"

"Judith works as a volunteer for a domestic abuse hotline. I work there too. That's where we met, actually. Judith gave me a job when I left my husband. Anyhow, she likes to keep it private. We were both in the office on the Saturday evening Matilda Rutherford passed."

I closed my eyes in embarrassment. "Oh my god. I was only worried about saving my behind and about keeping my job. I accuse this woman of murder, and she turns out to be a saint."

Esme laughed. "Not quite a saint. Judith has her faults. But she's not a murderer. She has a strict moral code. And an alibi."

"Gotcha." I gave a deep sigh again before opening my car door.

Walking up to the rental property, I felt like the worst amateur detective ever. But I had become one out of necessity, not choice. And however painful it had been, at least I could strike Judith off my suspect list.

If I took Esme's words to heart, I could definitely strike Gina and Emerald off too. If my daughter and my cat-slash-great-aunt vouched for them, I should really trust them too.

That left me with Jason Bullwart. His motives still confounded me, but Ellie had as much as said that he was the killer.

I'd have to tell Jamie about it, hoping he would take the investigation further. Maybe I could rely on the police for this, once I nudged them in the right direction.

CHAPTER THIRTY

The last thing I needed that evening was another hate message.

My kids ran out of the cottage when they saw my car pull up, in order to warn me, but it was hard to miss. This time, the perpetrator hadn't broken another window. They'd smeared their message in big bright letters on our front door.

It must have happened earlier today, because my children told me it was there when they had gotten home from school.

"We didn't want to disturb you at work," Blake said. "We tried to wipe it away, but it won't come off."

I stood a few feet away from the door, examining the slur. "That's actually good. This time, I'm telling the police about it."

I lifted my cell phone to take a picture but then stopped myself. I stepped forward and bent to examine the writing more closely.

"What is it, Mom?" Audrey asked, wrapping her arms around herself. "You didn't see a ghost, did you?"

"Hmm? No!"

I tilted my head, staring at the G in WITCHES GET OUT. It was unusual, with the top end curling all the way back to meet the middle, so it almost looked like a B.

I had seen this G before, but I couldn't think of where or when.

Stepping back again, I lifted the phone to take a few pictures and then called Jamie Rees.

"Can you come over, please? We're victims of a hate crime…and, well, I have a pretty good idea who might be responsible. Maybe for the murders too."

To my surprise, Jamie didn't chide me for acting upon hunches again. Instead, he sounded keen. "I have something to tell you as well."

We went inside, and I dug out the note that had been attached to the brick, comparing the G in CRIMINALS GET OUT to the image on my phone. The G looked the same, but that's not where I'd seen it before.

I closed my eyes, trying to remember. A knock on the door interrupted me. "Come in," I called out.

Jamie stepped into the cottage.

"That was fast," I said.

He looked troubled. "I'm assuming that's the hate message you talked about, on the door? I thought you meant you got a nasty text message or something."

"No, this bully is old school. And it's the second time. I didn't report the first one." I pointed at the still boarded-up window. "They threw a brick the other day, with this note attached to it." I handed it to him.

Jamie's eyes widened. "I almost asked you about this the other day when I was here for dinner, but I just figured you were having necessary repairs done. This is an old house. It was a brick through the window? That's serious, Liv. Why didn't you report it?"

I shrugged. "There was a lot going on at the time, you know, with Farrow's interest in me… I thought it would be better to keep my head down, not draw attention to myself. You know, like you told me in the car that evening."

Jamie rubbed his beard stubble, the expression in his brown eyes completely crestfallen. "Oh, I'm sorry, Liv. I shouldn't have said those things and made you feel you can't come to the police with this sort of thing. That you can't come to *me*." He held my gaze for a moment.

I got a little hot under the collar, and, remembering my kids were in the room, cleared my throat.

"Yes, I should have reported it. And I'm reporting it now. I'm done hiding. And I'm done feeling like I've done something wrong." I turned to my kids. "Blake, Audrey, please go upstairs so I can have a private conversation with DS Rees."

Audrey looked like she wanted to protest, but Blake nudged her, and they went upstairs.

I waited until the creaking of the stairs stopped, then I said to Jamie, "Like I said on the phone, I think I've finally worked out who did this. You told me not to play detective, and I have to admit that I suspected all the wrong people for the wrong reasons. I clearly suck at sleuthing, so you're getting your way, and I won't investigate this anymore."

Jamie started to say something, but I stopped him. "No, I mean it. But today, I received information about someone… The hows and whys aren't quite clear to me, but I thought I'd better let you make sense of it."

I told Jamie about my strange conversation with Ellie Bullwart. "It sounds like he did this, right?" I ended. "I'm not sure why he would kill Matilda Rutherford, but maybe he's working with someone—"

"No, I don't think Jason Bullwart is the culprit," Jamie interrupted me. "Maybe he's responsible for this." He pointed at the note. "And the message on your door. That seems like Jason's style. But the murder…" He grabbed my shoulders. "Liv, I think I finally figured it out."

I stared at him in suspense.

"It's about the jewels!" he said with triumph in his voice.

I shook my head in confusion. "The jewels…" Then I remembered that Tracy Martens had accused me of stealing Matilda Rutherford's jewels. "Oh. Did you find them?"

"No. That's just it. It looks like the jewels were stolen. That's the motive!"

"Ah! Then it could have been Jason. He could have killed Matilda for money."

Jamie shook his head. "Forget about Jason for a minute. I think it's Stanley."

I blinked. "Matilda's husband? He's dead!"

"That's what I figured out. Stanley is alive. Matilda let everyone believe he passed away. There was even a funeral. But there's no evidence. Nobody in Fairwyck could tell me how Stanley died, or when, exactly. More importantly, there's no death certificate."

I was stunned. After a moment of silence, I said, "You know what's weird? I had been under the impression Stanley was still alive in the beginning. When I met Matilda, she made it seem like that. The way she was talking about him… She still organized her life as if he'd come back any moment. Keeping the same hairstyle he liked, and so on. Maybe she did have hope he'd return home one day."

Jamie nodded vigorously. "And Matilda always refused to sell the jewels. Or give them to her niece. It's because they were Stanley's. What if Stanley came back for them? Matilda hoped he'd be back for her, wanted him to stay, was maybe holding out on revealing the hiding place to him. That's when he killed her."

"Hmm." I gently extracted myself from Jamie's hands. They were still on my shoulders, and I found I couldn't think clearly if he stood so close to me. "But that scenario would make more sense if Matilda would have been…I don't know, bludgeoned to death or something. The murder was premeditated, though. Matilda was sensitive to cleaning chemicals. She always made her own organic ones. The killer must have brought the aggressive store-bought products, intending to mix a cocktail with dangerous fumes so Matilda would die. And they brought the gas mask."

"Maybe…"

"And what about Phyllis? Remember, she saw the killer with the gas mask? How unlikely is it that her death was an accident? Someone must have doctored her medication."

"No reason to think this someone couldn't have been Stanley." Jamie rubbed his aquiline nose.

"If he's been gone all this time, how could he have known about Phyllis's heart condition? On the other hand, Stanley was the love of Phyllis's life. She would have welcomed him with open arms if he'd turned up on her doorstep. She might have told him, or he charmed or tricked her into…I don't know, taking too much of her medication?"

I gave Jamie the lowdown on the Phyllis-Matilda-Stanley love triangle. Something suddenly occurred to me. "What if she knew it was Stanley? She might not have turned him in if she was still blind with love. That could have been the real reason she was conflicted about going to the police." I closed my eyes, shushing Jamie when he wanted to say something. "I'm thinking."

"Okay."

There was a line of investigation I'd wanted to come back to but couldn't. Asking Matilda Rutherford who the killer was would have been the most direct way to go about it. Her ghost was next door in her cottage, but I hadn't dared enter it, knowing Farrow would throw me into jail immediately if he caught me there.

Matilda had tried to tell me already who the killer was with her message, but I'd only been able to decipher a few words, not enough to figure it out.

Now I was trying to remember the words. It was something about close and love…If Stanley was the murderer, that part of the message fit.

I told Jamie about it, then took my Nikon from the shelf. "I need to get back into Matilda's cottage. There has to be a way to ask Matilda, to get her to confirm if this was Stanley—"

Jamie grabbed my arm to stop me.

"I can't let you go next door." He grimaced.

I groaned. "Let's just do this quickly. Farrow doesn't have to know."

But Jamie stayed adamant. "The reason I think this is about the jewels is that Tracy won't shut up about them. She's certain you stole them. Farrow is inclined to believe her. It would be a great motive for you. You need money. He believes with your criminal background—"

"Oh, man!" I groaned. "Not that again. I'm so sick of it. My husband is the criminal. Not me. I'm not a thief!"

"For some reason, Farrow is hell-bent on sticking you with this. I—"

Jamie's phone rang. He looked at the display and his eyes clouded over. "The station." He took the call. "Hello?"

The person on the other line responded, and Jamie said, "Shit!"

He hung up. "Apparently, Farrow is on his way here with a warrant to search your home for the jewels. If he catches me here, talking to you—"

"I know, your job is on the line. I'm so sorry."

Jamie was already at the door. "No, I'm sorry. I've got to go."

"Wait." I ran upstairs to grab the photocopies with Matilda as a ghost and the picture of the gas mask. I pressed them into Jamie's hands. "He'd better not find them here. Now go."

He rushed out and drove off with screeching tires.

Only moments later, after I'd had just enough time to warn my children about what was coming, Farrow barged in with a warrant.

The kids and I sat huddled on the sofa while he and his men rummaged through our belongings.

We were all shaking. I had to tell Blake and Audrey that I was a murder suspect and warn them about the possibility that the police might take me away.

Audrey cried, and Blake turned deathly pale, their sherry eyes looking even bigger in their heart-shaped face.

"He won't find anything," I kept muttering.

But deep down I worried Farrow would find a reason, any reason, to send me to jail for murder.

Only a few weeks ago, I'd thought the worst time in my life was over. I'd been so wrong. The worst was yet to come.

CHAPTER THIRTY-ONE

Of course, the police found nothing. But I'd been so worried, even considered Farrow might plant evidence, that I broke down crying after the DI and his officers left.

The day had been such a roller-coaster, I just couldn't pull myself together.

My children had to console me, and I cried even more about that. I should be the strong adult, taking care of them after such a traumatic event.

Blake persuaded me to snuggle up in bed and brought me a cup of tea. Audrey read to me from her favorite children's book—a story I'd read to her countless times when she was little. It made me even more weepy.

I squeezed my kids until they protested, but I was so grateful to have them. I felt guilty for not being the perfect mother and father for them, but then I stopped myself. It wasn't my fault they didn't have a father. And was it so bad that sometimes a mother had strong emotions she had to work through?

I wiped away my tears and smiled. "Thanks. You're

both such a help. I think I'll drink my tea and go to sleep early."

I told them they could have a snack in front of the TV for dinner, as long as the snack plate also contained some veggies.

I didn't fall asleep for a long while, since I had a lot to think about. But I wasn't fretting anymore.

Even though I didn't mind showing my kids that it was okay to be weak and vulnerable every once in a while, I didn't want to be a victim anymore.

I really was done being pushed around.

I'd rebelled against that role before, but I'd gone about it all wrong. The only way I'd been able to come out of that horrible situation Steven had left me in was by accepting the lifeline my great-aunt had given me.

Ever since arriving here, I'd been suspicious of everyone, suspecting them of murder. Sure, this was partly because of Farrow putting me on the defense with his ridiculous accusations. And I'd reached out to Jamie but had withdrawn immediately after his skeptical reaction to my ghost photos.

Maybe Esme was right. The whole thing with Steven had made me distrustful, quick to retreat within myself. It had made me convinced I needed to go it alone.

Esme had told me that, but really, my kids had demonstrated it to me. It was good to accept help. I needed help. I wouldn't survive without it.

It was time to rally up allies.

The next morning, Tuesday, Judith had put me down for a supervised shift in the afternoon again, so I had the morning off.

First, I called Jamie. He said nothing about the photos with Matilda's ghost that I'd given to him, and I didn't force him to talk about them. What if he needed a little longer to come to terms with the fact that I had supernatural abilities? I couldn't really blame him. Heck, my mother and I had tried to pretend something like this didn't exist my entire life.

Jamie clearly liked me and wanted to help. I liked and trusted him too, so I'd take it.

I felt bad when he told me he'd been put on desk duty, of course. "Be careful," I told him. "It's great that you're doing all these inquiries behind Farrow's back." He'd said he wanted to inquire about Stanley Rutherford with his last known employer, the post office. "Better use your personal computer and phone. I don't want you to risk your job for me."

He insisted it was the right thing to do. "For you, and Matilda and Phyllis."

After we said goodbye, I walked to the Sacred Salmon.

Emerald was at work, but I had a great open and honest chat with my great-aunt Gina about my current situation.

"Maybe your cards were right, after all," I finished. "My job is on the line. Farrow is closing in on me, and I always feel like I'm a smidgeon away from getting arrested. Definitely a being-stabbed-with-many-swords situation." I tried to make light of it. "Sorry I was rude when you told me. It came a little out of left field. Added to that, all my life I'd successfully repressed that part of me that you and Emerald kind of…represented."

Gina grimaced. "I know. That's why we wanted to give you a bit of space after arriving in Fairwyck. But then I pulled that card… Emerald told me afterward it wouldn't have hurt if we'd treated you with kid gloves. But you may have noticed by now, subtlety isn't my strong suit."

I had to laugh, but I soon became somber again, when she followed it up with, "This wasn't about *almost* losing your job and *almost* getting arrested, darling." Gina threw her wild blond hair back over her shoulder in a dramatic gesture. "The cards indicated something worse in store for you."

"What are you saying?" My mouth was suddenly dry. "That more terrible things will happen?"

"I'm afraid so."

I wanted to ask her what exactly was going to happen, but I knew she wouldn't be able to answer that. Plus, I had a pretty good idea what awaited me.

"If something happens…you know, where I can't look after Blake and Audrey…" I swallowed. "Would you and Emerald—"

I didn't even need to finish that sentence. "Of course," Gina said emphatically. "We're here for you. And it means a lot that you'd trust us with your children."

I looked around the medieval haunted pub we were sitting in. "Feel free to stay at my house if that happens. They might feel a little more comfortable there."

Gina laughed as if I'd made a joke.

I made a mental note to speak to Emerald about it too.

Then I told my great-aunt about the latest developments in the case. "We've been getting threats as well, and I thought they were linked to all of this, but they might not be." I sighed. "It would be good to at least solve that mystery. I'm so close to figuring it out too. One letter in the hate messages seemed familiar, but with everything that's been going on, my brain is too jumbled up."

Gina clapped her hands. "Ooooh. That's something I can help you with."

"What do you mean?"

"If the knowledge is somewhere in your head, I can help you access it." When I still seemed unsure, she added. "It's a spell, but it works a bit like hypnosis."

I took a long sip of tea to give myself time to answer. I'd decided to trust Gina and Emerald, but did I want my great-aunt poking around in my head? It felt a little like going from zero to a hundred in this relationship.

But if it would help me find the culprit of the hate crimes. I took a deep breath. In for a penny…

"Okay." I wanted to tell her more details, but Gina stopped me. "It's best I don't know any details, lest you think I'd put something in your head."

We went to the annex and did the session in the room where Gina received clients. It looked similar to the Victorian parlor we'd had tea in but not quite as crammed.

I sat down at the table and waited for Gina to get out all kinds of paraphernalia: a light blue candle, a bundle of herbs, and crystals.

She struck a set of matches and lit the bundle of herbs, waving it around and fanning the smoke with a feather. "Just a bit of cleansing before we get started," Gina explained.

Then she lit the candle. There was a larger clear quartz on the table, and she asked me to hold another, smaller stone. "Red jasper. It shows blockages and clears them. Once you access the memory, you can let go of it."

"All right." I was nervous. "What do I do? Close my eyes?"

Gina shook her head. "Look into mine."

I locked eyes with her, and within an instant, it was as if everything else around me blanked out. Gina said something, but I only heard it as a low rumbling sound, not the actual words. It was fascinating to see Gina's eyes turn from blue to a violet color.

Looking back, I probably should have been alarmed to be immediately bespelled by her. But it felt good—very calming.

My eyelashes got heavy, and I let my lids flutter closed.

It didn't take long for the image to appear. The G with

the funny curly top, so it looked like a B. Someone was writing it on a chalkboard.

I mentally zoomed out so I saw more than the hand. The person came into view.

It was Jason Bullwart.

Now the memory came back to me in full. I'd seen Jason write something on the chalkboard at the pub. GIN.

My eyes fluttered open again.

"Was it successful?" Gina asked while clearing away the magical ingredients.

"Yes. It's not a surprise, really. But now that I know for sure, I can confidently pass evidence on to the police, since they can compare this guy's handwriting."

"Okay, great! So who was it?"

"Jason Bullwart."

Gina stopped in her tracks, on her way back to the table from the cabinet where she'd stowed away the crystals and candle. "Oh no."

"What?"

Gina sank down in the chair. "He's been threatening us too."

"Really? He threw a brick through our window and wrote something on our door. Did he do something like that here?"

Gina nodded. "A couple of bricks with messages. Luckily, he's aiming for the upstairs rooms in the inn, the windows facing the back. I told you, nobody goes there. They're just occupied by ghosts."

"Still! Why didn't you report it to the police? Especially if you know who did it."

My great-aunt shook her head. "We're used to that sort of thing, unfortunately. DI Farrow isn't particularly sympathetic to Seven women, I'm afraid."

I snorted. "Don't I know it."

"If I went to Farrow, telling him that Jason had a

reading and didn't like what I told him, he'd only warn me not to scam people with my psychic act. Secretly, he'd even think I had it coming. Believe me, I've been there. I'm just sorry you got caught up in this by mere association."

"So that's the reason?" I asked incredulously. "Jason didn't like the advice you gave him when he consulted you as a psychic?"

Gina nodded. "He asked me if he should leave his wife, considering they owned a business together. He was afraid the business would fail as a result."

"Well, Ellie is doing all the work in that pub, so I'd say that's a valid question."

"He just wanted reassurances that the pub would still be a major source of income."

"What did you tell him?"

"What the cards said. That he didn't need to worry about it, because his wife was about to leave *him*." Gina sighed. "He got furious about that. Maybe I shouldn't have said it, but I always try to be true to what the cards tell me."

"He blamed the messenger. He went to you for absolution, and when it wasn't what he wanted to hear, he started a witch hunt. That's why he had such a powerful reaction when you came to the pub the other day."

"We shouldn't have come. But we wanted to say hello to you. We realized it was a mistake and left straight away."

"And then he found out I'm related to you. He transferred his animosity to me. That's why he didn't want me working in the pub." I shook my head. "I get why you don't want to report it. I almost didn't either. But Jason shouldn't be able to get away with it. He could have hurt someone, and who knows what he'll escalate to."

"Yes, you're right. I didn't know your children were in danger. We need to put a stop to it."

I called Jamie but only got his voicemail. I left him a

message telling him about my memory of Jason writing the G onto the board. "It's definitely him. You can do a handwriting comparison, can't you? And Gina and Emerald got targeted too. In fact, he started this witch hunt because of a tarot card reading that wasn't to his liking. Please come by Gina's, ask her about this, and collect the evidence here."

After I hung up, I got to my feet. "Thanks Gina, but I've got to go." I really wanted to make sure Ellie was all right, especially after everything I'd just learned.

I had enough time to stop by the pub before grabbing a quick lunch and heading to work.

I called Ellie on my way over to the Owl and Oak, but she didn't answer. The pub had just opened, though, so I went in.

I stopped as the door closed behind me. It was dark inside, and nobody seemed around.

"Hello?" I called. "Ellie?"

Someone stepped out of the shadows. I sucked in a sharp breath.

Jason Bullwart.

His face was a snarl. "What do you want, witch?"

CHAPTER THIRTY-TWO

Slowly backing away, I sputtered, "I'm looking for Ellie."

"She's gone. Thanks to that stuck-up tease, Judith Winters." Jason spat on the floor.

"Oh." At least he didn't seem to know that I had been here talking to Ellie yesterday too.

Jason Bullwart looked like an angry gorilla with his puffed-up chest and big, tense arms. A permanent scowl was etched on his face, and his dark eyes glittered dangerously.

I didn't relish being alone with him. I'd come here to make sure Ellie was all right. She'd said Jason had never hurt her, but still.

It sounded as if she'd left Jason. Judith had helped her, and according to Esme, my boss was in the habit of doing this sort of thing, so I could assume Ellie was safe. There was no reason to stick around.

Except… This was the bully who'd scared my children half to death. I wanted him to know that I wouldn't stand for this sort of behavior. We had proof that he was the perpetrator of the hate crimes, and I wanted him to know that he could expect to go down for it.

It probably wasn't the smartest idea to confront a violent man like Jason Bullwart. What if I was right, and his hate crimes were connected to the murders after all? Jamie suspected Stanley Rutherford, but that was just a theory.

Jason had been ticked off by Gina, then spouted off tirades against the Seven witches in the pub—and the person who'd wanted Matilda gone might've managed to entice him to do their dirty work. That meant Jason could be a killer, which was scary as hell. But he'd have been the hired gun and someone else the mastermind.

Jason was really worked up, maybe in a state where he might let something slip if I poked and prodded a little.

Edging toward the door, I said, "Thanks to Ellie's testimony and the confirmation of a handwriting expert, the police know it was you who threw the brick through my window and graffitied my door. You'd better leave us alone from now on, or it's just going to get worse for you."

Jason scoffed. "Can it get any worse? My wife left me."

"It shouldn't come as a surprise. Gina already told you she was going to during your tarot card reading. You were looking for a convenient way out, anyway."

Jason gave a derisive laugh. "The witch's prediction came true, didn't it?" He made a rude gesture and swore. "I changed my mind. I want Ellie back. I need her."

"Why, so she can work in the pub while you get drunk with your mates?"

That was a step too far. I wanted to provoke him a little, yes, but now he charged at me like a bull who saw red. "You witch! You and your ilk think you know everything…"

Thankfully, he was a little uncoordinated, and I dodged out of his way. I backed away farther.

My eyes went to the now faraway door, and I swallowed. If Jason attacked me, I had no chance to escape. I had to say something to startle him.

"No, I don't know everything. There's a lot I haven't figured out. Like why you'd even consider leaving your lovely wife." I said the first things that popped into my mind. Jason was now so close that I could smell the booze oozing from his pores, and I was cornered next to the bar.

My brain was desperately trying to come up with something, anything…

People left their spouses for someone else. I couldn't picture any sane woman wanting to have an affair with Jason. But if a woman had an ulterior motive…if there was a payoff, like getting Jason to do something for her.

"I heard you're having an affair with…Tracy Martens. Were you leaving Ellie for her?" I blurted out.

Jason stopped moving. He looked thoroughly confused. So my minor diversion had worked.

But I was surprised as well. I'd pulled the name Tracy Martens off the top of my head. I didn't really imagine she'd have an affair with Jason. But she was the only one left on the list of people connected to the little old ladies and their valuable real estate.

I hadn't really considered her a suspect before. Tracy seemed even less likely than Judith to get her hands dirty and mix chemicals and drugs to murder someone. However, she'd benefited from Matilda's death by inheriting the cottage. She'd also benefit from Judith's plan, and I'd heard she was keen to list the cottage with WLA.

What had irked me most about her was that she kept insisting I had something to do with Matilda's death and wanted to steal jewelry I knew nothing about. She seemed hell-bent on making me a scapegoat.

Jason pulled a face. "Miss High-and-Mighty? No,

thanks. I want a woman who wouldn't be above getting on her knees in front of me, if you know what I mean."

I wanted to gag. What had Ellie ever seen in this guy?

"She's very pretty, but maybe she's not your type." I soldiered on with my affair idea. If not Tracy, maybe someone else?

But Jason was still talking about Matilda's niece. "She looks good now, but she got herself into debt in order to get that face and that body, and I'm really not interested in financing the broad. Even if she claims she'll be rich soon, I'm not buying it."

"What do you mean?" I knew cosmetic procedures could be really expensive, I just hadn't thought about that before. Tracy had been working as a pharmacist and was now in fashion school. How could she afford her procedures and all the stylish clothes? "Did she tell you she's coming into money?"

"She was here a few weeks ago, getting sloshed. With her girlfriends, the whole man-hating, holier-than-thou gang. Judith Winters, Tracy, that librarian witch cousin of yours."

"They're a book club." Emerald had told me about it. "Maybe they sometimes get a drink after meeting at the library."

"Book club," Jason snorted derisively. "Sounds about right. They usually nurse a white-wine spritzer all night, or something lame like that. But that evening, Tracy was chugging back G&Ts. And she boasted about being wealthy soon, when her aunt Matilda croaked. Something about a plan Judith had, something with a pond? Typical woman, knows nothing about money or business. How much can you make by renting out a cottage? Not enough to cover the debt she has. Owes money all over Gloucestershire."

Jason's comments gave me a lot of food for thought. My eyes went to the clock above the door. I had to hurry if I wanted to get lunch at the village shop and ask some questions there.

I slipped past Jason. "Gotta go, I'm late."

"Hey," he shouted after me. "Tell Ellie there's nobody else, do you hear me?"

Once I was out the door, I cast a glance over my shoulder, but Jason wasn't following me.

I rushed down the road to the shop.

Inside, I grabbed a cheese-and-tomato sandwich and a soda from the fridge, adding a chocolate bar from the display conveniently placed next to the till.

"Hey, Michelle," I said, when she handed me my change. "Didn't you say Tracy Martens used to work here?"

"Yes, at the pharmacy." She looked toward that part of the store. "Why?"

"Is her old boss in today? I'd love to ask him a few quick questions."

"Sure. Anthony has worked here forever. I don't think he has any customers right now."

I smiled and made my way up the few steps into the pharmacy section of the shop.

I introduced myself to Anthony, a stooped old man with white hair. "I wanted to ask you a few questions about Tracy Martens, if you don't mind."

Anthony looked taken aback, so I told him I was in trouble with the police because Tracy claimed I was after her aunt's jewels. "The allegations are completely unfounded, though, and I don't know why she insists on it. When Matilda Rutherford died, I'd been in Fairwyck not even a week. I'd only met my neighbor once. I knew nothing about any jewels, and anyway, I have an alibi for the night Matilda died. Lots of people saw me in the pub where I worked."

Anthony nodded slowly. "That sounds like Tracy. She likes to make up stories. We had a lot of money and inventory missing while she was working here, and she was always quick to point her fingers at someone else. She blamed Michelle—and I've known Michelle since she was a little girl." He lowered his voice. "She can be a busybody, but she's no thief. Tracy sounded quite convincing in the beginning. It took me a while to figure out she was behind the missing money."

My eyes widened. "She just helped herself?"

Anthony shrugged. "To be fair, nothing was ever proven. But there was a pattern. Cash or drugs went missing, and it was only a matter of time before she turned up looking a little different."

"Ah, her cosmetic procedures?"

"Surgeries, dentistry, hair and beauty treatments… Poor thing was obsessed with Kate Middleton."

"Of course, Catherine—the Princess of Wales! That's who she resembles! And she used to look so different, didn't she? I've seen pictures of her as a child. Tracy changed to emulate her?" I couldn't believe it. I'd never heard anything like it. Sure, people dressed like celebrities, copied their hairstyles…but nothing as drastic as this. "And she went so far as to steal for this?"

I must have sounded incredulous. The old man said, "I know it seems unbelievable. She was a pretty young lass. Why she felt the need to change, I'll never know. I wanted to give her the benefit of the doubt. I let her get away with it for far too long. But one day it hit me when I saw this hungry expression in her eyes. In my line of work, I get to see that expression far too often, I'm sad to say. On the faces of addicts. Like an addict, Tracy stole and lied to get her next fix."

"The next procedure that would change her and get her closer to looking like Kate?"

"I realized I wasn't doing her any favors by keeping her on, especially when she started taking potentially dangerous drugs to sell on the black market. I had to let her go."

I tilted my head. "So she didn't leave to go to fashion school? You fired her?"

"Yes. She wanted to become a fashion buyer, like Kate Middleton had aspired to become before her marriage. I don't think she's going to school, though. All I know is that the Jigsaw store in Cirencester asked for a reference. I assume she works there now."

"You gave her a reference, despite everything?"

Anthony sighed. "I know. It's just a part-time sales assistant job in a clothing store, though. I felt sorry for her, I guess."

I smiled at the kind old man.

"I've got to run, to make it to work on time. Thank you so much for answering my questions."

Anthony waved a hand. "You're one of our own. I remember you coming in here as a child with your mother or Ethel. I always liked your family, and you were ever so polite."

That hadn't even occurred to me. "Oh. Sorry, I don't remember that."

"Well, it's nice that you finally came home."

It hadn't really felt like that until now, but hearing Anthony say it warmed my heart.

I smiled, thanked Anthony again, and waved at Michelle on my way out of the shop.

Then I drove to the rental property I was supposed to meet Esme at, eating my sandwich and drinking my Coke on the way.

I really wished I didn't have to work today so I could

look into Tracy Martens. I had a feeling I was finally on the right track.

But it would have to wait until tomorrow, when I had the whole day off. Later today, there was one very personal task on my to-do list that I really needed to tackle.

CHAPTER THIRTY-THREE

That evening, after the kids went to bed, I poured myself a fortifying glass of wine, sat down on the couch, and placed a long-overdue phone call to my mother.

I had to ask her for another small loan so I could pay for the new window, but what I really wanted to talk to her about was her connection with DI Farrow.

"He's made it his personal mission to stick me with the murders," I ended, after telling her about the near arrests and the police search of our home. "And I think the reason is…well, you!"

"Albert Farrow?" My mother sounded incredulous.

"I've got no idea what his first name is," I replied gruffly. "He's got a prominent mustache. Like Poirot."

"He still wears that? He always took pride in it, even when he started growing it at fifteen and it was thin as a thread." My mother sniggered.

"So you do know him?" I asked impatiently.

"Yes, yes. I grew up with him. He first proposed when we were both eighteen. I told him I was far too young to get married, but he wouldn't take no for an answer."

"Proposed?" I couldn't believe what I was hearing. "That man was in love with you? To be honest, I had the impression his feelings were veering in the opposite direction."

"Oh, yes, well, there's a fine line between love and hate for some people, isn't there?"

"Hmmpf." I took a big sip of wine. "So what happened?"

"I turned him down, of course. I went to university in Oxford, and three years later, just before graduation, I came back pregnant—"

"Yes, yes, I know all that." I was all too familiar with mom's affair with an Oxford professor, which had resulted in her becoming a single mother—I'd asked her about it often as a teenager, fascinated by this unknown sperm donor of mine. "What happened with Farrow?"

"He proposed again, letting me know he'd happily take care of me and the child."

"Oh my god." I closed my eyes and shuddered at the thought of DI Farrow as my stepfather. "Thank goodness you said no."

"I wasn't in love with him. He took it badly. Told me I was making a big mistake and nobody else would take me, knocked up with an illegitimate child—and a Seven to boot. He wouldn't even talk to me after that, pretended I didn't exist."

"Not quite. It sounds as if he kept tabs on you—and me." Ethel the cat jumped onto the couch, and I stroked her back until she'd circled the cushion a few times and finally lay down. "He knew my whole life story, including what Steven had done and that the FBI had investigated me. That bit of gossip spread in Fairwyck like wildfire, and he may very well be to blame for that."

"Oh, I'm so sorry, darling!"

I gave Ethel a good scratch under her chin, and she

purred. "Maybe Farrow felt validated that you raised me to be a criminal—perhaps thought that wouldn't have happened if you'd married him."

"I don't know, Liv… Surely, he can't still be that hung up on me. It's been forty years."

"Some people are very loyal when it comes to love—especially lost love." Ethel looked up at me with her slanted golden eyes, and I was reminded of Matilda and Phyllis. They had clung to the idea that Stanley was their soulmate, and they'd never managed to move on from him.

"Maybe you broke his heart, Mom. He was deeply hurt. That kind of pain can twist people up. Then you left, and he never got closure. I turned up here, looking like you…" I stared at Ethel, lost in though. It almost seemed as if the cat were nodding, agreeing with me.

"Hmm. Maybe I should call him, confront him about this."

"I don't know. It might be like pouring oil onto the fire."

"But if you want to work through something, achieve closure, you need to confront it." My mother's tone of voice changed. "You know, I purposely left Fairwyck behind. I thought it was the best for us, especially for you. But now you're back there, like you've come full circle, and you have to deal with everything all at once. It feels like that's always been in the cards for you, and I made it worse by taking you away. I must say, I'm impressed to hear that you're embracing your abilities after all these years—"

"What do you mean?" I interrupted. I stopped stroking Ethel and jumped up from the couch. I wasn't sure I was ready for *that* conversation with my mother. "Where did you hear that?"

"Gina called me. We've been talking quite a bit. I have to admit that I might benefit from working through a few things too."

I was too stunned to speak.

"In any case, I do feel a little guilty. I can't come over there and support you, Liv. I'm sorry. But if I can do anything for you from here, I'd love to. Like screwing that ridiculous police detective's head back on the right way."

Now she sounded like my mother again. I giggled with relief. "Maybe it *would* help if you called him."

Ethel meowed, and I sat back down to resume scratching her chin. It occurred to me that Phyllis had never gotten closure where Stanley was concerned, and how bitter the whole thing had made her. Maybe she would have eventually talked to and forgiven Matilda, but then Matilda had been murdered, and Phyllis never got that opportunity. DI Farrow's situation was a little different, but it seemed to me that he deserved closure too, so he wouldn't die with hatred in his heart. Especially if it would get him off my case.

I told my mother that, and she said, "All right, darling. I'll look up his number on the Gloucestershire police website, and I'll give him a call."

"Thanks, Mom. Oh, and…" I suddenly got a lump in my throat. "Maybe we can talk about what…you know, what I'm going through, some other time."

"I'd like that. Bye, darling."

I hung up and sat there for at least another hour, sipping my wine, enjoying the company of the cat, while mulling over that phone call.

∽

The next morning, I drove to Cirencester and got to the Jigsaw store just as the manager opened up.

I looked around nervously, but Tracy wasn't anywhere in sight. "Excuse me," I said to the store manager. "I have some questions about an employee. Tracy? She's not in today, is she?"

The older lady in a pink pantsuit furrowed her brow. "Nobody by that name works here."

"Oh." I was taken aback. "Was she fired for helping herself from the till?" I asked sympathetically.

"What?" The store manager now looked annoyed. "I don't know anyone called Tracy."

"That's so odd. Her former employer, the pharmacist in Fairwyck, told me he gave a reference when she applied here."

"Fairwyck?" Understanding dawned in her eyes. "I have an employee from Fairwyck. But her name is Catherine."

Now I was confused. "I'm talking about a young woman named Tracy Martens. I'm pretty sure that's her name. Everyone in Fairwyck calls her that, including her father."

The woman tipped a finger against her fuchsia-lined lips. "Ahhhh. Hang on a second." She grabbed a laptop from under the till and began typing, her long pink nails clickety-clacking. After a moment she said, "Tracy Catherine Martens. She said she preferred to be called Catherine in her interview. So I forgot about her other first name."

My brain took a few seconds to process that. Tracy had taken her obsession with Catherine so far as to rename herself. At least that was less invasive than surgery.

"Um…do you know if she has another job or if she's getting a fashion degree?"

The woman crossed her arms in front of her chest. "Why would I give you that information? What business is it of yours?"

I couldn't expect everyone to be as forthcoming and friendly as Anthony. "Um…"

"And why would you assume I fired Catherine for stealing money from the till?" Her expression shifted from mistrust to worry. "Has she done that before? You said you talked to her former employer. He wouldn't have given her a reference if she'd done anything like that, surely?"

"It just seems that Tracy…Catherine is in a lot of debt, and I'm trying to find out more about her, where she's getting the money for her surgeries and expensive clothes."

The woman's eyes widened. "Oh. I get it." She looked me up and down. "Are you from a debt collection agency? You don't look like you work for a loan shark."

"I'm not!"

"There were some unsavory people here before, talking to Catherine. I asked her about it, and she claimed she didn't know them. Now, *they* looked like loan-shark goons."

I nodded slowly. So Jason hadn't made that stuff up about Tracy owing money…and it also fit with Anthony's suspicions.

"That clears a few things up for me," I said to the manager, turning to go. "Thank you."

"Wait," she called after me. "Is Catherine in trouble? We don't need that here. She presents herself as a classy woman, but if she stole money…you never answered my question if that's true." She hurried after me, touching my arm in order to stop me at the door.

Despite Tracy's best efforts to set me up for taking the blame for her crimes, it didn't feel right to pass information on to her employer that would almost certainly lead to getting her fired. If Anthony was right, she was an addict. It meant she needed help.

On the other hand, Tracy had gone to some lengths to get money. Maybe even murder. Who knew what else she was capable of?

"Look," I said, extricating myself from the manager's grip. "It's not my place to say. But maybe call the pharmacist who gave her a reference and implore him to tell the truth."

A customer came in, and I took the opportunity to slip out the door.

On my way back to Fairwyck, I tried my very best to stay calm and rational about my new hunch that Tracy was the killer.

Wildly suspecting people and running around confronting them had not gotten me anywhere, except in trouble. I'd nearly gotten myself arrested, turned my employers against me, alienated my relatives, and cut myself off from allies.

So I clearly didn't have the best track record where this investigation was concerned. But this time, I really thought I was on the right track.

Tracy Martens was in debt. She constantly needed more money because she was obsessed with turning herself into Kate Middleton. I wasn't a psychiatrist, but she clearly had problems. At the very least, a severe case of body dysmorphia. I'd read that getting cosmetic surgeries could become an addiction, so Anthony probably wasn't wrong.

She'd gotten fired from her job. Her career in the fashion industry wasn't going anywhere… It seemed likely to me that the tuition money her father had given her for her fashion degree had also gone to turning herself into the Princess of Wales.

Thinking about her father reminded me of the conversation I'd had with Luther. I'd only gotten half the story, but it sounded as if Tracy had been abandoned by her father as a child. Maybe that had brought on her psychological problems.

Luther now wanted to make up for all that, giving her money and turning a blind eye to what she really did with it. Luther seemed to be a hard worker, very handy, and eager and willing to take on all sorts of jobs in his field. But that didn't make him exactly wealthy, so for Tracy, that well was only so deep.

She'd turned to her aunt Matilda. I was only guessing, but Tracy had likely known she'd inherit Matilda's cottage. It seemed as if she hadn't wanted to wait for nature to take its course. Knowing about Judith's plan, Tracy had been keen to turn the cottage into a profitable rental property, providing her with a steady stream of money.

When I got home, I called Jamie Rees.

He updated me on the Jason Bullwart situation. They had arrested him after Ellie had agreed to testify against him. "It looks like you weren't the only one who bore the brunt of his hate. You and Gina and Emerald were only his latest victims. Others have come forward, after Ellie tipped us off that this was his way of dealing with people he didn't like." Jamie paused. "During the interrogation, Jason flat out admitted everything. He told us he got bullied as a kid. Claims it's his right to do the same now. The tables have turned, he said. Survival of the fittest."

I sighed. "What an idiot. At least he's not getting away with it."

"Yeah."

"Sooo…" I grimaced, bracing myself for Jamie's reaction. "I think I have a new suspect. I know I've been wrong about this in the past, but this time, I think I have a pretty good case against this person."

I told Jamie about what I'd found out about Tracy.

"Huh," he said.

I was a little disappointed by his reaction. "You don't think it's her? Why not?"

"You're making a convincing argument, Liv," he said, clearly in an effort not to hurt my feelings. "I would agree with your assessment. We found out about her debts. It's too obvious. She was on our radar."

"Okay, so why didn't you arrest her?" I asked impatiently.

"Simple. She has an alibi for the night Matilda died. And, before you ask, also for the day Phyllis died. She was with her father."

"Pfffff." I let out a stream of air, rolling my eyes, even though Jamie couldn't see it. "Are you being serious?"

"What do you mean?"

"*I* have an alibi. A good one. Many people saw me at the pub. Even so, Farrow thinks I did it, and I live in daily fear of being arrested. And you're discounting Tracy as a suspect because her *father* gave her an alibi? A father who's so wracked with guilt about abandoning her as a child that he now does everything for her? Please!"

Jamie stayed silent for a while. "Okay, maybe you're right. I'll look into it while I'm still on desk duty."

"I'm sorry. I know you're doing what you can. It just makes me mad that Farrow is so unreasonable. Couldn't you go to a superior? Farrow is only a DI, and your higher-ups would surely rein him in. If Farrow is targeting me because he hates my mom, that's not right. His personal feelings are impeding the investigation."

"You're right. I didn't want to make a big ruckus out of it, thinking it'll surely just be a matter of time until Farrow wakes up. I hoped I'd be more successful doing my own investigating—under the cover of desk duty, so to speak. But I'll take action as soon as we have indisputable evidence. Something that even Farrow can't ignore. A credible witness, forensic proof, you know what I mean. Now, I'm still thinking Stanley could be the culprit. I've contacted the post office, and I'm waiting to hear back from them. I'll do what I can to look into Tracy. If you get any information, let me know, okay? I don't think you should go around asking any more questions. It can be dangerous. And I don't need to remind you what could happen if Farrow finds out you're snooping or incriminating someone else. I'm afraid he'd use *any* excuse to put you behind bars."

"Believe me, I live with that fear every day. But I don't want you to risk your career over this either. I appreciate you helping me, but I don't need that on my conscience too. More than anything else, it feels good to know you're in my corner."

"I'm definitely in your corner, Liv." His soft voice sent a delicious shudder down my spine.

"I'm so grateful for that. I can't let you take care of this for me, though. I will not let others incriminate me either, sitting back and waiting patiently for Farrow to see reason. He's given me no indication he's capable of that. I'm going to take care of this myself."

Jamie groaned. "Liv, just be careful, okay?"

"Don't worry, I'm not going to jump the gun this time. I'll make sure Tracy is the murderer before I go after her."

"I don't know if I like the sound of that."

"First, I want to make sure you're barking up the wrong tree with that Stanley theory. It should be fairly easy to find out if he's dead or not."

"Really? How?"

"I know someone who can contact him from beyond the grave."

CHAPTER THIRTY-FOUR

That evening, I had Gina and Emerald over. I'd gone to visit Gina earlier to inform her of my plan.

I would have loved to have done this without my children present, maybe while they were still in school, but Gina had insisted we needed to do it at night.

Apparently, the moon was just right for it.

Blake and Audrey were far too excited about holding a séance to contact a potentially dead person. I couldn't tell them to go to their rooms, especially since they had Gina and Emerald on their side.

"They haven't grown up with these practices. It'll be good for them to see how these things are done," Emerald said.

"I don't know. Do they really need to know?"

"There is absolutely nothing to be afraid of," Emerald tried to reassure me.

"Besides," Gina added. "The more witches to contribute energy to the circle, the better."

"We're hardly witches," I scoffed. "We have some minor paranormal abilities."

Gina and Emerald exchanged a glance.

"Honey, you're still not ready to embrace who you are," Gina said. "I know you're getting more comfortable with your ability to photograph ghosts. That's only part of the whole story. Seven women are witches. Deal with it."

I looked at Emerald, who just nodded enthusiastically.

I let out a long sigh. "Let me get through all of this first, okay? Solve the murders so we can move on, really get started on settling into our new lives. Let's close that door, and then, maybe, I might have the capacity to embrace my inner witch."

My great-aunt and cousin looked at each other again in that knowing way.

"What?" I said, exasperated.

"Embracing your true identity *is* how you get through this, darling," Gina said softly.

"You've got to go all-in to get out of this, so to speak," Emerald added.

I bit back a comment about fortune-cookie advice. I really had no time to argue. "Whatever," I said. "But first things first. Let's try to contact Stanley to see if he's dead or alive. And while we're at it, we can also contact Matilda and ask her if I'm right about Tracy."

"Oh, that's your part," Gina said cryptically. Before I could ask her what she meant, Emerald cut in.

"To contact Stanley, we need something of his. An important item, something that meant a lot to him."

"You're telling me this now?" I said, my annoyance flaring up again. "I don't have anything like that. But I had all afternoon to come up with something if you'd told me earlier."

"We thought it would be better to sneak into Matilda's cottage after dark to find something of Stanley's."

I shook my head. "Absolutely not. I can't go into Matilda's cottage. The police forbade me to go in. If Farrow catches me there, he'll arrest me on the spot. I wouldn't be surprised if he's placed a camera inside, just to set a trap for me."

Audrey, who had been stroking Ethel the cat on the couch, now put in, "We don't need to go into the house."

I looked at my youngest in confusion. "What do you mean?"

"Ethel knows about an item we can get from Matilda's garden."

I stepped up to the kitchen window and looked across the fence to Matilda's property. "I don't know. It's still trespassing, isn't it?"

"You don't need to go," Emerald said with a firm voice. "I'm going." She tucked her hair under a black woolen cap. Her pants were black, and she had a dark windbreaker on, almost as if she'd known she'd need to be a stealthy burglar today.

"Are you sure? What if someone sees you? If Farrow has cameras outside Matilda's house too? I don't want you to get into trouble."

Emerald waved it off. "I'll just say a frisbee flew across the fence or something like that."

I wanted to protest, but she'd already opened the back door, calling Ethel. The ginger cat nimbly jumped off the couch and followed my cousin outside.

I bit my nails, waiting for Emerald to come back, while Gina explained to my children about all the paraphernalia she'd brought along for the séance.

"I've got it!" Emerald called out triumphantly upon her return. She took off her dirty boots at the back door, and we all crowded around her in the kitchen.

She opened a small Ziploc freezer bag, pulling out a little box. "What's in—" I started to ask impatiently, but when I saw the contents, the words got stuck in my throat.

It was a jewelry set. A pendant necklace with diamonds

arranged around a large teardrop-shaped ruby. Teardrop earrings with rubies and diamonds in the same design. And a gold bangle bracelet with diamonds and rubies interspersed.

"These must be Stanley's jewels," I said, when I could finally speak again. "They're a family heirloom, and Matilda never sold them, even after Stanley supposedly died. Tracy accused me of stealing them—or wanting to steal them. Jamie Rees has the theory that the jewels were the motive for her murder, that Stanley murdered Matilda so he could get them back."

"Well, here goes that theory," Blake said. "Nobody stole the jewels."

"No," Emerald said. "I found them in a tree hollow in the old oak in Matilda's garden."

"Yes, Ethel knew Matilda hid them there." Audrey explained.

We all looked at the cat, who was leisurely cleaning itself, as if she had nothing to do with the whole thing.

It made sense that Ethel knew about Matilda's hiding place—she was her best friend.

"Couldn't she have told us earlier?" I asked, a little exasperated. "And what else does she know? Why did Matilda hide the jewels there?"

Audrey knelt down to communicate with the cat, who stopped licking her paw and focused on Audrey.

"Tracy pressured Matilda to sell the jewels and give her the money—or give her the jewels." Audrey relayed Ethel the cat's thoughts. "Matilda got increasingly worried about her niece. The way she had changed and everything. She felt Luther was too soft and that he wasn't doing Tracy any favors with the way he coddled her. She didn't want to give Tracy any more money."

"That makes sense," I said. "But she still had Tracy in her will as the sole heir."

Audrey conferred with the cat again.

"She wanted to change the will," Audrey told us. "Leave everything to the Postal Workers Benevolent Fund. She died before she had a chance to do that."

My mind was racing. Where had I heard that before, the Postal Workers Benevolent Fund? Yes, Luther Martens had mentioned it. Matilda must have told Luther, and Luther had informed Tracy about Matilda's plans. Tracy would have had to act quickly, do away with her aunt, so she'd still inherit the cottage.

"Can she tell us anything else?" I asked excitedly. "Does she know who killed Matilda? Was it Tracy? Is there evidence?" I bent down to lean over the cat.

Ethel's ears flattened, her pupils got bigger, and her whiskers twitched.

"Mom," Audrey protested. "You're stressing her out."

"I'm sorry." I backed off. "It's just…if she knows something…"

"She's still a cat," Audrey cut me off in a matter-of-fact tone. "Yes, she's also Aunt Ethel, but she's not… I don't know how to describe it. She's not an old lady with a human brain and memories, just in cat form. She's an animal with Ethel's spirit or essence or whatever. Most of the time, she's thinking about catching mice and getting you to feed her more tuna and taking a nice nap."

"All right," I said, a little disappointed.

"Talking to cats isn't like talking to humans either," Audrey further explained. "Although Ethel and Gina and Emerald's cat *are* special, compared to other animals I've tried to communicate with."

"They're familiars," Gina said. "Although Ethel is a special case."

"And Ethel wants to take a nap upstairs in your bed now, Mom," Audrey informed us. "This has taken a lot out of her, and she's tired."

I just waved my hand. I hated cat hair on my pillow, but Ethel had earned it. And it didn't sound as if she could give us any more information right now. "Take her upstairs."

I refocused on the jewels, still in Emerald's hand.

"What do we do with those now?"

"What do you mean?" Gina said. "We can use them for the séance. They're perfect."

"Noooo," I protested, widening my eyes. "We need to get rid of them immediately. Put them back where they were, before anyone else touches them. If Farrow finds these here, he has his evidence for arresting me. And Tracy will have succeeded in pinning the murder on me." I huffed in exasperation. "I can't really give the police any clue where to find them; otherwise, I'll just cast suspicion on myself. On the other hand, it's important that they find them. It means Stanley wasn't here to steal them. He isn't the murderer. He wouldn't have killed Matilda before she'd told him where they were. I don't think it's even necessary to do the séance now, do you?"

I was frantic with worry, half expecting Farrow to burst in at any moment and catch me with the jewels.

"Calm down," Gina said, rubbing my back.

"We're not doing the séance?" Audrey said, who was just coming back down the stairs. She sounded disappointed.

"Does it even matter if Stanley is dead or not? I really don't think he has anything to do with the murders." I shook off Gina's hand and started pacing between kitchen and living room. "Unless we can contact Matilda with these jewels. Ask her directly who the murderer is. Should we?"

I stopped and looked at my relatives.

"Honey, you don't need the jewels or a séance for that,"

Gina said gently. "Matilda is waiting for you in the cottage next door, ready to tell you. You know that."

A cold shiver ran down my spine. I'd been toying with the idea of going to the cottage with my camera. Even though it was dangerous for me to be caught there.

Matilda had left me a message that I hadn't quite pieced together. I'd thought the words "love," "change," and "close" fit Stanley. But they also fit Tracy, the niece she had once adored. Tracy had changed so much.

I hadn't been able to figure out the message yet, so I felt like my gift was pretty useless. Taking photos of ghosts wasn't really like communicating with them. The poorly deciphered message just proved that. Truth be told, it felt like a stupid and inadequate gift, compared to what the other women in my family could do.

But I realized now that there would be a way to ask Matilda if Tracy was her murderer. The way she'd pointed at words in her home to relay a message told me she wanted to communicate.

I'd convinced myself that going over there and trying to photograph Matilda's ghost again wasn't worth the risk.

The ice-cold fear that was gripping my stomach as I decided I had to do it, after all, told me that there was another reason I'd refused to do it thus far.

I was dead scared.

Scared of what it meant that dead people turned up in my photographs. Overwhelmed at the thought of them being all around me, just waiting to get a chance to communicate with me. It was a heavy burden, a responsibility I wasn't ready to take on right now. I already had too much on my plate.

The camera was a filter between me and the world of the undead. It was a window through the veil.

All my life, I'd kept the shutter closed. It was scary to

even open it for a few seconds at a time. I didn't want to let too much from the other side in.

What if the shutter didn't close properly anymore? Actively seeking ghosts to photograph might signal to the universe that I didn't need the medium of a camera anymore, that I *wanted* to see.

Ever since Steven had left me and all his sordid secrets and lies had come to light, I'd sworn to myself that I wouldn't run around with blinders on anymore. I think I was managing to do that, facing what I needed to face—in *this* life.

But was I ready to open my eyes to the entire afterlife as well?

I swallowed hard, and my gaze went to my Nikon, where it was sitting, as always, collecting dust on a shelf.

This wasn't about all the other dead people trying to get to me. This was about helping one person, my neighbor, Matilda Rutherford. She hadn't deserved to die.

If I could help her, then I needed to do it.

I grabbed the camera. "Hand me those gloves," I said to my cousin. "I'm putting the jewels back, and I don't want my prints on them. I want them out of here—they really can't be found in my home."

"I can just put them back in the tree, if you want," Emerald said, but she was already taking off her gloves.

I shook my head. "I'm not sure the tree is the best place. The police need to find them somehow. I'll think of something. But first, I have to ask Matilda Rutherford a few questions."

Blake furrowed her brow. "Do you want us to come with you?"

"No. You and Audrey stay here with Gina and Emerald." I turned to my great-aunt, tugging on the gloves Emerald gave me. "Are you okay to stay with them until I get back?"

"Of course. But, you know, if you need support over there—"

"I know," I cut her off and grabbed the jewelry box Emerald had put down on the table. "I definitely need your support—here, to watch after my children. And you've already helped me understand I need to embrace my gift. This next bit, I'll have to face alone. I'll be all right."

CHAPTER THIRTY-FIVE

I walked around the front, taking the stone path to Matilda's door. I didn't want to leave my footprints all over the garden, and in any case, I wasn't sure if I should put the jewels back in the tree. Nobody had discovered them in there yet, and I needed them found, so Tracy could no longer accuse me of being a thief.

Only when I lifted the planter did it occur to me that the key might not be there anymore. Tracy or the police would surely have removed it after I'd broken in the last time.

But the key was in its hiding place, which left me equal parts relieved and worried. I had easy access to the cottage and could go ahead with my plan—but it might very well be a trap.

I only hesitated a moment, though. My mind was made up, and there was no going back. Matilda held all the answers. And she needed me to know them.

Determined, I stuck the key in the lock and turned it. The door swung open.

I held my breath. The house was dark and silent.

I stepped inside, pulling the door shut behind me.

As light-footed as possible, I moved down the hallway, peered into the living room, and then stood at the bottom of the stairs. I contemplated checking the bedrooms. But then I decided against it. There was no living soul in this house. I could feel it.

And I didn't know how much time I had, so I was better off going straight to the scene of the murder. The kitchen. It was where I'd encountered Matilda's ghost for the first time. I silently prayed that she was still there, waiting for me.

Nothing had changed. It was tidy and clean, everything in its place. For all I knew, nobody had been in here since I was caught by Tracy a week ago. I placed the box with the jewels on the kitchen table.

Staring at the tiled floor where I imagined Matilda's body had been found, I suddenly got a little dizzy. It was such an awful thing to contemplate. A life had been snuffed out. But worse than that, if I was right, a niece had killed her aunt—coldly orchestrated the death of someone who'd loved her dearly.

I shook off the sentiment. I couldn't allow myself to be overwhelmed by it.

Closing my eyes, I focused on my neighbor. "Matilda, are you here?"

I tried to sense her—and I thought I did, even though I strongly considered the possibility that I was simply imagining it.

There was one way to find out for sure.

Opening my eyes again, I lifted the Nikon. My hand shook as I removed the lens cap. I took a step back for a wider angle and pressed the button.

Click.

My heart raced when I looked at the digital image on

the screen. A strange gargling sound escaped my throat. There was Matilda, in her sensible beige clothes, the cat's-eye glasses, and the old-fashioned beehive hairdo.

"Hi, Matilda," I said. "It's so nice to see you."

I zoomed in on her face, and reading her expression made my heart beat even faster. She didn't look pleased to see me at all. At least she didn't seem happy or relieved. Instead, she looked alarmed. Her eyes wide, her mouth open, cheeks flushed.

"Matilda, I'm so sorry I left it so late to talk to you again." I didn't know if I should be speaking to the image on the camera or to the empty space in the middle of the kitchen where her ghost was standing—according to the photograph.

I felt foolish and inadequate. I didn't know how to do this.

I forced myself to slow down my breathing, to temper the panic.

"But I'm here now," I said, maybe more to myself than to Matilda. "So let's figure this out together. You tried to send me a message last time, pointing at words. I wanted to piece those together, but it was harder than I thought. I figured out a few words, like close, love, and change, but when I was here the second time, taking a closer look at what you'd pointed at in my photographs, I was caught by your niece, Tracy. She called the police. I couldn't come back here, since DI Farrow remained convinced I had something to do with your murder. So I tried to investigate on my own, identifying a couple of suspects who turned out to be innocent. DS Rees, who is a friend of mine and has been helping me, is convinced Stanley might have… um, done this."

I faltered a little, knowing that Matilda had a high estimation of Stanley. If Jamie was right and Stanley was still alive, then he'd left his wife. Unless he'd actually faked his death, which I couldn't imagine, because if he'd succeeded in that, there'd be an official record. Matilda had preferred to present herself as a widow to the world. Most likely because she hadn't been able to cope with the fact that her soulmate had fallen out of love with her.

Just the idea of Stanley murdering her might send Matilda's ghost into a tizzy. And I really didn't want her angry. Horror movies were full of angry ghosts, so I had an inkling of what could happen if Matilda exploded ghostly energy in a rage.

"But I don't think Stanley did this," I blurted. "DS Rees's theory hinges on the fact that Tracy claimed the jewels had been stolen. He thought Stanley might have wanted to reclaim his heirloom, and you, um, stood in his way. The jewels were still in their hiding place, though, in the old oak. Ethel showed us. Your message might have fit Stanley, but it might also have fit someone else. The person I'm now convinced is the killer. It's really horrible. So if I'm wrong, please don't be mad at me, Matilda. But…I don't think I am. I need you to confirm it for me, somehow."

I took a deep breath. "Matilda—was it your niece, Tracy?"

I listened to the deafening quiet of the kitchen, and a few seconds passed before I remembered Matilda couldn't actually answer me.

I lifted the camera again and took another picture.

The image didn't look different from what I saw with my own eyes.

An empty kitchen. Matilda wasn't in it.

Panic rose inside me. I probably shouldn't have told her all of this. Maybe I was wrong, and now Matilda was pissed off at me. She wouldn't show herself to me anymore.

I'd never find out for sure who the murderer was. I

could never present any evidence to the police. Tracy would get away with all of it, including making me the scapegoat. They might arrest me after all, and there was nothing I could do about it.

Tears sprang to my eyes, and I wiped at them furiously.

I couldn't give up now. I'd doubted how my paranormal abilities could be of any use to me all along. It was one thing not to fear them anymore. Why did I expect they'd help me solve a murder?

Photographing ghosts was a weird talent to have. I didn't begrudge the other women in my family, including my children, their stronger and more useful abilities. They could still help me investigate. And the rest might have to be done with old-fashioned detective work, even if I seemed to be the worst sleuth in the world.

I'd spent the whole day doing research, and one of these lines of investigation would pan out. I needed to keep at it.

I put the lens cap back on my camera and left the kitchen, making my way to the front door. When I passed the living room, a cold draft hit me.

I stopped and turned my head.

Again, I thought I felt Matilda's presence.

I squinted into the semidarkness of the living room. Something odd was going on in the corner, where the framed photographs were arranged on the sideboard. Almost like there was a lamp on.

I stepped into the living room, slowly approaching the sideboard.

There was no lamp or other light source visible, and the glow slowly dimmed down until it disappeared completely.

I took the lens cap off my camera again and snapped away.

On my camera display, Matilda was standing in front of the sideboard, pointing at a frame.

It saw it on the camera, but to make sure, I stepped closer to inspect the framed photograph.

The one Matilda had pointed at was that of a little girl. Round face, freckles, blue eyes, red curly hair. It was Tracy Martens, before she'd turned herself into Catherine, Princess of Wales.

"So it *was* Tracy who murdered you?" I asked, wishing desperately that Matilda could answer me.

I had an idea. The point of a Ouija board was to communicate with ghosts straightforwardly. They could answer yes or no and even spell out an answer, shifting the planchette from letter to letter.

At least that's what I'd learned from watching TV, because I'd never seen one in real life. I doubted Matilda Rutherford would have one lying around either.

But I could make my own rudimentary version of it, to get the clear answer from her I was seeking.

I pulled open drawers to find a pen, paper, and Scotch tape.

Then I wrote YES in large letters on one piece of paper, and NO on the other.

I pulled the couch away from the wall—the only one with enough room for what I had in mind. Then I taped the paper on the wall, spacing YES and NO a foot apart.

I moved around the couch and the coffee table, facing the wall some distance away from it.

"Okay, Matilda. I'm sorry, but I need to be really sure, because I've been wrong about it a few times. Is your niece Tracy the person who murdered you?"

I waited a few seconds, then lifted the Nikon to take a picture.

I stared at the display, waiting for the digital image to appear.

There it was.

Matilda was standing in front of the wall, between the two pieces of paper.

She clearly pointed to one of them.

YES.

I exhaled slowly in relief.

But my relief only lasted for a few seconds.

Focused on thinking about other questions I could ask Matilda in order to find evidence against Tracy, I didn't hear the front door.

Suddenly the light turned on, and DI Farrow stood in the living room.

He looked like the cat who got the canary.

"Well, well, well, who do we have here?"

I closed my eyes.

This couldn't be happening.

I'd convinced myself that a quick visit to my neighbor's cottage wouldn't do any harm, that it would stay under the DI's radar.

Even though I'd known the whole time that coming back here would be the nail in my coffin, suspecting that DI Farrow—or Tracy, who wanted me to go down for this—had means of alerting them if I entered Matilda's cottage again.

I didn't know how. I hadn't seen a camera or a burglar alarm. Maybe it had been a case of a patrol car surveilling Matilda's cottage at night.

It didn't matter. I'd been busted.

I had faced my fear of using my unique talent and communicating with Matilda's ghost. I'd even gotten my answers. But had it been worth it?

As DI Farrow got out handcuffs, informed me of my arrest, and told me my rights, I was trying not to panic. What could he charge me with? Breaking and entering, most likely. A murder charge wouldn't stick, because I was innocent. I had an alibi, and there was no evidence, no motive that explained why I had wanted to kill my new neighbor.

Except, now there was, I realized with a sinking feeling, when the officer stepped into the living room, holding up the jewelry box.

"Look, boss, what I found in the kitchen."

CHAPTER THIRTY-SIX

Just over a year ago, I'd narrowly avoided jail time after it had come to light that my husband had run a Ponzi scheme and absconded with his ill-gotten gains.

I vividly remembered the phone call from the FBI agent the day I'd been cleared of any criminal misconduct.

By that point, I was out of money and out of options. If my mother hadn't taken us in, I don't know what would have happened to us. We might have ended up on the street.

But at the moment of the phone call, none of that mattered. I was free, and that meant more than anything. I could start fresh.

And as dire as our financial situation had been, I wouldn't have traded it for what we had before. A luxury life paid for with other people's dashed hopes and dreams. An illusion of wealth, really, not at all what a truly abundant life was all about.

I'd meant what I'd told my former best friend on the phone the day we'd moved to Fairwyck. It was a relief to me that I could make an honest living, working, living within our means—focusing on what really mattered.

Even though I had done nothing wrong in the eyes of the law, I would forever live with my moral failings—I should have noticed what Steven was up to, and I should have turned our lives around and onto the straight and narrow sooner.

But I was here now, living that honest life, doing everything right. I'd thought the days of dealing with law enforcement were behind me.

And now, mere weeks after we'd started our do-over, I was in jail.

I'd been handcuffed, put into the back of a police car, and driven to the police station in Cirencester. My camera, phone, and keys, my earrings and necklace, had been taken away. They'd even taken my shoes. I'd had to stand against the wall to have a mug shot taken.

Then I'd been led into a small, tiled cell with a low-lying bed fitted into the wall. There were flat blue cushions as padding, but the plastic cover felt disgusting on my skin, and I couldn't help but think about the fact that the material had been chosen because it was easily wiped down and cleaned—because all sorts of body fluids probably ended up on that bed.

Even though it smelled strongly of disinfectant, I thought I could detect the faint scent of blood and vomit and body odor underneath.

The only other items in the cell were a small sink and a toilet, which I held off using. There were notices written on the wall, including a warning that the cell might be monitored with CCTV.

They'd turned off the light, since it was nighttime, but it was far too loud to sleep. Half of the other cells seemed to be filled with people who'd been booked for being drunk and disorderly, and they made quite a racket.

The truth was, though, that I couldn't have slept, even

if the cell had been furnished like the penthouse apartment of a luxury hotel.

My thoughts revolved around how unfair it was that I'd ended up in a cell like this, after all. My worst nightmare had come true.

All throughout my investigation into Matilda's murder, I had been telling myself that as long as I took action instead of turning a blind eye, everything would work out okay.

I thought I'd figured out what I needed to do differently in life. I wasn't the old Liv anymore, and however bad things were, at least I was empowered.

I'd been wrong.

Life wasn't fair. There was no scoreboard that counted honest work and good intentions. There were no medals for doing the right thing.

My criminal husband was free, probably enjoying cocktails on a tropical island, while I was in jail for something I hadn't done.

There was nothing I could do to change that. I felt more helpless and disempowered than ever.

I was lying there, wondering if I'd changed at all, if that was even possible—and if it mattered in the grand scheme of things. Until the lights went on.

Shortly after, there was a knock on the door. A uniformed police officer passed me a tray with a polystyrene cup of weak tea and what looked like a microwavable meal with the plastic lid still on. Two sad sausages were swimming in tomato sauce with beans.

I stared at the sad excuse for a breakfast. While it might be true that I couldn't do anything about the larger situation, that didn't mean I had to take everything lying down.

"Excuse me?" I called the officer back who had moved on to the other cells. "Excuse me, can you come back here, please?"

He finally opened the door with raised eyebrows.

"Can I please get a cup of coffee?"

"We're not a hotel, you know."

"I know." I hadn't used my big-golden-eyes routine since college, and I'd been young and pretty back then. Add to that a night spent in jail, which meant I hardly looked my best. But I wouldn't survive in here without coffee, so I batted my eyelashes as if I'd just won a beauty queen pageant. "I'm not asking for anything special. Not cream or sugar, even. Just chuck this in the sink and fill the cup up with whatever comes out of your staff-room coffee machine."

It worked. So the first thing I learned in prison: It never hurt to ask.

The grumbling police officer soon came back with a steaming cup of coffee. It wasn't too bad.

"What happens next?" I asked before the officer left.

"DI Farrow will be here soon to talk to you. Your duty solicitor will also be here. There's a bail hearing this afternoon."

I sighed. Before putting me in this cell, I'd been offered a phone call to my lawyer. I'd looked up a few law firms online in recent days, but the bottom line was that I couldn't afford one. Now I was fretting about how good or bad this court-appointed duty solicitor would be, but I'd hardly finished my coffee when the officer returned and told me the bail hearing had been moved up.

He cuffed me and walked me to a different part of the building. On our way, DI Farrow crossed our path, probably just on his way to interview me.

He looked equal parts confused and livid. "What's going on? Where are you taking her?"

"Bail hearing, sir."

"Are you daft? That's this afternoon. I arranged it with Judge Peters myself."

The young officer turned red. "No, Peters moved it up himself, sir."

Farrow studied me with narrowed eyes.

"Who is your solicitor?"

"Um… I only have—"

"Henson, pleased to meet you." A tall, well-dressed gentleman with a full head of gray hair interrupted us.

Farrow looked even more disgruntled. "Should've known," he murmured.

"I'm your solicitor, Ms. Grantham." Henson gave me a dazzling smile.

"Ooo-kay." I found it hard to keep up. I didn't know how these things went usually, where this solicitor had come from, or what I was supposed to do. But I didn't really have time to figure it out either.

Mr. Henson whipped out a cell phone and pressed a button. "There's someone who wants to have a word with you, DI Farrow."

Farrow frowned but took the phone. "Just leave it at reception for me when you're done," Henson said, then turned to the police officer. "We're running late."

I was whisked off to court before I heard who was on the line for Farrow.

There was no time to ponder it, either, because I was more preoccupied with when I was supposed to stand up and when to sit down again, hardly listening to the short and legalese-heavy exchange between Henson and Judge Peters.

Then the judge announced I was released on bail, citing a staggering amount of money.

"Congratulations," Henson said.

"Wait!" I pulled him back down in his seat. "I don't have money like that!"

"Oh, don't worry about that," he said. "My client is posting the bail money."

"Who is—"

"Please come with me, Ms. Grantham." A different police officer than the one who'd brought me to court now dragged me away. I wanted to protest, but then I was told that I was getting my things back. I was mainly concerned about my camera. Nothing had happened to it. I even got my SD card back.

I would have loved to see Farrow's face when he studied the images of Matilda's ghost. But I loved getting released even more.

My solicitor was there to escort me out, and I wanted to ask again who'd hired him, when Gina, Emerald, and Blake rushed toward me.

"Oh my god!" I gave them all big hugs. "What are you doing here? Where's Audrey—at school? Why aren't you at school?" I asked Blake.

"I wanted to be here, Mom," they answered.

"Of course. I'm glad you are."

Gina and Emerald were talking to the lawyer, who explained how things had gone in court.

"Did *you* post my bail money?" I interrupted them.

"No," Emerald said, "your mom did."

"Oh my god." I was mortified at the thought of owing my mother even more money but also immensely grateful to her. "Did you call her and ask for it?"

"We've been in touch recently." Gina said. "Calista called me last night, worried because she'd been unsuccessful in contacting Farrow. You'd just been arrested, we were all in a tizzy, and so, naturally, I had to inform her of it. She stayed remarkably calm, only said to leave it to her because she knew someone who could help from way back when."

"That would be me," Mr. Henson said.

"Wait, so that was my mother on the phone to Farrow just now?" After the arrest, the night in the cell, and the whirlwind of the bail proceedings, I found it hard to keep up with everything. Something occurred to me. "Mom's not using her retirement money for my bail, is she? She's comfortable, because my stepdad was fairly well off, but still…"

Gina patted my back. "Don't fret about it, darling. Your mother doesn't mind. In fact, I think she's a bit bored as a lady of leisure in that retirement community. She's asked me a lot of questions about my business model, and I think she intends to make extra cash as a soothsayer."

"*What?*" I rubbed my temples. I almost felt sorry for coldly dismissing Phyllis's alien theory and not being able to apologize to her anymore. Now I was inclined to believe in extraterrestrials, since they must have switched my mother. "I just…ahhh, can we just go home? I need a few hours of sleep in my cozy bed, to let this sink in before we move on and deal with everything."

Mr. Henson said goodbye after promising to call later.

Everyone else just stayed rooted to the spot, and there was tension in the air. Why weren't we going home? Something was going on.

My gaze went to Blake. They looked very much subdued. At first, I'd figured picking up their mother from jail might be the reason for that, but now I saw panic in their eyes.

I suddenly got a horrible feeling in my belly.

"What's wrong?"

Emerald pulled me to the car and opened the passenger door. "Get in. Let's not talk about it on the street."

I tried to catch Blake's eyes, but they wouldn't even look at me.

My stomach cramped.

Blake got into the back seat, so I didn't resist when Gina gently pushed me to get into the passenger seat.

When Gina and Emerald were seated too, I turned around to look at everyone. "Can someone please tell me what happened?"

"It's Audrey," Gina said.

Blake's eyes filled with tears.

My mouth was suddenly really dry. "Isn't she at school?"

"We drove her to school this morning. We didn't tell her much about the arrest, and we thought it would be better for her to be preoccupied at school instead of worrying too much. Blake changed their mind about staying at school and drove back home with us, though."

"Okay, so Audrey's fine?" I was confused.

Gina took a deep breath. "No. Tracy took her."

"What?" I shook my head. This couldn't be true.

"She dressed up as a police officer, just walked into Audrey's classroom and claimed she needed to take Audrey to the station because her mother had been arrested."

"And they just let her take her?" My voice screeched.

"Well, the principal called the police station to make sure. They confirmed that you'd been arrested, so…" Emerald shrugged.

"I can't believe it!"

"Well, you know that Tracy. She can be very persuasive," Gina said.

I shook my head. "Has she contacted you?"

"Yes, she called your house, which is how we know it was Tracy," Emerald explained. "She must have known we were staying there. She left a message for you."

"What's the message?"

My hands were balled into fists so tightly, my nails were digging into my skin.

Gina and Emerald exchanged a concerned look. "Just tell me!"

"You're supposed to confess to the murders of Matilda

Rutherford and Phyllis Bishop," Gina said. "You have until tomorrow morning to come up with convincing evidence for DI Farrow and make your confession. Or Audrey will be harmed."

CHAPTER THIRTY-SEVEN

There were a few minutes of silence in the car.

Eventually, Gina asked, "Liv? What do you want to do?"

"We need to find Jamie Rees."

"So you want to involve the police in this?" Blake sounded skeptical.

"I told you it would be the most sensible thing to do," Emerald said gently. "Kidnappers always try intimidation tactics. Because they know the police are likely to catch them. But we need all the resources and expertise we can get."

"What if Tracy harms my sister, like she said?" Sheer panic tinged my child's voice. "If she knows the police are on her trail, and she has nothing to lose, and Audrey is no use to her anymore—"

"Shhh." I reached across the back seat to take Blakes's hand. "I will not report this to the police. Don't worry."

"You won't?" Emerald said, confused.

"No. But I do need to speak to Jamie urgently. He's on desk duty, so he should be in there." I pointed at the building I'd just walked out of. "Do you mind getting him,

Emerald? And tell him to bring what I passed to him before the police searched my house. That's important, okay?"

Emerald turned to open her door, but I could tell my cousin was struggling to comply with my wish. Maybe she worried the stress of the arrest and the pressure of what I needed to do to get Audrey back had done a number on me.

"Trust me," I said. "I have a plan. And now hurry, please!"

Emerald nodded and got out of the car.

"I still think informing DS Rees of the kidnapping is a good idea. He can take it to the right people, people who are trained to deal with these sorts of situations," Gina put in her two cents.

I wondered if Mom talking to Farrow had changed anything. Even so, I couldn't risk it. I shook my head. "Farrow's got too much skin in the game. He's arrested me, and I don't think he's the type who admits to his mistakes. I'm afraid if we report Audrey missing, he'll twist it into some strategy I came up with to make myself a victim. I mean, there's a chance he changed his mind, and sure, there's a good chance the higher-ups will understand if Jamie goes around Farrow. They should. But what if that's not the case? What if it takes too long to convince the right people? I don't want to waste time with this—time we don't have."

"So what are you going to do, Mom?" Blake asked anxiously. They wanted to be reassured that I had a plan.

I didn't really have one yet, and there was no guarantee I was doing the right thing. But I couldn't tell them that. So I said the one thing I felt sure about.

"Don't worry. Tracy must have caught wind of my investigation. Maybe the manager at Jigsaw told her. She knows it's just a matter of time before her house of cards breaks down. She has Farrow in her corner and set me up as a suspect. But despite the arrest, she has to know that evidence and truth will most likely prevail and that a talented lawyer would get me off. Eventually, even Farrow is going to have to concede that I'm not a murderer. The only way this might still go her way is if I confess and present some concocted evidence to Farrow. Tracy might be cold-blooded, but kidnapping a child? That's risky and reeks of desperation. She will not harm Audrey because she needs her in order to pressure me."

Even though I believed what I said and sounded calm on the outside, my insides were churning. Every cell in my body clenched in despair at the thought of something happening to my little girl.

But I couldn't let it debilitate me.

Once all of this was over, I could break down and let myself feel. Right now, I had to numb myself. Tomorrow I could break down. Now I had to be rational and methodical, use the few hours we had wisely, to build a case against Tracy that nobody, not even Farrow, could dispute.

Just then the car door opened, and Jamie Rees slipped into the driver's seat. Emerald got into the back, squeezing in next to Gina.

"Hey, I'm glad you got out so quickly," Jamie said, concern etched into his face. "I called Gina, and she told me about your lawyer—"

"Thanks," I interrupted. "I appreciate it. We don't have time to talk about that now, though. Remember, before the police searched my house, I gave you the printouts and a piece of paper ripped out of a magazine. Do you have it on you?" I asked, trying not to sound too impatient.

"Um…yes, I have it here." He got a folder out of a backpack he'd brought with him. I snatched it from his hand and opened it. "What's going on, Liv?" Jamie asked.

I breathed a sigh of relief when I saw the small picture I'd found in Phyllis's kitchen of the gas mask.

"I really think you should tell him," Gina urged from the back seat. "Surely DS Rees can help, even if it's not in his official capacity as a police officer."

I hesitated, looking into Jamie's earnest brown eyes. He worked for the police, but he was also a friend, and I needed all the help I could get to find Audrey.

"Audrey has been kidnapped by Tracy Martens," I told him.

His eyes widened in shock.

I gave him a summary of what had happened. Before he could respond, I said I wouldn't report it to the police because we had no time to waste. To my surprise, Jamie didn't even attempt to argue with me. He simply said, "This is your call. What do you need me to do?"

"Can you talk to Luther Martens? I hate to ask it, because I know it's going to get you into trouble if it comes out, but if you pretend you're questioning him in an official capacity, maybe threaten him a little, he might cave and tell you the truth. He's Tracy's alibi for the night Matilda got murdered, and the Tuesday morning Phyllis died too. But he must have lied. I know that Luther still feels guilty for abandoning Tracy as a child and tries to make up for it. He does everything for her. Matilda thought he was an enabler. She'd recognized that Tracy had gone off the deep end, with her cosmetic surgery addiction and obsession with turning into Catherine. But Luther can't see it. You need him to admit that he lied for his daughter. Preferably convince him to go to the police station and tell them right away."

"Okay," Jamie Rees agreed.

I could tell from Gina's face that she was dying to butt in. Now she blurted out, "Luther Martens was at the cottage this morning, while we were waiting for news from

Mr. Henson. He installed your new window. I thought it was odd, but you'd hired him, and you needed that window replaced, so…"

"Hmm. Yes, he came recommended, and at the time, he probably wasn't aware that I was a murder suspect. Or he didn't care because he needed all the jobs and all the money he could get. But he must know by now since Tracy was so vocal about it, telling everyone I wanted to steal Matilda's jewels. Maybe Luther heard I was arrested and thought it would be a good time to get the job done without bumping into me."

"Mom and I wondered if he was working with Tracy, even," Emerald said. "You know, maybe he overheard our discussion about whether the kids should go to school. We might have said the name of the school. That's how Tracy knew where Audrey would be." Emerald turned red. "Of course, we didn't think him capable of something like that when he got there; otherwise, we wouldn't have let him in."

"Don't worry," I cut in. "Tracy probably had already been prepared. I don't think Luther would willingly go along with harming a child."

"No. Like I said, Emmy, I didn't get that vibe from him," Gina agreed.

"Luther does Tracy's bidding, but I think he's just a father trying to protect his daughter, blind to her faults. He doesn't recognize that Tracy needs help of a different kind."

"There's something I just remembered," Blake put in with a small voice. "With everything that happened, it totally slipped my mind." They frowned. "I'm not sure it matters, but now that you're talking about the man who put the window in today... Audrey told me something, and he might have overheard. I'm sorry I didn't say anything about it earlier."

"That's okay, sweetie. You're telling us now. What did Audrey say?"

The furrows on Blake's brow deepened. "She said something about a witness that saw the person responsible for Phyllis's death. But that the witness was wearing a disguise. I said to her, 'No, you're mixing everything up. Phyllis was a witness to Matilda's murder but couldn't see the person's face because of a disguise.' Audrey got all red in the face. You know how she gets, Mom, when she feels like she's being treated like a little kid, not taken seriously. She just muttered, 'You're so not getting it,' and then stomped up the stairs to get ready for school."

"That's very odd." I mulled it over for a second. "She might have mixed things up. But she might not have. That would mean she'd have new information about a witness we know nothing about. Where would she have gotten it from?"

We were silent for a moment. Then Emerald exclaimed, "The cat!"

"That fits. She was conferring with the cat before breakfast," Gina said matter-of-factly.

"You mean Ethel could have seen someone on Tuesday morning? Someone who would have witnessed Phyllis's murderer…maybe breaking in? Why wouldn't Ethel have mentioned that earlier?"

"Remember when Audrey explained the cat was Ethel but also a cat?" Gina said. "Ethel clearly knows stuff and is much more aware than other animals, but she might not have understood the significance or the urgency. Who knows, right? Who can look into the mind of an animal?"

"Audrey," I sighed. "It would be really useful if she were here and we could ask the cat again. If there's a witness, we need to find them."

"Slow down, everyone," Jamie Rees put in. "I'm not

following here. Audrey knows this from a cat? Or Ethel? You mean your late great-aunt?"

"Both," I said absentmindedly, then remembered who was asking. I looked at Jamie. "It's nothing you need to wrap your head around right now. The important thing is that Luther might have overheard that Audrey knows there's a witness to Phyllis's murder. If he told Tracy, that might explain why she resorted to such extreme measures. She needed to nab Audrey before she could tell anyone. It was more urgent than ever that I go down for the murders and that nobody would question that outcome."

Jamie nodded. "I agree. And I also think putting pressure on Luther is important. Aside from retracting his alibi, he might have valuable information that would help us build a case against Tracy and find Audrey."

Gina got her cell phone out. "Why don't I call him and ask him to come to your house, Liv? I could say that there's something wrong with the window he put in. If he's reticent because he knows what Tracy is up to and suspects a trap, I'll tell him we won't pay until this is fixed. It seems to me money is the biggest motivation, since he's been bankrolling Tracy's surgeries."

"And also, if he asks if I'm there, tell him I'm at the police station, being questioned again by Farrow," I suggested. "That should put him at ease, and maybe he'll even report back to Tracy. Hopefully, she'll think her plan is working out."

"That's a good idea." Jamie agreed. "I can work on Luther better if he's not on his own turf."

"So where are you going to be?" Emerald asked. "Not at home?"

"No. Blake and I are going to investigate something else." I held up the picture of the gas mask. "We're going to establish who bought this mask."

CHAPTER THIRTY-EIGHT

After remarkably persuasive efforts from Gina, which had me wondering if my great-aunt could hypnotize people over the phone, Luther Martens agreed to come to the cottage to fix the window within the next hour.

We all sat in the car, holding our breath, until Gina hung up.

"Okay," I said, a little relieved. "That plan's set in motion."

We agreed Jamie would take his own vehicle and drive to my house with Gina and Emerald, and Blake and I could use Emerald's car.

After saying goodbye, I shifted over to the driver's seat, and Blake got in next to me.

"Where are we going?" they asked.

I fished my phone out of my purse, but after a night in lockup, the battery was dead.

"Shoot. Look something up for me." I told Blake the name of a store. Luckily, a fifteen-year-old could always be trusted to have a charged cell phone on them.

"What is this place?" they asked, after telling me the

address I'd asked for so I could input it into the car's navigation system.

"It's an army surplus store."

While I followed the instructions to the store just outside Gloucester, I told Blake about the research I'd done yesterday while anxiously waiting for the séance to take place.

"To be honest, I was aimlessly running internet searches to pass the time, anything to do with this case that came to mind. And one thing I researched was gas masks. Jamie had the picture, so I relied on my memory. The gas mask in the magazine picture looked a little different from the one you'd drawn, but it was still an older model. While looking up gas masks, I realized the one you'd seen in Phyllis's head had to be an older model, which resembled an alien. Modern respirator masks look much sleeker. The one Phyllis described had a long, snout-like thing and round eyes. And it was a dull gray. So I was trying to figure out which type of gas mask the murderer had used. I found all sorts of sites that sold old gas masks, but I figured the perpetrator wouldn't have ordered something on the internet because, if the investigation ever went that far, there'd be a money trail. There was a chance they already owned this gas mask—maybe they'd found it in an old attic. But if they bought it, they would have done it with cash. I searched the internet for places in the area that sold secondhand stuff like these old masks."

I pulled up in front of the store. "This is what I found." I turned to Blake. "Do you have your sketch pad on you?"

"Of course." Blake patted their backpack.

I smiled. "That's what I thought." Any fifteen-year-old could be relied upon to have their phone on them, but my kid also always carried something to draw with. "Bring it with you."

The army surplus store was narrow and long, with lots

of camouflage clothing items on racks lining both walls. The till was at the end. It was manned by an older guy with gray hair, glasses, and wrinkled skin. He was built like someone you'd imagine being in the army, with broad shoulders, enormous arms, and a ramrod-straight posture. Aptly, he was dressed in camouflage.

"Excuse me," I said. "Are you the owner of this store?"

He said he was, and when I asked if he had other people working as sales clerks, he said it was mainly him but that he had help on the weekends.

"Why?" he wondered. "Are you looking for a job for your kid?" He looked at Blake dubiously.

"No." I smiled. "We're looking for someone you might have sold a gas mask to." I asked Blake to show the man the sketch of the supposed alien.

"It's an old-fashioned gas mask, isn't it?"

"Yep. I can't be sure, but it looks to me that this is a Russian GP-5 gas mask kit. The Soviets issued those to the population during the Cold War. They produced way too many of them, three times more than there were people living in the Soviet Union at the time. So we have them floating around every once in a while."

"Okay." The store owner definitely seemed to know his stuff. "Do you sell them too?"

"We sell everything, including GP-5s, if we get them in."

"And did you sell one of these recently?"

The store owner nodded. "I had a whole bunch of them a few weeks ago. Put them up on this table." He pointed at a display next to the till. "People recognize these types of gas masks from movies, and I get impulse buyers who think it might come in handy in an emergency." The store owner shrugged. "I don't tell them there are much better, modern respirator masks out there. Gotta shift the inventory."

I smiled and nodded, secretly thinking that there might also be customers who didn't want to draw attention to themselves, so they didn't ask, but preferred to buy second-hand items on display.

"We're looking for a woman who might have come in and bought one of those gas masks. A well-dressed young lady who would have looked out of place here?"

The store owner narrowed his eyes. "Maybe there was such a customer. But why should I give you this information?"

My gaze slid over to Blake, who was drawing furiously. The image on her sketch pad got more and more detailed, showing a woman with long hair in an elegant coat.

"Did she have brown hair?" I kept asking to make the store owner think about his customer more.

"Like I said, I don't feel comfortable telling just anyone which customer bought what. Why are you asking?"

I looked at the sketch pad again. The woman Blake had drawn now bore an uncanny resemblance to Tracy Martens.

I grabbed the counter with both hands. I was so relieved, all the tension went out of my body, and my knees were buckling.

Now I just had to convince the store owner to identify Tracy as the person who bought the gas mask.

The man eyed me with concern. "Ma'am? Are you all right?"

I nodded, trying to hold back tears.

After taking a shaky breath, I could speak. "That customer might not have looked like it, but she's a criminal. A murderer. In order to divert attention from herself, she cast suspicion on me. Right now, she's holding my young daughter hostage until I turn myself in. I need to find evidence against her so the police will believe me that it was in fact her who committed the crimes they're accusing me of."

The store owner's gaze shifted to Blake. "That's a wild story."

Blake said, "It's true."

"I know you're probably thinking you should call someone to pick me up, so I can have my mental health assessed." I tried a wobbly smile. "But I'm not making this up. This is really happening."

The store owner still seemed unsure, and I couldn't blame him. "I don't know. Either way, I should call the police."

I didn't want him to get on the line with Farrow, who'd probably confirm his suspicion that I was crazy or a liar before their conversation ever got around to the fact that Tracy Martens had bought the gas mask.

"I'll tell the police about this," I said. "A police officer with a badge will come by and ask you to identify the customer. That would be all right, wouldn't it?"

"Well, yeah." The store owner relaxed visibly. "I'd tell the police if they asked. To be honest, it wouldn't be too difficult to describe her. She looks like a certain celebrity everybody knows. For a moment, I thought it was her. But her eyes were different."

"A bright green?" I asked. "Sort of unnerving."

He nodded.

"Okay, well, the police will be by soon. Bye, and thanks!"

I could tell Blake was excited, and when we got back to the car, they said, "That went well, didn't it? Can we go to the police now and tell them about Audrey?"

I pulled a face. "Not yet, honey, sorry. It's great, but it's only one piece of the puzzle. Even if the police established that Tracy bought the gas mask, we only have your drawing to prove that Phyllis saw what Matilda's killer with the gas mask looked like. She never gave a statement to the police, remember? It's our word against Tracy's lawyer's that the gas mask used during Matilda's murder was a Russian GP-5. It's suspicious she bought one, but it could be regarded as circumstantial evidence."

"Oh," Blake said, deflated.

"It's still going to help our case, I think. Let's not give up yet. Can you give me your phone?"

Blake passed it to me, and I called my landline number. Emerald picked up.

"How's it going?" I asked.

"Hang on." I heard creaking stairs and assumed Emerald was going upstairs to talk in private. "Not that great," she continued. "Jamie is good. But Luther is not giving his daughter up. He admitted to a lot of things. Tracy's psychological problems, that he knows she's not enrolled in fashion school but using the tuition fees for her surgery and beauty treatments instead. He even told us that Matilda was concerned about Tracy, that she told him not to give her any more money. But he's not budging where the alibi is concerned."

My stomach clenched, and I thought I was going to throw up. "We really need him. If he'd go to Farrow and tell him all of this and that he lied for Tracy, the DI would finally have to concede that she's a more viable suspect than me. And if we then send the school principal to him, telling him that Tracy kidnapped Audrey, they'd have to help us look for her."

"I know," Emerald said with sympathy in her voice. She could probably tell how desperate I was. "But I don't see Luther caving in anytime soon."

"Don't let him leave." I said through clenched teeth. "We're coming."

"Mom?" Blake asked, tears streaming down their face. "What are we going to do?"

"I'm going to use my ability to persuade Luther to go to the police and give Tracy up."

CHAPTER THIRTY-NINE

Just before we got to Fairwyck, I asked Blake to call the house again. "Ask Gina to come outside."

When I turned into my driveway, I could already see Gina with her poofy blond hair and colorful caftan, hugging herself to ward off the chill.

She rushed toward us when we got out of the car. "Everything okay?"

"Just a question I hope you can answer. Do you know if Tracy Martens's mother died in her own home?"

"Actually, I'm very familiar with how Janine Martens died. She came to me for a psychic reading shortly before she passed."

That didn't surprise me. I had a feeling Gina knew a lot about the people of Fairwyck. It seemed as if nearly everyone here had consulted her—and told her their secrets. Which was why I'd hoped she'd be able to help me out—my next port of call would have been Michelle.

"Janine was terminally ill, you see. She'd been fighting cancer for years. This was the end stage. Her doctors wanted her to go to the hospital. Tracy thought it meant her mother could continue the fight. But Janine knew she wouldn't have long, and she wanted to stay at home, where she was comfortable."

"Did the cards tell you Tracy's mom would die soon?" Blake asked, fascinated.

"The cards only confirmed what Janine already knew. She'd made peace with dying, and I told her to follow her heart and stay home. She passed a few days later."

"Is Luther living in the same house?"

"Yes, they'd bought the house together and never divorced. Luther left the family after an affair had been made public. He didn't have contact with his wife and daughter, but he kept paying the mortgage. After Janine died, Luther returned to Fairwyck. I'm not sure how Tracy felt about it, but the house was legally his. She was a minor, and he wanted to make up for everything."

I thought for a moment. "Luther still feels an immense amount of guilt. He can't get over having abandoned his family, so he gives Tracy all the money he can, enables her cosmetic surgery addiction, and even lies for her. He can't do this for his wife, because it's too late. Luther probably feels even worse where Janine is concerned."

Gina raised her eyebrows at me, waiting for me to expound.

"If Janine told him he needed to give Tracy up to the police because it's for Tracy's own good… He'd do it, right?"

"I'd imagine so."

I nodded. "Then we're going to have to make him believe that she's telling him that."

My great-aunt gave me a skeptical look.

"I know it's not exactly ethical. But let me tell you something. All my life, I've been worried about coloring inside the lines. I never stopped to think who put those lines there in the first place. And look where it got me. Heck, I've been stressing about little white lies like passing off store-bought baked goods as my own. I even felt guilty about not being more suspicious of my husband, as if I could have changed anything he was capable of. I tried to do everything right here, and it feels like it doesn't matter. Even finally embracing my gift, conquering my fears, and contacting Matilda didn't help. If my gift can be useful for once, I'm not above using it."

Gina frowned. "But do you think this is what your gift is for? Tricking someone?"

"I don't know—and right now I don't care. This is about my daughter's life. I have no guarantee that Tracy is going to release Audrey, especially if my daughter has incriminating evidence against her. I might be coloring in gray areas, but I'm going to do what feels right to me and not worry about what anyone else thinks. Tricking a man who's shielding a ruthless murderer and kidnapper—well, that's right in my books."

Blake stared at me, open-mouthed.

Gina smiled and said, "All right then. Let's do it."

We walked into the cottage, where Luther sat at the kitchen table, looking red-faced and very uncomfortable.

Jamie, who was leaning against the fridge, looked a little worn out too.

"Hey," I said and smiled. "Thank you, Luther, for the window. Please send me the invoice, will you?"

Luther looked at me in shock. I remembered that he expected me to be at the police station, turning myself in.

Jamie understood I was cutting Luther loose. "Um…so you don't need to talk to Mr. Martens anymore?"

I smiled at Luther. "No. But I'd like to pay this invoice as soon as possible. Get that squared away before…" I let the sentence dangle and made a sad face, hoping it suggested to Tracy's father I still expected to go to jail soon. "So if you could go home and get that invoice ready for me, that would be great."

Luther staggered to his feet. "Sure. Um, okay…" He looked at Jamie, who didn't stop him.

"I have a plan," I mouthed in Jamie's direction as Luther rushed to the door.

He nodded and called after Luther, "I'll know if you're not going straight home. I have someone tailing you in case you *do* know where Tracy is."

I was really glad Jamie understood that it was vital Luther go home, because my plan would fall apart if he now disappeared on us.

I'd barely given Jamie a quick summary of what I'd learned at the army surplus store and asked him to go there to take the owner's statement when his phone rang.

He frowned at the display. "I'll quickly take this, if you don't mind?" I nodded, and he stepped outside the back door.

This gave me time for a quick strategizing session with Gina, Emerald, and Blake. We were in our jackets, ready to go, when Jamie came back into the kitchen.

"Remember I reached out to the post office, Stanley Rutherford's former employer?"

I nodded, even though Stanley had slipped my mind, since we'd learned who the murderer was.

"The post office wrote him a job reference when he left. He didn't die, like I suspected. Stanley did a runner, found another job in a different part of the country."

I pressed a palm against my heart. "Ahh, poor Matilda. She couldn't handle getting dumped by the love of her life, so she turned herself into a widow, with a fake memorial service and everything. At least he didn't take his family heirloom. He must have had too much of a bad conscience to leave her high and dry. But Matilda never even cashed the jewels in, keeping them as a last sign of hope for Stanley's return."

"Maybe he wanted a clean break, with nothing to tie

him to the past. More people do a runner like that than you'd think, starting a completely new life somewhere else from scratch. Although, according to the post office, they wrote him a reference for a new job at IPS. A private parcel service—not too much of a change there."

Suddenly my alarm bells were ringing. "IPS?" I grabbed Jamie's arm. "There's this old guy hanging around Fairwyck. I've seen him in the pub. He's there every Saturday night, according to Ellie. In fact, he was there during my first shift, the night Matilda died. Could it be Stanley Rutherford?"

"Well, we know Stanley isn't the murderer—if he was there that night, he'd have the same alibi as you. Why would he suddenly turn up here, after all this time? If he has nothing to do with this? That would be a bit of a coincidence, don't you think?"

The gears in my head churned. My intuition told me there was something to it. "Yes, but coincidences happen. Maybe he's been working up the nerve to talk to Matilda... or Phyllis, for that matter. Someone said something about the mail deliverer leaving parcels, ringing the doorbell and running away... And I've seen the man in the IPS uniform hanging around. I didn't notice a resemblance to Stanley in the old pictures, but he has a gray beard that covers half his face, and he always wears these big aviator sunglasses, even in the pub, which could be an attempt to disguise himself."

My heart beat faster as I said this. I knew I was on the right track. "Audrey said something about a witness in a disguise who saw Tracy entering Phyllis's house, right? What if it was the IPS guy—Stanley? He'd have a reason not to come forward with the information. He might not know how relevant it is. And he's trying to stay under the radar."

My enthusiasm was tempered by Jamie's reaction. "I

guess it's possible…but it's a bit of a reach. I mean, Stanley was a few years younger than Matilda and Phyllis. I found that out when I looked for his death certificate. He's still in his early seventies, though. Would he still be working?"

"If he needs the money, he might. You've got to find the IPS guy and question him," I insisted. "If he really saw Tracy on the day of Phyllis's death when she claimed to have been with her dad, we can definitely go to Farrow with it. And who knows what else the IPS guy saw—no matter if it's Stanley or not! Add that to the fact that Tracy bought a gas mask… If we can now persuade Luther to recant Tracy's alibi for the night of Matilda's murder too…

"Okay, I'll follow up with the army surplus store and check out the IPS guy," Jamie said.

"We really should go," Gina interrupted. "Luther hopefully went home to write your invoice, but what if he leaves after?"

We hurried out the door, and I shouted over my shoulder. "IPS guy first. It's important."

"All right, don't worry, I'll take care of it," Jamie reassured me.

"Let's take your car, Emerald," I said outside. "My camera is still in it."

"Okay, but can you drive?" My cousin rubbed her temples. "I have a terrible headache. Maybe the stress is getting to me."

It was a short drive to Luther Martens's house, but in the car, Emerald's headache got much worse. Gina seemed concerned. "That's not normal, is it?"

I saw Emerald shake her head in the mirror. "I've never had this before. It's almost as if…" she trailed off.

"Can you focus on this?" I asked her, because we'd just arrived in front of Luther Martens's house. "Or do you want to stay in the car?"

Emerald shook her head. "I'll be all right. I want to help you any way I can."

I grabbed my camera from the floor of the passenger side.

Luther certainly looked surprised when he opened the door to us.

"Hey, have you got that invoice ready?" I blew right past him, and the others barged in as well.

"Um…yes. It's still sitting in the printer." He pointed toward a room next to the front door that looked like an office.

"Can you get it for me, Emerald?"

I pulled a dumbstruck Luther farther down the corridor, to an open-plan kitchen and living room with a large glass window looking out into the garden.

"How lovely," I said, then turned toward the kitchen. "Aren't you going to offer me a beverage?"

"Um, I guess…"

"Coffee, black, please."

Luther actually went into the kitchen, but he said, "Listen, I already told DS Rees everything there's to say about my daughter. You're not going to convince me—"

"Oh, I know. The very first time we had a chat, I knew you'd do anything for Tracy. You have a lot to make up for."

Luther was clearly taken aback, but he was still making coffee—as if he'd forgotten who he was making it for.

Blake, Gina, and Emerald came into the living room. Blake was holding the invoice. When Luther spotted it, he said, "You got what you came for, didn't you? I think it's best you leave now."

"Luther, I'm not here because of the invoice. I'm here to talk to Janine."

CHAPTER FORTY

Luther Martens's face blanched.

"Is this supposed to be a poor joke? You know my wife is no longer with us!"

He turned to Gina. "Ah, is this your doing? I know what you are... What you claim to do. Tracy told me Janine consulted you just before she died, and you told her to give up on her treatment. Why do you insist on meddling?"

"Mr. Martens, your wife's days were numbered. She'd known that even before I confirmed it with the cards, or else I wouldn't have told her something like that. She just wanted to spend her final days in comfort." Gina spoke in a very gentle tone, but her words seemed to rile Luther up, nonetheless.

"That might be true, but if you think I'm falling for your scam like Janine did back then, you're mistaken. You can claim to be in contact with my wife all you like. I know you're just trying to pull wool over my eyes."

Meanwhile, I had taken the cap off the camera lens and started taking pictures. "Janine," I whispered. "If you are still here, please show yourself to me."

I could have had a lifetime of learning about ghosts, how they showed up on my photos, figured out how I could best communicate with them. I hadn't, so all this was new to me.

On TV, it was only people with unfinished business who stayed on as ghosts—if their situation got resolved, they could move on. Into the light, Heaven, or, presumably, some peaceful state.

If that was the reality, and Janine Martens had made peace with her time on Earth running out, maybe she'd moved on long ago. There was a chance her troubled daughter had kept her tethered to this place, though. As awful as it was, I really hoped so.

Gina spread her tarot cards on the dining table, and Luther protested, so he was preoccupied enough not to notice what I was doing at first.

After a short while, though, he gave up on Gina and her cards, maybe deeming them harmless. That's when he paid attention to me again.

"Why are you taking photos? What's the meaning of this?"

Luther Martens was clearly out of his depth. As much as he adored his daughter and was blind to her faults, he'd lied to give her an alibi. So he had to at least suspect that Tracy had something to hide. This was about the murder of his own sister.

That's why he hadn't just thrown us out. He didn't know what to do. He might have been devoted to Tracy, but I could see his steadfast intention to be loyal to her at all costs crumble.

"Luther, you already know that Gina is a psychic, and you, like most of the villagers, might have heard that this kind of talent runs in the family," I said. "All Seven women have a unique paranormal talent."

Luther made a derisive sound, but the look in his eyes

betrayed him. He'd heard about it, all right. And despite what he'd said to Gina earlier, at least a part of him believed it.

"My talent has to do with photographing ghosts," I said. "That's how I communicated with your sister, Matilda. She gave me a message. She told me who her killer was."

Luther's eyes widened, and red splotches appeared on his face.

"But you don't need me to relay the message," I said, as gently as possible. "You know what she said."

Luther shook his head.

"It was Tracy. She killed her aunt, just so she could inherit the cottage and rent it out. She murdered Matilda for money. Now she's kidnapped my daughter Audrey. She's only nine years old, and she must be scared to death. Tracy is doing this to pressure me to turn myself in. So she herself won't go down for the crimes she committed." I tried to stay calm, but talking about Audrey made me so anxious, my voice rose. "You must know something about it, having given your daughter false alibis. Even so, you keep lying for her."

Suddenly, there was a beeping sound. We all jumped, except for Luther, who stood stock-still.

"What is that?" Blake exclaimed, looking around wildly, like everyone else.

I remembered. "Luther's blood pressure monitor. He usually has pills in his tool belt."

Gina went over to him, found the pills, and shook one out of the bottle. She spoke to him in a soothing voice, walked him to a dining chair, and got him to sit down.

The beeping stopped.

"Have you counted your pills recently, Luther?" I couldn't stop, even if this man's health was in jeopardy. I had something higher at stake: my daughter's life. "Did you have a feeling the bottle seemed lighter? I think Tracy took some of them. She knew about Phyllis Bishop's medication. When she still worked at the pharmacy in Fairwyck, she used to fill it one Tuesday a month. She also knew Phyllis always went to the shop on Tuesdays. She could safely enter Phyllis's house on a Tuesday morning, your crushed pills in her pocket. Tracy added the pills to Phyllis's oral solution of propranolol, causing the old lady to overdose that same afternoon."

When Luther still didn't say anything, I spoke to Janine Martens again, this time loud enough for him to hear it.

"Janine, what do you think of all this? Tracy asked her father to tell the police she was with him on Tuesday morning—and on the Saturday night Matilda Rutherford died. Luther has a lot to make up for after abandoning Tracy as a child. But do you think he should aid and abet murder and kidnapping?"

Now Luther stood up. "Janine can't help me with this. She not here anymore," he shouted with a booming voice. He had tears in his eyes.

I flinched, but then looked at the display of my camera, flicking through the last images I'd just taken. My voice croaked. "You're wrong. She is here."

I showed him.

In the images, there clearly was a gaunt-looking woman with long brown hair. She had dark circles under her eyes, and she looked crestfallen.

Luther put his hand in front of his mouth. "Oh god, Janine."

He looked up and his gaze wandered around, as if he expected to spot her. "Wh... Where is she?"

I took a few more photos and then pointed at a space in front of Luther. "She's right here," I whispered.

Now I could feel Janine Martens's presence like a chill in the air.

Luther sobbed. "Janine. I'm so sorry… Oh my god, I regret leaving you." He stretched out a hand, as if he wanted to caress his wife's cheek.

He looked at me. "What is Janine saying? What does she want me to do?"

I swallowed. My plan had been to lie about this. I wanted to make up something, pretend that Janine told Luther to come clean to the police and give Tracy up.

But now, being part of this emotionally charged moment between two people who'd never made up and achieved closure, I couldn't be disingenuous.

No matter what the circumstances, my ability had allowed for this reunion to happen, for a catharsis of sorts, and it felt like I would be betraying my gift if I now made something up.

I hesitated a couple of moments, then the decision was taken out of my hands.

Luther's blood pressure monitor beeped again.

Emerald, Gina, and Blake looked at me in alarm. "What do we do?" Gina said. "We already gave him a pill. Can we give him another one?"

"Maybe we should call a doctor?" Emerald suggested.

"Wait!" Blake called out. "It's not a normal beeping sound. There's a pattern."

"What?" I stared at them. But they were right, I realized. There were shorter and longer bursts of beeps coming from the monitor on Luther's arm. There was something familiar about it.

Luther came out of his daze and looked at it. "It's not showing anything on the display. It's never done anything like this before."

"It's Morse code!" I shouted.

Luther's eyes met mine. His mouth stood agape. Then he said with a hoarse voice, "You're right. I know Morse code." He looked around, then pointed at a notepad and pen on the counter. "Hand me that."

Emerald grabbed it and passed it to him.

Luther put the pad on the dining table and hunched over it, writing down the letters.

I took pictures. On the display, I could see Janine at Luther's side. She was doing something to the monitor on his arm.

"It's Janine," I said excitedly. "It's a message from her."

When Luther was done taking down the message, his hand shook so much he dropped the pen. It clattered onto the floor, and the sound seemed too loud since we all stood there in tense silence.

Luther sank down on a chair, put his head into his hands, and cried while I looked at Janine's message.

Thor Let T suffer consequences Love always J

CHAPTER FORTY-ONE

We learned that Thor had been Janine's nickname for her husband. Luther might have questioned his wife's image on the camera display, but he knew this name that none of us could possibly know about was proof Janine was really there.

Luther agreed he couldn't protect Tracy any longer, that she needed to live with the consequences of her actions. No matter how bad he felt about the past, he was not responsible for the fact that his daughter had murdered her aunt and Phyllis Bishop.

He agreed to go to the police immediately, admit that he'd lied about Tracy's alibis, and inform them of everything he knew.

Unfortunately, there was one thing he didn't know.

Where Tracy had taken my daughter.

"Could she have barricaded herself at home?" I asked. "Where does she live?"

"She's staying here," Luther said. "Ever since she enrolled in fashion…umm…she moved back home a few years ago."

Luther was willing to let the police search his home, in

case Tracy had left any clues to where she might have taken Audrey.

I suggested Emerald accompany Luther to the station —I didn't trust him to go there by himself, just in case he changed his mind on the way.

But Emerald's headache had worsened, so Gina went with Luther instead.

I wanted to call Jamie, see if he had any updates. Before I went to the station myself, I needed to have all my ducks in a row. I couldn't risk Farrow getting tunnel vision at the sight of me, explaining away the evidence. There needed to be no doubt in anyone's mind, even Farrow's, that searching for Audrey was the only priority.

When Jamie picked up, he didn't even say hi. "It's Stanley."

"The IPS guy?"

"Yep. It wasn't too hard to find him. I contacted IPS, and they gave me the GPS location of his van. Get this. Stanley returned to the area a few weeks ago. He's staying in Meckham. Fairwyck is on his IPS route, though. He's retiring this year, and that made him rethink his choices in life. He wanted to clear the air with Matilda but couldn't psych himself up to do it. Then she passed. He thought about coming forward, but he knew what it would look like, him turning up in the area just before her death."

"Was he gearing himself up to speak to Phyllis too? Was he hanging around her house that Tuesday morning?"

"Yes. He figured if he couldn't make things right with Matilda, at least he could apologize to Phyllis. But he observed what kind of person Phyllis had turned into and he was, well…scared of her."

"What a coward that guy is! Never mind that, though, the important thing is: Did he see Tracy?"

"Yes. He saw her breaking and entering. I'm driving

him to the police station now, where he promised he'd tell the truth about everything."

I exhaled with relief. "We got Luther to recant the alibis he provided for Tracy."

"How did you do that?" Jamie seemed amazed.

"I'll tell you another time. The important thing is that he's on his way to the station with Gina right now."

"Great. Shall I drop Stanley off and then go to the army surplus store?"

"No, that can wait. I'd rather you go in with Stanley and make sure his and Luther's statements are being taken and all goes well with Farrow. I figure this should be enough for him to see that Tracy is a much more viable suspect than me."

"I should think so."

"So it would be okay for me to come in and report Audrey missing?" Suddenly my voice got wobbly. I'd been so focused on getting Luther to admit he'd been lying for his daughter.

It was important that the police knew who the real killer was so that they'd no longer suspect me. But we still didn't know where Audrey was, or what Tracy might do to her. I'd done the opposite of what she had said. Would she take that out on my daughter?

My whole body started shaking.

Blake was by my side and gently removed the phone from my hand. "DS Rees? My mother isn't feeling too good. We'll come to the station now and meet you there."

They led me to the car. "Are you okay?"

I nodded, not wanting to tell Blake that it had just hit me what great danger Audrey might be in. Their mind was on taking care of me, and that's where I wanted it to stay.

Emerald was in the driver's seat of her car, taking deep breaths.

"Do you mind driving?" Blake asked. "Mom isn't doing well."

"I'm okay," I protested weakly. But Blake had already guided me into the back seat.

"Umm, I guess." Emerald rubbed her temples. "My headache is a killer. But I just found pain meds in the glove compartment. I hope it'll get better soon."

"We can switch soon. I'll be all right to drive once I stop shaking." I had to pull myself together for Audrey, so I closed my eyes and took deep breaths, which seemed to help.

Just when I'd achieved a relative state of calm, Blake's panic-tinged voice pulled me out of it.

"Where are you going? I thought we were driving to the Cirencester police station?"

My eyes snapped open.

"Emerald?" Blake called out, now very concerned.

I leaned forward between the front seats.

"Emerald, what's going on?"

My cousin had a strange expression on her face—as if she was very far away.

"Emerald!"

"It's okay," she mumbled. "I know what's causing my headache. They're all calling me—and it's too much."

"What's calling—" That's when I noticed Emerald's eyes behind her glasses had a green glow.

"Mom? What's wrong with her?"

I turned to face my child. "I think it's the books. Remember Emerald's special ability? Books talk to her. I visited her in the library the other day, and I witnessed it. A book in the upstairs section of the library called to her. This is exactly what she looked like when she answered the call."

By that point, we had passed the church. "I think we're going to the library."

Emerald parked the car and got out.

Blake and I scrambled to catch up with her.

"Emerald, honey, we don't really have time for this," I said. "We need to go to the police station."

But she kept on walking in a sleepwalker-like fashion.

I stepped in front of her and waved my arms, which at least got her to stop. Uncertainty registered on her face.

"Something's going on in the library," she said. "The books are in an uproar. They're all calling me."

I stepped aside and said to Blake, "Last time, the books told her something useful about this case. They helped. It wasn't that clear which suspect their clue led to, but I landed on Tracy in the end. So maybe the books are helping us now too?"

"How would they know where Audrey is?" Blake's voice sounded small, like that of a little child.

I shrugged helplessly.

Emerald was already at the front door. We hurried after her. The door closed behind us. As we moved into the open space with the reception desk and the children's books, Emerald said, "Shhh. One at a time. You're all talking over each other, and I can't understand you."

Suddenly, she froze and turned around.

Her face was white as a sheet.

"She's here. Tracy."

CHAPTER FORTY-TWO

I stood there for a moment, open-mouthed and frozen. Then I spun around, trying to take everything in at once.

The library was quiet, and there were no lights on.

I couldn't see Tracy anywhere.

Blake spotted the bundle in the children's story-time corner before I did. When they ran toward it, I didn't hesitate and followed.

"Audrey!" I gasped.

My youngest looked like she was asleep on one of the soft mats the kids sat on during story time, wrapped in a blanket. I shook her gently, but she didn't stir.

"Oh my god." I felt her pulse, and in my panic I thought there was nothing at first, but then I detected the faint rhythm.

"Is she okay?" Blake sobbed.

"Yes, she's fine. She's just unconscious." I rubbed Blake's back. "Maybe Tracy gave her something."

"Audrey, honey, can you wake up?" I stroked the blond curls out of her face and patted her cheeks. Her eyelids remained closed. She looked so young. I choked up at the thought of what my baby had been through.

Finding Audrey had completely diverted Blake's and my attention from Emerald's announcement that Tracy was in the library.

A loud thud pulled our attention away from Audrey, though. We spun around.

Emerald lay on the floor between the reception desk and the story corner.

Tracy was hovering over her, a heavy tome in her hand.

Emerald stirred, and Tracy whacked the book over her head again.

"No!" I rushed toward them. "Leave her alone!"

Tracy straightened. The powder-pink Alexander McQueen suit she must have changed into since kidnapping Audrey in a police uniform didn't even have any wrinkles.

The woman may have been able to maintain an effortless sense of style while drugging my child, hiding out in a library, and bludgeoning my cousin, but the snarl on her face revealed how grotesque she really was.

No amount of cosmetic surgery or pretending to be the kind, generous, and classy Princess of Wales could ever cover Tracy's true self.

"How the hell did you find me here?" Tracy called out in anger.

I stood straight and looked her right in the eyes. "The Seven women have skills. You should never have messed with us."

Tracy looked me up and down with disdain in her eyes. "Pah. You're a victim. I knew it the first time I laid eyes on you. The perfect patsy."

"I hate to disappoint you, but you're very wrong about that. I might not be a born sleuth, but I built a case against you. We found out where you bought the gas mask, and the store owner can identify you. There was a witness who saw you break into Phyllis's house. But you knew that, didn't you? Luther told you, which made you panic and kidnap Audrey. Well, we found that witness, and they're at the police station right now."

I'd been slowly moving toward Tracy, so she was forced to back up—away from Emerald. I could only hope my cousin was all right. A book couldn't do that much damage, could it? It would be really ironic if Emerald was seriously injured by a book, of all things.

"And you know who else is at that station?" I continued. "Your father. He's ready to recant the alibis he provided and tell the police everything about you."

"He would never," Tracy scoffed.

"Luther finally understood that he shouldn't protect and enable you anymore—your mother made him understand."

Tracy blanched. "My mother?" Then she gave a hollow laugh. "You're bluffing. I knew it. My mother couldn't have told Dad anything. She's been dead for years."

"Well, yeah. But remember, I told you about the special skills of the Seven women? Mine is to photograph ghosts." I lifted the camera I still had hanging around my neck. I had never taken it off—I might never take it off again after this. How I could have existed without it all these years was beyond me.

"I have pictures of your mom in your living room, and she communicated with Luther. Wanna see?"

Tracy's face showed she was torn for a moment. Then she took a step back. "This is a trick. I'm not falling for it. What do you plan to do? Strangle me with the strap of your camera?"

It hadn't even occurred to me. But now it seemed like an option.

I turned the camera around to show her the display. "See?"

Tracy inched closer, then bent forward. She narrowed her eyes at the small screen. Her voice was shaky, and there wasn't even a trace of the upper-class accent she usually affected when she said, "Looks like Mom in our living room. I've never seen this photo before. But it can't be from today."

She moved away again.

There was a sudden chill in the air—and the feeling I had begun to associate with ghosts came over me.

On impulse, I lifted my camera and took a few pictures.

Tracy lifted her arms to shield herself. "What are you doing? Stop that!"

I looked at the display—and gasped.

My limited experience with spirits had led me to believe they were tied to places…maybe the places where they'd died? But apparently I'd been wrong about that. It looked as if spirits could move around. Attach themselves to people, perhaps.

In the photograph, three ghosts surrounded Tracy.

Matilda, Phyllis, and Janine.

I slowly turned the display around so Tracy could see it. "It looks like your mom is here right now. Together with your murder victims. I wonder what message they have for you."

Tracy came closer. First slowly, but when she saw what was on the display, she threw caution to the wind.

She grabbed the camera and stared at the screen. "No! No, this can't be."

Her wild eyes turned toward me. I only noticed now that she hadn't put her fake green contact lenses back in again. Tracy's real eyes were big and blue and full of vulnerability.

"How are you doing this?"

I swallowed. There was a very scared little girl inside of Tracy. Something had gone really wrong with her. Maybe she'd known it, and that's why she'd dedicated her life to turning into another person, almost literally putting on a different skin. But she'd done horrible things, and I couldn't let myself feel sorry for her now. "Didn't you know? I'm a witch."

Books flew from the shelves, whizzing across the library.

Tracy screamed.

I looked around to check on my kids. Blake was covering Audrey's body, but the books didn't come near them.

Emerald was still out cold, so it probably wasn't her doing.

I'd automatically moved my hands to my head, in order to shield it, but none of the volumes hit me.

One hovered in the air, right between Tracy and me. It was an alphabet board book. It stayed there, slowly opening up to a page.

I carefully stepped around it so I could see what it showed Tracy.

It was the letter S.

Tracy's blue eyes were wide. She mouthed, "What the…"

The book flipped to a U, then back to an R. It closed, then showed the R again. In quicker succession, it proceeded to open up the letters E, N, D, E, R.

SURRENDER.

Tracy first looked at me, then her eyes moved around, as if she was waiting for the ghosts to materialize. But no spirit turned visible.

With a hopeful voice, Tracy said, "Mom?"

The book, which had dropped to the floor after spelling out the word, quickly rose again.

Tracy and I both flinched.

One letter after another, the alphabet book spelled out FORGIVE.

Tracy sank down onto the floor and started crying.

I had no idea what the message meant. Was Janine asking her daughter to forgive her father and her for messing her up in her childhood? To forgive herself for what she had let herself become—or for what she had done, even?

Or were Janine or maybe even the two murder victims telling Tracy they forgave her?

It didn't matter what Tracy read into it.

The important thing was that she did as asked: She surrendered.

I called Jamie Rees to tell him where we were and what had happened. "Tracy is ready to turn herself in," I said. "Audrey has been drugged, and she hasn't woken up, so please send an ambulance."

While we were waiting, Tracy only asked for one thing.

My camera.

She flipped through the photos of her mother again and again, staring at them, muttering at them.

The way she was sitting there, it almost looked as if she was confessing her sins to her mother.

Maybe she was. Or maybe she was just saying goodbye.

I helped Emerald when she came to, and then we sat with Blake and Audrey.

Shortly before the police turned up, the atmosphere in the library changed. It was…a few degrees warmer again. I didn't have goosebumps on my arms anymore.

Audrey fluttered her eyes open. "Mommy?"

"I'm here, baby." I took my daughter in my arms, and Blake and Emerald joined in the group hug.

I didn't have my camera, since Tracy was so preoccupied with it, so there was no proof. But I'd recently learned to listen to my instincts. And they told me.

The ghosts were gone.

EPILOGUE

With Judith's and Luther's permission, we were holding a memorial for Matilda Rutherford and Phyllis Bishop in the joint gardens.

It was a lovely day for spring in the Cotswolds, a cloudless and sunny sky, and the guests didn't seem to mind circumnavigating the mysterious sheep dung and climbing over low fences.

Well, we had advised them on the invitation to wear wellies.

Judith Winters, who had forgiven me after a long talk, sported the most stylish pair of rubber boots of all. They were leopard print and in a cowboy-boot style. A perfect accessory to her Stella McCartney leopard-print trench coat.

Audrey was in awe.

I made a mental note to search for a budget version of those wellies. Audrey had a birthday coming up.

Obviously, I wanted to coddle and spoil my youngest after everything she'd been through, so I needed to restrain myself.

I also had to keep myself from asking her how she was

feeling all the time. Yes, the kidnapping must have been traumatic. But luckily, Audrey had really thought Tracy was a police officer, and there had only been one short moment, when they'd stopped the car and Tracy had turned to her and pressed a funny-smelling rag against her mouth, that Audrey had actually been panicked and afraid.

Drugged, Audrey hadn't been aware of being brought to the library. She hadn't witnessed anything that had happened there. She'd woken up in the hospital, and she'd felt fine.

I was sending her to a child psychologist anyway. And Blake, who'd been through just as much, if not more, was seeing the therapist too.

Obviously, my children couldn't tell the therapist everything. I had yet to find a psychologist who specialized in dealing with ghosts, their spooky messages, and all the emotional turmoil those hauntings brought on for the bereaved.

So I told my children they could ask Gina, Emerald, and me anything, even though we might not always have the answers.

Audrey asked a lot, maybe because filling in all the blanks helped her feel in control. And she randomly came at me with questions in the oddest situations, like today, at the memorial service.

I was fetching bowls and cutlery from the kitchen when she trailed after me. "Mom?"

"Hmm?"

"Why did Tracy take me to the library, exactly?"

"Umm… I think she knew the building from the book club. There's a book club on Monday nights at the library. So she probably also knew that Emerald didn't work on Wednesdays. The police found a broken latch on one of the bathroom windows, so they assume that's how she got in. She might have been familiar with the broken latch from her book club visits, and maybe she thought she was being clever, hiding you right under my cousin's nose."

"Ah. Makes sense."

I tried to be patient, even though I was a memorial service hostess and had a million things to do. "Any other questions right now?"

"No. Can I help you carry stuff?"

I exhaled. "Sure. Here, why don't you bring this bowl of water to Ethel? She's not touching the tuna I already put next to her chair. Maybe she'd like to drink something."

Ethel the cat was a guest of honor. We were mourning the death of her former best friends, so it seemed appropriate. I'd draped blankets over an old garden chair and put that next to the large, framed photo from Ethel's album.

The one of the three friends in their youth, arm in arm, laughing. Before bleeping Stanley Rutherford had entered their lives and ruined their friendship.

I wanted to believe that all that was forgotten in death. Maybe the FORGIVE message had been for each other as well?

I knew that Phyllis and Matilda had been inching toward making up in the last few months. I'd finally discussed the Judgement tarot card with Gina—the one Blake had plucked out of Phyllis Bishop's head and that we had asked Gina about during that first afternoon tea at the Sacred Salmon Inn.

Gina had admitted that Phyllis had been a client. "She was a curmudgeon, make no mistake, but after Ethel died and Matilda contacted her, she got a crisis of conscience. I believe, if the former best friends would have had more time, they might have found it in their hearts to put the past behind them. The Judgement card had Phyllis rethinking her past behavior."

We couldn't be sure that the cat was conscious of the

fact that Matilda and Phyllis had passed and that we were remembering them today, of course. But Ethel stayed in the chair and ignored the most expensive tuna I'd ever bought. That made me think she was too sad to eat. I could've asked Audrey to find out, but then I decided to let the cat grieve in private.

I walked over to the table we'd set up for the potluck buffet for the human guests and put the bowls and spoons down.

I'd contributed store-bought Chelsea buns in Phyllis's honor, as well as homemade scones. Luther had found Matilda's recipe and given it to me. I could say with confidence that they tasted as if they'd come right out of Matilda's oven. Mine had turned out just as dry as hers had been.

Luckily, there were guests with better culinary skills than mine. Gina had brought her delicious lemon bars. Michelle had turned up with baskets full of sausage rolls and pork pies. And Ellie Bullwart had made her famous chili, for which I'd brought the bowls and spoons.

"You should be the first to try it," Ellie said to me.

I hadn't eaten anything yet, too busy greeting guests and making sure everyone was all right, and I suddenly realized how hungry I was.

"It's such a shame I never got to try your cooking at the pub," I said, as I topped my bowl with a generous dollop of sour cream. Then I stopped mid-stir, realizing I'd put my foot in it.

Anxiously, I looked up. But Ellie wasn't crying at the reminder that her life as a pub landlady was over. She was smiling.

"Oh, I already have a new project in the works," she said. "And I wanted to talk to you about it." She looked around, a little more subdued. "Oh, sorry, I guess this isn't the right time."

I waved the hand holding my now-empty spoon. "Hmmm," was all I could say until I'd swallowed the mouthful of chili. "Don't worry about it. A memorial service is about saying goodbye. Of course it's sad. But in the end, they tend to turn out joyful."

"Yes, because people get drunk." Ellie smirked and looked over my shoulder.

I turned around, following her gaze to Matilda's garden, where we'd set up a bar. Luther Martens and Stanley Rutherford had already had words and aired all their grievances before the memorial service. Since they both had abandonment of their wives and regretting it in common, they must have figured they might as well become pals. Now they were boozed up, singing melancholy songs in oddly cheerful voices, celebrating the lives of Matilda Rutherford and Phyllis Bishop.

I raised my eyes at Jamie, who was manning the bar. He lifted a jug of water and the vodka bottle and winked. I took it to mean that he'd already started diluting their drinks.

I turned to Ellie again. "Not just because of the alcohol. Endings are also beginnings, in a way, and memorial services remind us of these inevitable circles of life."

Ellie nodded. "True. It's a new beginning for all of us. For me, certainly. And for you."

"Yes! Now that this murder investigation is over, I can finally move on and get started on building a new life for us." I suddenly got pensive. "Actually, I think we've already moved on and started building this new life."

I looked over to Gina and Emerald, who were chatting with Anthony, the pharmacist.

"I would have never cleared my name and gotten Tracy to confess if I hadn't realized that I had friends somewhere along the way. Allies who would help me, if I only let them into my life. Maybe the hardest part is over already. How did that happen?" I laughed.

Ellie smiled. "I'd like to be an ally."

"Oh, you are." I touched Ellie's arm. "You were my first friend here in Fairwyck. You gave me a job, and without you, Judith wouldn't have hired me."

"Of course we're friends. I wouldn't have known what to do if you hadn't turned up that day in the pub. You called Judith, who helped me leave Jason."

"Well," I said, "it was actually Esme who called Judith."

Ellie waved a hand. "Anyway, you were there for me when I needed you. So I'd love for you to be my partner. I've decided to renovate and run the old Fairwyck theater. It's been empty for years. And it's much more in line with what I always wanted to do. The pub was Jason's dream. I enjoyed working there, but I always wanted more. We both put an equal share of money in, so he has to buy me out. And Judith told me about loans women business owners can apply for, so financing this endeavor shouldn't be a problem. I'm envisaging a bar-style eatery where theatergoers can have a light dinner and snacks before and after the show. I'd be in charge of all that. But I'd need someone to run the theater. I know from your résumé that you majored in arts administration. How about it? Let's become business partners!"

Ellie's enthusiasm was contagious.

"Wow, that sounds like a dream. I'd love to work in a theater. But…" Reality sank in, and I self-consciously smoothed a hand down the black wrap dress I'd bought for the occasion. "That degree was a million years ago. I don't have any experience, remember? And I need a steady job with a good income to support my family. A new business like that is too risky."

"I'm sure we can work something out. You can still do

cleaning shifts at WLA and then dial those down as things pick up at the theater. And it's going to be a while until it gets busy. We need to renovate first."

I was torn between being reasonable and saying yes—because I really wanted to.

Ellie laughed. "I know you're the right person for it. But you don't have to agree to it today."

"Okay," I said in relief. "I'll think about it."

"You'll come around, I just know it."

I made a noncommittal sound, my mouth again full of chili. At that moment, Esme came around the garden path.

"Please excuse me, Ellie."

I put my half-empty bowl on one of the bistro tables as I walked toward Esme.

"Hi, Esme!"

"Hey." We hugged, and I showed her where she could set up the chips and dips she'd brought along. Then I introduced her to Gina and Emerald, who were coming over to the buffet table.

Gina took me aside. "Looks like everyone is here. Do you want to make a speech?"

"Oh. No." I hadn't even thought about that. "I'm not good at speeches. But you're right, someone should say something. I'd rather take pictures." I grimaced and lifted the Nikon I had around my neck.

When Gina didn't say anything but continued to look at me, I caved. "I could welcome everyone and then invite anyone who wanted to say something to take the floor."

"Good idea."

I grabbed a spoon and clanked it against a glass bowl. "Gather around, everyone."

Jamie brought the guests from the bar over, getting someone to help tipsy Luther and Stanley over the fence.

When they'd made it to where I was standing, Jamie

pressed a glass of Prosecco into my hands. "Thanks," I mouthed.

I cleared my throat. "Thank you all for coming today. We're here to celebrate the lives of Matilda Rutherford and Phyllis Bishop, my neighbors, who sadly passed away before I could really get to know them."

Pointing at the large, framed picture, I said, "Back in the day, my great-aunt Ethel—who also recently left us—Matilda, and Phyllis were best friends. Unfortunately, a rift occurred that left Phyllis bitter and lonely. Matilda's and Phyllis's lives ended tragically, and it seems particularly ill-fated that this meant they never had to a chance to make up. But we don't know what happens when our lives end, and I'd like to think it wasn't too late for reconciliation."

Some guests looked confused, but I was focusing on Ethel the cat, giving her a smile. Audrey was next to her, stroking her head.

"Ethel agrees with you, Mom."

Everyone laughed.

"Cheers to Phyllis and Matilda." I lifted my glass and took a sip before putting it down on the buffet table.

Then I lifted my camera and took a photo of my daughter and the cat.

After everyone had raised and clinked their glasses, I said, "Please tell us your fondest memories of Matilda and Phyllis, or just say goodbye to them, if you want to."

The guests clapped, and I was relieved to be able to give the floor to Judith.

I went over to Gina, Emerald, and Blake and showed them the photo I'd just taken.

There was a cat in the chair next to Audrey. But when I tilted the camera a little, the display showed a woman. My great-aunt Ethel, smiling and crying at the same time, surrounded by two shining spheres of light.

Emerald put her hand in front of her mouth, and Gina got misty eyed. "Oh, Ethel, it's so good to see you."

"That's so cool," Blake exclaimed. "Do you think the lights are Matilda and Phyllis?"

I shrugged.

When Judith had finished saying a few words and Luther geared himself up for a drunken speech, I said to Gina and Emerald, "You know, all this time I never asked. What was Ethel's ability?"

"She didn't have one," Emerald said.

"What? You said all Seven women are witches."

"They are. But abilities can skip a generation, can't they, Mom?"

Gina tipped her head. "Ethel always maintained she didn't have a gift, but I had the suspicion she was just keeping it a secret. The cards told me it had something to do with her home."

I looked over at our run-down cottage. "You mean this house…my home?"

Gina nodded.

"Maybe that's why Aunt Ethel stayed on as a cat, instead of turning into a sphere of light," Blake suggested.

"Maybe. Audrey could ask her," I said.

Gina gave a mysterious smile. "I have a feeling Ethel the cat is going to reveal it to you when she's ready."

"Hmm," I hummed. "I thought once this murder case was solved, our lives would return to normal. Even though everything has changed for us, and we still have to figure out what our new normal is. But I'm just now realizing: With our special gifts, there's no ordinary life, is there?" I pulled a face. "It's just going to be a series of strange events, one after the other, isn't it?"

My relatives laughed. "That's one thing you can count on," Emerald said.

Gina put an arm around me. "And on us."

AFTERWORD

Thank you for reading SNAP, SPIRIT, MURDER, the first GHOST PHOTOGRAPHER MYSTERY. I hope you enjoyed reading it as much as I loved writing it. If you did, I would greatly appreciate a review on Amazon or your favorite store or book review site. Reviews are crucial for authors as well as for readers who are looking for their next book—even just a line or two are so helpful. Thanks!

I love to chat with my readers, so if you'd like to contact me, visit felicitygreenauthor.com.

Are you excited for another GHOST PHOTOGRAPHER paranormal cozy mystery? CLICK, CURSE, CORPSE is coming up next.

If you would like to know more about my books, learn about my SCOTTISH WITCHES MYSTERY series, and get information on latest releases, please sign up for my newsletter on felicitygreenauthor.com.

You'll receive a free book, NO REST FOR THE WICKED WITCH, and get access to free short stories and bonus scenes.

Happy reading!
 Felicity Green

www.ingramcontent.com/pod-product-compliance
Ingram Content Group UK Ltd.
Pitfield, Milton Keynes, MK11 3LW, UK
UKHW041112110325
455992UK00004BA/203